A
FORGETTABLE
MAN

Set me as a seal upon thine heart,
as a seal upon thine arm:
for love is as strong as death...
Solomon's Songs
Ch8, verse 6

Robert Golden

ISBN: Print: 978-1-9998181-6-6

Cover Design by Robert Golden

Published by WriteSideLeft Ltd, UK

www.writesideleft.com

PART 1

CHAPTER 1

The cracked bell vibrated against the corroded chrome hammer, rattling the wooden wall it had been hung on thirty summers before. Years of sand billowing in from the arid street and years of cooking oil spume from the café beneath David's rented apartment blunted the telephone's once clear chime.

One ring, another and it stopped. Would it ring again? David held his breath. Life or death announced by a broken note on an ancient telephone in a tin pot dictatorship. David sniffed at the irony.

He rose from the tired teak chair, limped to the French window and looked down on the narrow street below. White haired Muhammad, unshaven as usual, plied his fennel-perfumed dough into small rounds to be cooked on his humpbacked pan into thin, soft breads he would stuff with mincemeat, tomatoes, green chillies and shredded herbs. Nearby, the middle-aged woman from the key shop, sweeping the pavement as always against the ever-present sand, glanced up and smiled to herself.

"I never asked her name." David looked away. The cobbled street was increasingly crowded with early morning shoppers, a middle-aged man rushing to get a sweet bun before work, children on their way to school, battered taxis and even now, in the early twenty-first century, a donkey cart piled high but with polythene crates rather than wooden barrels. The gaunt gnarled drover was wearing patched trousers. Oranges hanging on the drooping trees and baskets of bright yellow lemons added intimations of hope in the dun coloured world of sand and dust.

Would the phone ring again?

David steadied himself against the chair and eased his hand down his back, feeling the dampness of the spring heat soaking through his cotton shirt. The discomfort in his lower spine and his right shoulder were lasting mementoes of his profession: cameras tugging around his neck, a heavy equipment bag banging on his right side, a backpack slung over the other shoulder while running towards or away from the riots, swinging batons and rifle rounds, and then crouching behind walls or fences as armoured cars stalked past. The ache in his left thigh, a harsher memory of things past, penetrated more deeply. He shoved his knuckle into the centre of the muscle, searching for an acupressure point to relieve the pain and growled, "Miners with lung diseases, subway drivers with the stress of another suicide, soldiers with their nightmares." His lips tightened. "Next to them, I've no right to complain."

It happened. The cracked bell argued again with the peeling hammer and slapped the wooden wall. Once only, time suspended and then silence announced his death.

David glared at the phone, stood very still for a moment and nodded, confirming what was an indisputable pronouncement. He clinched his fists and assured himself, "Stoical is good". He glanced across the room further into the shadows, confirming his box of memories was still present.

He thought, 'All the conflicts and crazy violence, but still I imagined there was everything to live for.' He closed his eyes. The haunting memory of ammonia and ether, the miasma of pain and drugs, and there it was, the end of a dream; he could no longer touch her.

With a whiff of self-pity, he whispered, "Can I say I've really lived if, in the end, I still have not become fully conscious of who I am?" His lips relaxed enough to allow what could pass for an ironic smile.

David sank slowly onto the chair. It took his weight but creaked. "Should I have been silent?"

He was an outsider with only a few friends and a small group of aficionados around the world who still remembered him; now a nobody with little fame and less money. The regime will silence him as they have their own journalists, artists, intellectuals, trade unionists and human rights lawyers, all of who have disappeared one by one over the past weeks since the renewed crackdown began.

He slapped his hands against his cheeks.

Amongst the disappeared were friends – good people. First they'd have been tortured to surrender names, maybe raped, then a bullet in the back of the head, a shallow grave. Ignominious, final but the next morning the sun still rose, sand still seeped into the city, surf still pounded against the broken sea walls and the people of that forlorn capital were still somnambulant within their fear and pity.

Muhammad will bake his breads and the sweet key shop woman will sweep. For the majority, a life of sorts goes on.

He shook his head like an irritated bull loosening the flies from his face and searched his memory.

In Sarajevo, after the Bosnian war, which he had reported on, David waited for Goran to arrive. The restaurant specialized in national dishes. David, sitting outside in the sunshine, ordered a begova corba - a chicken soup enriched with egg yolks and sour cream, sharpened with lemon juice. As he watched the passers-by, his eyes were drawn up to the restored minaret rising elegantly above the hubbub of the old marketplace and to the mountains beyond. The city nestled between the mountain's steep sides as though taking refuge in the valley. From their rocky crevices, several years earlier, Serb irregulars bombarded the city, pummelling it day by day like eternally hungry buzzards pecking the body of their defenceless victim. David still held within his nostrils the stench of burnt wood, blood and excrement. He was certain that any of the passers-by who had been present during the siege would, like him, forever recall the odour on those streets.

Goran appeared, tallish with a Van Dyke beard befitting a Balkan poet, accompanied by his pipe and his twinkling eyes. Goran and David embraced. They gossiped about all the people they knew in common; they ate Bosnian polenta covered in sour cream and a helping of boiled spring greens, they drank the local beer and then they talked about poetry.

Goran, who had been in the city for the entire siege, seemed often to be involved in an inner dialogue, occasionally emerging to engage the world. He looked up from his plate, his eyes shone. "Poets almost inevitably live their lives in opposition. It's our condition."

David squinted at his friend who was silhouetted against the sun, which was just peeking out from behind the minaret. He knew Goran hid his pain behind mirth and rarely spoke without levity. David smiled, uncertain if this was another of his friend's humorous tales.

"I'm serious." Goran laughed in his stuttering way and laid his pipe onto the edge of the thick glass ashtray. "Poetry leads to dreams and dreams lead to the desire for change and change leads to challenging the status quo. So you see, if you dare begin to dream you end in opposition."

David concentrated on Goran's formulation. "Good", he murmured. "The poet's psyche, human aspirations and revolution in one sentence."

The flickering upturn at the corner of Goran's lips belied how pleased he was. In the silence that followed, Goran hid his pleasure within renewed interest for the remaining polenta.

David watched the light dance across the plate. When Goran finished the last buttery morsel and after he took another sip of the hop-flavoured beer, David spoke quietly. "Do you think we invent love as a dream? That it's not something real; just a passing fabrication all mixed up with lust, sex and loneliness; that its transience, its mutability forces us to suicide or poetry?"

Goran tapped his pipe and using his thumb, forced some Old Holborn shag into it. He studied it a long moment as if appreciating something of beauty. He looked up, directly into David's eyes. "You will grieve for many years. Maybe you should stay here. It's now a city of grief; we are specialists in it."

An impatient honking from the street below brought David back to his present problem: survival.

'Serbian, Bosnian, Arab, what does it matter? How could I have kept silent amongst these people? It was my choice; I'm a big boy, I knew talking would lead me into trouble.'

The phone had rung twice and once again; that was the warning signal his friends had decided upon.

He chastised himself aloud. "This isn't a game. I've two hours before they show up, two more hours at the end of my life to live my destiny as I choose. And then the uniforms will rush in, beat me, throw me from my balcony onto Muhammad's scalding griddle or drag me off to a worse fate." The sound of his voice gave him comfort and the need, because of speaking aloud, to form complete sentences, concentrated his mind.

His fists jerked closed and blood palpitated in his temples. He rasped, "Okay, I'm old and sore, but somehow I can still resist. I have choices, perhaps limited but choices. I still have shreds of freewill."

He became aware of the vegetables and lamb cooking odours rising from the café beneath his rooms.

'People are like a stew made of divers elements but, when you cook it down, only the essence of what they are is left. Mehmet and Suleiman … my comrades, my friends, they should be able to help.' He frowned. 'But in this oil-free sideshow to the region's unending melodrama, who really cares? Anyway, it would be irresponsible to endanger them.'

His eyes narrowed and after a moment he tapped the table forcibly. 'I can wait to be arrested or maybe murdered on the spot.'

Again he smacked the table. 'I can try to escape but in my condition on my own, with few resources, it seems unlikely.'

He rapped the table's edge with his knuckle one more time. 'That leaves a quiet, anonymous, self-inflicted extinction. The rest of the world would soon forget I existed; unlike for Martin Luther King or Mozart, there will be no lasting memory of me.'

He sighed deeply and murmured, "A forgettable man".

He exhaled a short sharp breath as if expelling poisonous air. 'I've always sought a meaningless eternity. Bizarre, infantile. Nothingness is nothingness.'

David gazed at the stained white ceiling. 'I need to be matter of fact. I must not allow myself to smother my dread of extinction by hoping my photographs will provide lasting memories of me.'

"Crap," he shouted, "it's all pure crap, decorations over the abyss." He moaned again. "Pure ego."

Sweat poured from his forehead and into his eyes. Fear banished remorse. He struggled to stand upright but nausea swelled through his gut, the same nausea he felt when photographing the violence he had borne witness to around the world. As then, he knew the antidote was movement and action.

The rising heat of the morning and his pumping blood allowed him to move more easily through the steamy shafts of light streaming in from the increasingly busy dusty street below. He crossed the ancient tiles to the grey cardboard box sitting on the table next to the threadbare divan. He picked the box up and weighed it in his hands. "Not much heft for a whole life."

Suddenly tears poured along the arroyos between his nose and cheeks. Of all the photographs, all the memories, all the people, she was what had made his years a life and now, in his end game, it was only she that he wished to hold onto. Neither his box of prints not his threatened life meant much in relationship to his memory of her beauty, her warm skin, her crooked smile, her being who she was. More tears. "Her crooked smile, her warm skin."

His energy drained from him. 'I'm still the kid wondering what the heroic decision should have been. I knew I'd never recover from grief. Goran had been correct.' He tapped his forehead. 'It's been weighing down the bookshelves of my memory, forcing me to prop them up until now, when still it fills me with remorse…but maybe a little sweet comfort too.'

His hand smoothed the surface of the box. 'What about all my grand notions, what about the prisoners and desperate children I helped? My work always rationalized my existence until I met her.' He looked at the box and out towards the pale blue sky. He faded again. His hands rose to support his head, sinking as it was towards his chest, deflated by the hollowness of memory.

A deep unconscious moan which rises from people when they fall to sleep and sometimes when they expel their last breath, a sound previously unknown as one of his own, escaped his lips like steam from a freighter's funnel…lonely, echoing against an empty sea, bouncing off scudding clouds. There could be no response but from within himself, from the source of the sound.

His shoulders heaved with a Sephardic gesture; his head nodded slightly to the side, hands raised, palms up as if even he, an atheist, was showing God that he had nothing to grip, that his grasp was empty. 'Life's like this, unfathomable, endlessly mysterious and too complex for me to figure out with so little time left. I guess I'm pissed off. I thought I would have figured it out and I would have drawn tidy conclusions before the end.'

He glanced at his box and whispered, "This way, it's not right; I object." He looked up, his eyes searching as if trying to establish if he could be heard. He all but shouted, "This is not how it should end."

He remembered someone telling him about Job complaining to God, "Why me?" And God answered, "Why not?" And Job cried, "But what have I done to deserve this?" And God said, "Nothing."

Carefully he placed the box on the little table he used as his writing and dining surface and walked to the bathroom. He opened his small bag of medications and took from it the bottle of sleeping pills Doctor Suleiman had recently handed him. He looked at the blank label, the blank instruction's space. He remembered Doctor Suleiman's calm smooth voice as he surrendered the bottle to David.

"They're strong, very strong. Don't make a habit of them and no more than two at a time." He mewed his urbane all-knowing laugh. "Could kill you."

David flipped open the stubborn plastic top, poured the small shinny white pills into his hand and quickly counted. them.

He looked into the peeling silvered mirror, a distant relative of the 1970s telephone, and studied his face. 'Not so bad for my late sixties.' Little remained of his once thick black hair but his tanned skin hid a myriad of discolorations, dry patches and liver spots. He shook his head as if to dismiss any further consideration of his corporeal existence, looked at his watch, judged the time the pills would take to work and moved back to his eating table and the light of early morning pouring through the open French windows which led to the small balcony.

'Sure, they may shove me off. I'll die breathing in Muhammad's fennel-scented dough. There are worse ways. But how public would the authorities want my death to be? At such a delicate time, would they risk the ire of the Americans and British?'

Because he carried both passports, he had made certain, after his first contact with the opposition, the two embassies knew he was in that God-forsaken country. The Americans warned him, "Be careful, don't be seen with suspicious people. Something's brewing; we can't protect you." The Brits said, "Look after yourself, any bother give us a ring between nine and five."

David placed a glass of water between the sleeping pills and the box and slowly opened its lid. There lay sixty photographs, his testament, a history of the world he had witnessed, neatly piled, proclaiming all that he was and all that he had become. The earliest photograph was on top, the most recent was at the bottom, and somewhere in between, she was waiting with her beauty frozen in silver greys, inky blacks and finely detailed whites.

He'd time it: his entire existence in one hour and forty-five minutes. A lifetime of memories to enjoy before they would pound on the door as they had in Mussolini's Rome, in Stalin's Moscow, in

Hitler's Berlin, in Petain's Marseilles and on and on through Bosnia, Tunisia, Syria and Chile to detain and destroy the dreamers.

He picked up the top print and looked at the face of a woman in a farmer's market, from a time before supermarkets, from a time in his life of innocence. It was his first true documentary photograph. He was all of fifteen when he shot it. He held the beautiful print in his hands. The black and deep grey inks proudly sat on the surface of the semi-glossed paper. He thought, 'the greys are so beautiful'.

•••

It was spring or at least warm. A celebration of some kind surrounded him. It was his second birthday, seven hundred and thirty days from the moment he had been born which, coincidentally was the same moment American troops entered Dachau.

Years later, in high school, he would learn Lavoisier's law of the conservation of mass - that matter is neither created nor destroyed but transformed from matter to energy and back again in a constant cycle of creation and change. It pressed him to ask if a part of the ashes and a part of the pain from the war and the camps, even though an ocean away, had been breathed in by his mother as she carried him in her womb and that they had become a part of him. He lived his own life and with the suffering of others as if in a persistent clinched dance that nagged at him like the Greek furies he had read about.

It was the twenty-ninth of May 1947, in the boundless American Midwest. Palestine and Italy were in turmoil. The President of the United States signed the Truman Doctrine officially starting the Cold War, a war of potentially mutual annihilation. David and his generation lived with that threat for most of their young lives, knowing that at any time, on any day, a madman or a calculating politician could, within hours, wipe out all of them and their loved ones because of a whim, because of an ideological or religious tick, because of an emotional weakness or a desire for control. This threat alone would be sufficient to drive many of his generation into asking dangerous questions about hierarchy, power and wealth and many more into a private hedonism. "Hell, there's nothing to hope for and anyway, we may be dead within the hour." That threat would, in his teens, give him partial admittance to manhood.

But for now, in his last moments of innocence, the air was scented with the perfume of budding roses and growing grasses thriving on the moisture of an earlier shower and from earth tumbled thick with worms.

Men's voices, his uncle Marvin's thick liquid tones and his father Harry's remote, curt notes, as always they would be - flat, joyless - were nearby and familiar. There were also gentle birdcalls emitted by tiny creatures, unknown to him but not worrisome. David's stem brain said all was calm and safe, no reason to cry out, no threat from giant reptiles, sabre tooth tigers or other dangers. The sounds should have meant safety. They were not of the thing creeping towards him, plot in mind, the devil in his eyes.

"Dirt", said his father, looking down at the scrappy grass beneath the barbecue. "I jes' call it dirt. Earth? You call it that? I don' know. Anyway, not worth talking about."

Marvin, used to Harry's abrupt pronouncements and then his cascade into silence, didn't mind. He liked having an audience. He was a clothing salesman. His wife Bernie said proudly, "Sure thing, my Marvin's got the gift of the gab. He could sell a poor guy his own shirt." She always laughed at that and added, "Not much else though, but hey, what's a girl need 'sides a pretty word or so?"

Marvin, undaunted by Harry's silence, went on. "Calling it 'dirt'... it's like somethin' disgusting, to wash away, to protect yourself from. No sir, not the earth of seeds and life but dirt- kind'a like an alien thing." He watched as Harry turned the burgers on the grill and the ideas in his mind. "Not saying this is you or anything but the fear of the earth that'll finally hold you, maybe like a fear of the worms and wood lice is all 'cause it's really a fear of becoming something else in the endless cycle."

Harry looked up from his burgers towards Marvin. He nodded.

Marvin continued his dissertation on life, caring little that his audience was more concerned with the state of the hundred percent chuck on the fire-licked grill. "Little do most Jews know that the word 'barbecue', in French or Spanish or whatever the hell language it is, means skewering the porker from his 'barb' or moustache to his 'cue' or bottom to be roasted on the spit."

Harry gulped down more sweet lemonade and said, "Unha".

They were American Jews of several generations who frankly couldn't care less; their identity macerated in the great continent's patriotic stew. Pork, scallops, inobservance of the high holidays, Christmas all rolled into the same ball of opalescent wax to create lives guided by the conservative establishment's mores and Hallmark card emotions. The myths and legends, ghosts and traditions of the old country were lost to their families, replaced by their fragmented existence in an alienating housing tract and by the reconstituted truths of ABC and CBS new programs.

In his cot, David's eyes followed the sunlight dancing across the ceiling's wooden slats. He was still closer to the earth than the social world; for his time of infancy and into childhood, he accepted things as they were. Colours to be gazed at, shapes to be eaten, touched or toyed with, some of which were worrying and some of which brought comfort. And the incomprehensible and ungraspable joy of light from the bright thing in the sky, from the silver thing at night, from glowing balls and thin blue strips he saw while carried in his mother's arms. For that moment, in his cot beneath the wooden ceiling, there was comfort in the bird song floating in the warm late afternoon air and from the shifting sunbeams playing on the ceiling, walls and window screens of the enclosing porch.

He was captivated by his hands learning how to hold and pull and even to feel things through the still thin skin of his fingertips. The cot was bluish, firm but comfortable.

Now, punctuating the murmuring voices of his father and Marvin and the sweet songs of the creatures, that other sound, scrapping, panting, slowly approached his domain.

The thing, three years older than David, known as his brother Joey, popped his head over the edge of the cot. His brother's eyes darted around searching for something or perhaps making certain that the something or someone could not see him. Satisfied he was safe, his narrow-slatted eyes settled on David. Joey's face went puce but with hardly a change of expression he flung his arms upward, suspended them at the apogee of the move and slammed down the flats of his palms on David's forehead and cheeks. David was more surprised than frightened, at least at first. This was an unknowable event. But his brother, egged on by David's startled silence, struck again and again, enthused by his ability to get away with it. He slapped and flayed and smacked and struck over and over until something red spurted from David's nose. The insides of his eyes were slashed by pain. Shocked, he let out a wailing scream, an incomprehensible curse that would echo all the days of his life. Joey, the thing known as his brother, who, for that moment, had become another Cain in the abused history of humanity, disappeared. A few seconds later his mother's shocked face loomed above the cot.

In the future David would be bloodied by boys his own age, he would see men on huge horses riding people down, trampling them, slashing at those fleeing with crowbars and with hammers attached to canes, their victim's blood spattering across pavements, shirts, hair and terrified faces. One day he would meet children traumatized by war, all of whom had blood in their nightmares. And one day he would witness his own death.

CHAPTER 2

The heat thickened across the town, foretelling the approaching summer, which would scorch the bricks and clay roof tiles that sheltered its citizens from its onslaught. The heat was oppressive; it bruised and burnt the people as did their arrogant bureaucrats and their arbitrary politicians and police.

David arched his back, attempting to elude his pain as he continued to study the photograph of the woman in the farmer's market. For most of his picture-making career he preferred fast shutter speeds, long lenses and wide apertures, a technique which freezes the subject against an out of focus background. This clearly reveals the subject in an otherwise random and uncaring world. Of course, as in all of his documentary pictures, the world was present. Behind the woman was the stolid upper torso of a man leaning towards a crate of vegetables reacting to his own ordering of the day. And she, seeming exhausted, stared without interest or hostility towards the camera's lens and therefore towards the young David. The woman was neither giving herself nor holding back. The ambiguity seemed innocent.

In the moment of photographing her, he learned that he had the ability, perhaps a power, to creep into people's souls, achieving an unconscious bond of confidence. From then on he decided that in exchange for their trust he was responsible to honor the wellbeing of those he photographed. This allegiance would lead him into conflict.

The woman had been silent. As so many other people he would photograph with pain in their eyes, whose voices had been stilled by frustration, fear or simply the exhaustion of work, children or poverty, he hoped he could help them to have a presence in history, to bring to other's attention their quiet dignity and the oppressive plight of their lives. He smiled a soft, gentle smile to himself. "Ohh", he murmured, "How naïve I was."

David placed the print face down on the open lid and looked at his watch. Minutes had passed in his reverie. He could smell the lamb and garlic more distinctly from the boiling pots in the café below and remembered the first time he met Mehmet.

The café was almost empty. David occupied his usual table in the cool shadows, half leaning against the cool stucco wall, painted a dense blood red up to shoulder height and from there a pale yellow, the colour of Cornish clotted cream. The owner sat on a high stool across the room at the bar, leaning over his newspaper. The ancient colour TV, suspended above the bar on a lazy iron bracket, blared a Turkish soap opera, much loved throughout the region.

David's fingers were covered with oil as he scooped with a thin flatbread, the generous melting hunks of lamb from a deep bowl filled with potatoes, French beans and paper-thin slices of tongue-searing red chilies, all in an aromatic and silky sauce.

A solid young man entered, looked around, wove through the tables away from the bar and even though the café was not busy, he sat down, uninvited, across from David who looked up at him.

The man had watery brown eyes with dark Mediterranean rings of exhaustion hanging like half-moons from his lower lashes. Mehmet was well fed, broad shouldered but not threatening. He smiled at David as he watched him scoop a chunk of lamb. "You like our food." It was more an announcement than a question, pronounced in good but accented British English, which rolled across the table in deep soft tones.

David, appreciating the sound, smiled and wiped his fingers carefully on several white squares of thin paper, which passed as napkins in that part of the world.

Mehmet smiled again. "We know your work." Mehmet waited for whatever reaction his words would pry loose from this odd stranger who, inexplicable, was living in Mehmet's troubled country.

David remained expressionless and waited.

"Your work in Egypt, Cambodia, well, you know the list everywhere including in your own country."

David still waited.

Mehmet, usually unfazed by other's opacity, stumbled, "We need help."

'Cop or revolutionary', wondered David. 'A plant, a provocateur, a fifth columnist?'

Mehmet nodded as if making a decision. He looked around to be certain he could not be overheard and then, leaning across the table, he spoke quietly. "I understand that no one can be taken at face value in a country like mine at a time like this. A trusted person today can be tomorrow's informer, sometimes bought, sometimes saving a relative from a terrible destiny, sometimes keeping our sister's child in school or protecting a daughter from rape." He looked away, through the café window for a moment, his eyes slightly misted.

David scrutinized him like a bird of prey.

Mehmet gathered himself and carried on, still watching the window. "Our political leaders, like their brothers in Zimbabwe, central Asia, Tibet and too many other places, have learned well from uncles Joe and Adolf." He looked back at David. "Yes", he assured himself, "politics as criminality".

Mehmet paused to see what affect he had upon this quiet man and then added, "Our mutual friend Doctor Suleiman mentioned me … I'm the film director."

David sat back, folded his hands together and nodded.

Mehmet took out a neatly folded square of paper. "Here, from the Doctor."

David took the piece of paper and looked at the note written in what he remembered as his friend Suleiman's terrible scrawl. 'Typical doctor's writing'. David placed the note on the table and looked into Mehmet's pool-like eyes. "So?"

Mehmet smiled. "We need photographic testaments for what's going on here, published by your friends in London, New York and other places. Maybe published in on-line blogs."

"I'm not here for that. I'm not working, nor do I have many influential contacts left."

Mehmet nodded, as though he expected this reaction. "Okay, I studied in London. I've seen in the faces of people I knew, prejudice against men with, as they said, 'towels on their heads and fancy face furniture'; I saw they were disgusted by the screaming into the press cameras, the waving of the leader's pictures and the flag burning of that week's enemy, of whom there seems to be an ever evolving list."

David dipped his head in agreement. "Sure, it all plays to people's prejudices, but I know there's something stirring here, something that needs to be supported. It's in the air and it makes it smell fresher."

Mehmet hesitated, uncertain that David had leapt ahead of him or had perhaps agreed with him.

David continued. "You know as well as I, that as yet there's no real news here. Religious leaders and politicians using blood curdling imprecations means little now; we've heard it all before. You saw it yourself. The Western audiences are tired of being blamed, as true as it may be that we, or at least our governments and corporations are partly responsible. But blame and guilt have a sell-by date and now people no longer want to know. They're worn down by the endless wars, murderous tribal spats between Irish Catholics and Irish Protestants, Tutsi and Hutu, Sunni and Shiite, Walloons and Flemish, Basques and Spaniards, Turks and Kurds, war lords and villagers, Muslims of the north and Christians of the south and on and on, night after night, news bulletin after news bulletin. Your people have become the 'other', strange inhuman beings of no interest." David hovered his still oily hand over his heart. "It is not my belief but that's how…"

Mehmet butted in. "Okay, it's true that I can only offer lank haired Western aid workers, thin men wearing sandals and sometimes a nun to be interviewed who have any concern or idea about what's going on here."

David appreciated Mehmet's candour. "Sure, that'll have the media eating out of our hands, lapping it up. More Empathy-Sans-Frontiers." He paused and peered through the muzzy dimness of the café's cool gloom and into the young man's thoughts. "Anyway I came here to answer questions for myself, not to document another revolution."

Mehmet, discouraged, went silent and melted into a heap like a beaten child.

David returned his attention to his cold lamb-pot with its now congealed fat.

At last Mehmet quietly spoke, as if from miles away. "Even if you have little success in placing stories, any contribution on your part will help my friends - members of the underground - to feel they're not alone. This is important."

David gave up on his lamb. He studied Mehmet as he reflected. 'So much for my retirement, for running away from memories, for being able to concentrate on the last few questions I wish to answer about the human plague.'

As David mused, Mehmet ordered a Turkish coffee. He sipped it, again looked around and leant forward with a melodramatic gesture of secretive complicity but abruptly stopped as the café door banged open behind him and footsteps echoed against the plaster walls.

Two men entered the café and sat halfway between David's table and the bar. One man un-rumpled a newspaper to the sports page as the other ordered two cups of chai from the grumpy owner.

Mehmet and David both understood. If they were what people called 'crows', two of the thousands of local spies, it could be a coincidence. or it could be that Mehmet had been followed. But now, trapped at the back of the café, they could only carry on, as if in a business meeting. Mehmet, whose eyes skittered from place to place and began to perspire as if fevered, leant closer and spoke even quieter.

"Our rulers rely upon most people's willingness to accommodate themselves to the terror around them by living in a moral vacuum. It's not that our people are evil or cowardly but just that their lives are so hard they cannot see beyond the borders of their own pain." He sipped again and continued. "Ultimately this eats away at their souls and their bodies."

He savoured the final dregs of coffee, letting David absorb his words. "Your friend," he tapped Suleiman's note, "told me that hypertension, heart disease, cancers - these are the children of stress which take their toll on many of his patients. It's the stress of not being able to forget and pretending to be blind to the fate of their neighbours."

Mehmet waited for a reaction. "Whoever knows if they're safe?" He nodded his head slightly towards the two men. "Are you and I safe now?"

David dipped his head to assure Mehmet that he was listening and understanding.

Mehmet wondered if this understated reaction was the normal, cold calculation of a man who had witnessed too much. He decided that for the moment it did not matter. What counted was to enlist David's loyalty. Anyway, Mehmet worked day by day with actors and was pleased to provide a performance of his own. "It's ironic but our leader's madness confirms for me the people's goodness and it gives me faith."

David continued to watch him but he too became distracted by the leather coated men sitting quietly, without conversation, as if listening to either the Turkish soap opera or to what they could hear of his and Mehmet's conversation.

Mehmet, shifting on his chair, looked closely at David. "My comrade, my friend, do you think this is crazy, somehow dirty?"

David placed his clean left hand on Mehmet's fist, shook his head from side to side and spoke quietly. "I've known many people in many places who found their moral compass in odd ways but the important thing was to realize its value, no matter the route to discover it. And anyway, I'm a photographer because I want to be a witness, not a judge." He concentrated on Mehmet's thick, sensuous lips. "You're a director; you know about process."

Mehmet was surprised but pleased at David's response. He slowly shook his head in agreement but looked away, disguising his turmoil.

David went on. "All of us are fleeing from danger while rushing towards tragedy. Because of this mess we're in, everyone is suffering. In that, you're not alone."

Mehmet was certain about his belief in the need for change, but less clear of his analysis, which was more a complaint than a theory. He spoke, looking into his coffee cup. "They're destroying…", he hesitated, his face drawn and concentrated, "…they're ruining all of our lives." He looked up. "How do we let them get away with this?"

David smiled as much as he ever did. "Think about it. Your corrupt establishment is like our political right; so staunch in their defence of greed and their sociopathic kleptomania, only a long, slow and terrible demise lies ahead."

Mehmet's bitterness brazed his words. "Yes, and as always, the innocent suffer most."

"Hmmmm," hummed David. "Afterwards the few who remain will call this period 'the failed age of Homo Sapiens', that moment when one particularly flawed species had been dominant. It lasted roughly twenty thousand years and fell, like all civilizations, into the tide of arrogance and ignorance."

"And avarice", added Mehmet.

"And avarice", agreed David.

Behind them the two men stirred.

Mehmet appeared desperate to David, perhaps because he was genuinely confused or perhaps because he was so conscious of the men behind him. He dropped his head into his hands and, looking blankly at the table, he hoarsely asked, "What allows us to do this to each other?"

"Age has not made me particularly wise. I accept that what others are capable of, so am I. Love, kindness, stupidity, cruelty are in the vocabulary of possible actions we all share. To my mind, the evil parts are a consequence of some kind of human plague. Before I die, I want to understand it."

As Mehmet's eyes raised towards David he continued, "Globalization has intensified our preoccupation with materialism.

Wealth has become a narcotic. Now, in this horrible sleep, all of our irrational shades are mustered."

David paused as the man with his back to them, turned his attention from his newspaper to glance over his shoulder at Mehmet and him. David noticed his dead eyes and looked back towards Mehmet. "In short, the avarice and all the rest of it, is simply human. I think it is an expression of our inability to become conscious of who rather than what we are." He paused, saw the man had looked away, and continued. "No wonder they hate the intellectuals and the artists."

Mehmet was filled to the roots of his short-cropped hair with disgust for the corrupt officials, the twisted and hollowed out ruling generals and party members. In his anger at the recent arrests and disappearances, he grasped David's arm and seethed, "The politicians and the military leaders know, above all other things, how to mobilize fear and stupidity".

The crows pushed back their chairs and rose. Both turned and looked at David and Mehmet as if filing their features in an insidious charnel house vault. With neither a word nor sign of intention, they left without paying.

David, convinced he must offer some aid, imagined that with his camera he could try again to understand the dimensions of the human condition. Little did he think that instead of observing he would become his own subject.

Later, when David returned to his flat above the café, for a moment he leaned against the French window, catching the timid breeze. To his surprise he saw Mehmet in conversation with the two men. There seemed to be neither friendship nor hostility between them.

David shook off the memory of that remote meeting, placed the print on the box and shuffled to the window, as if repeating the earlier event, and looked down on the increasingly crowded street. Still no sign of the secret police filtering along the street, casually leaning against walls pretending to read newspapers.

He recalled an aphorism told to him by a Russian friend. "Under Capitalism man exploits man; under Communism it's just the opposite." Was this humanities fate everywhere; was this simply how we are? Was this the pox upon us, the thing that gave birth to our plague?'

His eyes scanned slowly upwards and outwards, taking in the crumbling plaster, the faded paint of old signs and then the purple crags of distant cliffs and the ever-thickening morning sunlight. Between the edge of the town and the hazy mountains, date palms glistened in the breeze.

David returned to the box. Slowly his eyes caressed the luminous forms of the second photograph. This one was a problem; its stillness and quality of light reminded him of things past.

•••

On a summer's day, still living in his parent's first house in the vast American Midwest, on the eastern edge of the Great Plains, his father and brother were painting round rocks that separated the border of the property from the rutted street running along the side of it. Beyond lay a grid of other houses, pine and elm trees, strangers, barking dogs and rattling pick-ups.

David stood near his father, mesmerized by the broad black bristled brush as it spread thick layers of white paint across the smooth grey stone. David precariously leaned over the paint bucket as the brush was dipped into it, penetrating the creamy surface and emerging with dollops of shiny liquid leaking into thin triangles as they drizzled onto the undulating surface below.

"Move away!" snapped his father to David. The five-year-old looked from the perfect world of the paint bucket up towards his father's irritated face. He stood still, hands by his sides, not knowing what to make of the tone of voice. "Go on, get into the house."

David was confused. What had he done? His eyes instinctively darted towards his older brother who was happily painting the next rock along. Joel stood up and walked to the bucket carrying his now dry brush like a weapon in front of him, bristles pointing at David. As he neared the bucket, he knocked into David and hissed, "Go away".

Their father seemed not to notice this latest in the endless pinching, slapping and bumping assaults by his brother and carried on painting his smooth grey stone. The viscous white shining paint oozed across the surface and dribbled onto the grass patch below. Tiny flecks spattered onto his father's trousers. "God almighty, what next?" His father again glared at David. "I said get into the house."

"But Joey's helping; why can't I?"

His father abruptly dumped his brush into the bucket and with his left hand grabbed David by the arm and shoved him towards the house. "Do as I tell you."

David stared at his father. Something stirred in him. His stomach rippled. He grasped his chest as pain fluttered across it. He tried to object but chocked as his throat constricted.

His father's eyes narrowed. Joel snorted a triumphant laugh.

Tears welled, diffusing the sharp light of midday behind a mist of mucous and histamines. The white of the stones and the high summer clouds turned purple as blood filtered the backs of his eyes.

David's fragile world of childhood assumptions seeped out of him in the tears rolling down his cheeks. He had known since the bloodied nose that his brother was something to be wary of, but now the man, his father, with whom he had but the slightest contact, had turned on him, rejected him. He too had assaulted David. His hand had grabbed him, shoved him just as Joel continually hurt him.

David did not need being told again. 'He loves Joey more. Papa and Joey are two of a kind? Maybe papa loves God more than me? Maybe papa, who's close to God, knows I'm bad?'

Day after day throughout his childhood, David experienced the same course of events. His father returned from work in the early evening, a silent brooding man entering the front door. Although David might be in the room, his father ignored him. He went to his bedroom, changed from his suit to a pair of slacks and a short-

sleeved shirt, he emerged, sat in 'his chair', took out 'his Bible' and the lessons sent to him once a month from the Christian Scientists, and then he read, disregarding his youngest son's presence. David snuck looks at this father; sometimes he would stir, hoping to gain his father's attention. At times he would ask his father if he would like a cup of coffee. Always his father carried on reading and with hardly a nod of his head, he would indicate he wanted to be left in silence. It was like living with a shell, a rumour of a man, a poor caricature of a father. David grew wary of God and religious people.

On that summer's day, as David walked away from the glistening white stones, he knew his brother's eyes were on his back, smiling at this turn of events and that his father, as always, had all but forgotten his presence. In that short walk thought the midday heat to the screen door, his breath tightened, and his temperature rose further. Looking down, he saw edges that divided each from the other and from the invading weeds and grasses around them. David stopped and stared at the way the pavement was distinct from the first wooden step up to the screen-door.

Behind him he heard his father's raised voice. "Go on, get inside."

Several weeks later, his mother put David and Joel in the back of the car and drove to the furniture shop where their father worked. It was late afternoon. She explained that she needed the car that day so they were picking their father up and would return home for an early supper.

David was in awe of the big shop filled with dining tables, what seemed like hundreds of couches in all sorts of colours, wooden and stuffed chairs, even desks with leather tops and stamped gold trim and a field of beds. His father, in the distance, approached a young couple looking at one of the beds.

"You two jes sit here and be good", said his mother.

She moved away to speak with her husband's boss. Joel skipped off and David, sitting on his own, looked around at the cavern and began to feel chilled and alone. He slowly stood up and unnoticed, walked near to where his father was.

"Can't do better than this, the new Sealy Posturepedic mattress. Best thing ever. Yer body just fits into it yet it gives total support. Yes sir, jes like the advertising says."

David was amazed. He had never heard his father speak so many words in so short a time. Was he dreaming? Was this really happening? Was it really his father?

"Well, dunno", said the young man. "It's a little above our budget."

"Now you don't worry 'bout that," said his father with a broad grin. "We got ways to help you out. I mean, sometimes you gotta think 'bout what's right for you and yer misses here that's about yer health. And yes sir, health comes from good food and good sleep."

"Well, I don' know; still more than we wanna spend."

"What kinda price would make it work fer yer budget. You jes tell me and I'll go talk personally to the boss and see how far he kin bend the branch."

His father did not get the sale. They drove home in silence.

Later, with the low sun still streaming into the breakfast-nook with its round table, covered with a yellow oilcloth, David sat across from Joey, between his mother and father.

In front of him was a plate of mashed potatoes, frozen peas and a piece of flat blackened cow's liver. David had tasted it; he disliked it. He looked up at his father.

"Papa, mama taught me to tie my shoes today. I can do it, can't I mama?"

"Yep, good too, now eat yer food", said his mother.

"So what", said Joey, "Any stupid kid kin tie his shoes".

"Papa, do you think it's good, I can tie my shoes?"

His father looked up at him, glanced at his plate and said, "Eat yer liver".

David continued to eat everything but the liver. He thought the smell was horrible.

Joel said, "Look, he ain't eating his meat like I am".

His father watched David for a moment.

David felt his eyes glaring at him.

"What did I jes tell you? Eat yer liver."

"Papa, I can't. It makes me feel funny."

"You don't have a right. That's God's food. It's an offering and you can't refuse it."

"Yea', said Joel, "he don'care about all the starving in India."

David looked down at the piece of overcooked organ on his plate. He had no idea it was the messenger of so many things. But the idea of eating it, chewing the tough dry stuff, taking in the smell of steel and blood, disgusted him. He felt his skin was flushing and perspiration beads were gathering on his forehead. His fingers grasped the table edges to steady him.

"You jes quit messing around and eat", ordered his father in a raised voice.

"He's stupid, can't even tie his shoes until now and won't eat God's food."

His mother snapped at Joel, "You keep outta this." She turned to David. "Go on, take a mouth full, it's good fer ya."

Through the tears forming in his eyes, he looked up at her. He knew she did not mean him any harm but he felt trapped and queasy. "Mama, I can't."

At that, his father leant across, stabbed a piece of liver and thrust it at David. "Eat it. Don't make me wait fer you."

David was snared; he had no choice. He looked up at his father and as tears ran down his face, he took the piece of organ into his mouth. He chewed and almost gagged and then stored the pulverized mash in his cheeks.

"Look at Davy, he's like a stupid rabbit."

"Swallow," yelled his father.

"But papa…". He swallowed. Something fulminated in his gut and rushed up through his stomach into his throat. Violently he vomited onto his plate.

Joel laughed. His father threw himself from the table shouting at his wife, "You take care of the brat." His mother rushed for cloths and a sponge.

David remembered a scene from a Western film he had recently seen where a wild horse, which had been rounded up and forced into a corral, waited until all the cowboys were gone, and then he ran the full length of his log prison and leapt over the bars to freedom. He gagged again and was sent to bed.

CHAPTER 3

David whistled through his teeth and placed the print face down on the back of the first one. Here he was, in a land of airless summers, broken only by the annual sirocco and the occasional dust storm, and here he was, with not only the seasons and the years, but now the minutes flying by.

He had looked at two pictures and was none the closer to those prints of his beautiful lover. His need for order made him resist clawing down into the neatly stacked file to find the images of her. Picture by picture he would reclaim a lost life and finally savor his time with her.

The next photograph was luminous. He had travelled with a friend to New York when he was seventeen. On the way they veered into Montréal where he photographed the elaborate Notre Dame Basilica. The gold altar, smothered in bas relief and fully rounded sculptures like a wedding cake designed by a deranged baker, was set at the eastern end of the long aisles whose thick stone walls were punctured with glowing stained-glass windows. As he walked into this extraordinary place, unlike anywhere he had ever been, he began to understand how its radiance could overwhelm those wishing to believe. The light tiptoed across the space and folded itself around every sculpted detail. All of it glowed as if from an inner illumination. He stood rooted to where he was; he gazed, silently wondering about people succumbing to the supernatural. Slowly he raised his light meter, took a reading and exposed one frame.

'This is not God, this is light I am photographing. This is beauty used to confuse people, to overwhelm them and force them to submit. There's something wrong here. I hate the people who do this. And why is the space so dark. Why don't they let the sun in? Why is it so cold here? It's like death. All those agonized Christ paintings; they celebrate death.'

He placed the beautiful orange and golden print down. 'Men created that space and the sculpted extravaganza as they created myths of power, mysteries and mayhem. Even then I felt rising impatience with human foolishness.'

He snorted a half laugh. 'I've paid for turning my back on men's fortified mystical establishment.' He nodded to himself. 'I've paid for turning my back on men's constructed myths. I said "no" to the newspaper publishers and "no" to the broadcasters, I will not conform to your view of whom others are and who I should be.'

David's eyes opened wide and then narrowed. He leaned forward, allowing his forehead to gently caress the back of the third print. 'Are my beliefs as simple and silly to die for as those of these local rulers?' Aloud he complained to his prints, "Who cares what happens to me? Acch", he scoffed, "I'm feeling sorry for myself."

He lifted his head. 'In the scale of things, in history's near infinity of unrecorded events, if I sacrifice myself for Mehmet's and Suleiman's cause, will it mean anything? Will it contribute to the wellbeing of others? Is my suicide not a meaningless action flaunted against history by an insignificant soul?

'My dreams of childhood demanded that I called upon myself to do worthwhile things. My dreams instructed me to help change other's lives for the better. And yet here I am, a man barred from the corridors of fame and position and therefore influence because I rejected the status quo. Had I been less insistent on doing things my way, living up to my needs, perhaps I could have done more, helped more people.'

He rocked back and forth. 'Am I now, at this murderous moment, going to be overwhelmed by my long held moral stance; am I about to capitulate to the local rulers or to my ideologically motivated friends? And is this not all nonsense?'

He stroked the back of the print. 'I was convinced that my true interests lay outside of myself in the world of others who were mostly powerless men and women. I recorded their world. I believed that good and evil, oil and fire, rulers and ruled were all of a oneness; not a sameness but a part of a world of material, social and psychological states which were tied together in a horrible dance, one which should have been a joyful dream but was indisputably a living nightmare.'

He locked the fingers of both hands together. 'Naturally I attempted to integrate diverse elements, forms, actions and inner states exhibited in front of my lens into a rational, balanced, well-composed image. The act of making sense out of chaos, creating order out of confusion and beauty out of ugliness assured me that if I could do this, so could others, and if others could then perhaps there was hope that love and beauty could be created in the world. My caring and rationality were testaments to what being human could mean.'

His fingers relaxed and he withdrew them from the lock he had constructed between them and he smiled. He was, a friend had told him 'a mensch', a person filled with humanity. David shook his head slowly from side to side. He whispered, "Who knows anything?"

The glass of water glinted in the light, its surface undulated to David's slight movements. It gave him a moment of pleasure.

He whispered, "So innocent". He stared at the next image.

'I looked for truth. I was self-critical. I viewed what I captured, I listened to what the frozen, two-dimensional world could tell me. Did the image express the moment's truth, did it reveal the rationality I sought, did it expose emotional reality? Was it representative of what had actually happened or was it a romanticized, humanistic overlay of my imagination? And if so, was I listening only to my own song.

Was it not true that the frozen moments were simply matters of fact and not of interpretation? Brutality could be explained by the minutia of current political tensions but in the end, it was always and only another moment of Cain striking Abel, another manifest act of the human plague.'

David's breathing shortened and came in shallow gasps as though panic was beginning to inhabit his body. His forehead beaded with sweat. 'All my fancy words, ideas, notions were simply an expression of my need to elude the conclusion that I and the rest of humanity are trapped in a limitless horror.'

He glanced at his watch. The minutes seemed to be flying and dragging by at the same time. He gently tapped the back of the print again. 'My dialogue with my pictures invariably led me to ask how I might cauterize my own haemorrhaging remorse.' He jerked his head up and seethed, "Love and bile, bile and lust, lust and remorse, remorse and love. A circuit surrounded by chimera silently watching my private dance towards death.

He glanced at his watch. 'Yes, the minutes are seeping away.'

At that very moment, somewhere in the scalding downtown of the increasingly hot morning, a middle ranking party functionary stamped an arrest warrant and handed it to the waiting security service Sergeant. The pale-eyed functionary looked up at the thin-faced officer. "Well, what are you staring at? Take it to your Colonel." The functionary sensed something: dumbness, stubbornness or worse, rebelliousness. He snapped: "Immediately!"

On his way to the Colonel's office, which was at the far side of the stone paved courtyard, the lanky Sergeant diverted around the dented, unmarked and supposedly anonymous dark brown cars and the plain brown lorries, which every intimidated citizen recognized as the vehicles of the most feared of the security services. Once hidden from view, he ducked into the gaping dark armoury behind the cars. At that time of the morning it was empty and cool. Quickly he pulled out his forbidden private mobile phone, usually hidden in his padded shirt's inner pocket, and tapped in a number. He waited for the receiving message to end. His eyes darted around. He was still safe. Finally, the bleep.

He croaked: "Red Dragon", and disconnected. He redialled, e-mailed two jpegs and quickly disconnected again. The lean Sergeant looked into the darkness, wiped the call record and the jpegs, buried his phone deep into his clothing and continued to the Colonel's office carrying in his hand a death warrant for a man who was supposedly a stranger to him.

•••

When David was eight, he was nominated as a gifted child by his elementary school's art teacher to attend Saturday drawing and painting classes at the city's Museum. Although he was fascinated by drawing and painting he did not understand why he had been chosen.

"Mama, why me?"

She put her cigarette down and looked at him thoughtfully for a moment, seeing something she had not previously recognized in her youngest son. She leaned forward and whispered, "You ask too many questions."

He didn't understand. "Is one question too many questions, mama?"

"Don't be a smart-aleck or I won't take you."

His mother was present but always distracted. She spoke three times a day to her cousin who lived around the corner and several times a week to her brother, who lived around another corner. Every Tuesday she would go out to lunch with the 'girls', a mysterious group of people David only knew as part of the family mythology. His mother seemed impatient, ill at ease as if she needed to go off and do something, especially when David approached her with a request or a question. Like many children of his age, his head was often full of 'why this, 'and 'how does that work'. As his mother probably had children because it was what was expected rather then what she wanted, she had little interest in either of her sons.

David looked at her with his unflinching grey eyes and asked, "Mama, what's a smart-aleck?" She kissed him on the forehead and told him to go and play.

He walked away and sat in his room with his toy soldiers. He knew their fates were easier to understand than his own within his family. He could construct the story of the day: who were the good and bad guys, around which table leg, pile of books or egg carton boat would they fight and die, who would lose and who would be the hero.

Those encounters followed his invented script until his brother invaded David's private battlefield, often with a friend.

"Hey, what'ja doing little piss-face? Playing toy soldiers?"

Joel turned to his skinny friend Norman. "Look, all on his own. Ain't got friends." He looked down at David. "Ain't got friends huh?"

There was nothing to say. There was never a response that made sense to his brother. Sometimes, although rarely, if David stayed silent, the worst would not happen. But that day, he could see the glint.

Norman pretended to be interested and, using the tip of his gym shoe, he knocked over soldiers one by one and laughed. "See Davy, I kin play too. Look, I kin kill 'em good."

"Don't", shouted David. "Don't. Leave them alone."

"Oh look, he's a cry baby." Joel tuned his attention back to David. "Gonna cry, huh, gonna?" With that, Joel swept his foot across the floor, knocking over and throwing David's carefully constructed set piece into disarray. He laughed. "See, me and Normy's playing too." He moved quickly across the room to where David was squatting against his bed. Joel leant down and grabbed his brother by his short hair and pushed his head back, forcing David to look at him. "You like us playing with ya? Huh? Tell me. Ya like it."

David pushed his brother's hand away and shouted, "Leave me alone. Get out and leave me alone."

Joel stood up and turned to Norman. "See, I told ya, he's nasty like this all the time."

David closely watched his brother, certain of what was coming.

"Hey, Normy, ya think he needs a lesson in respect?"

"Let's go Joey, fore someone comes."

"Sure." Joel laughed, turned towards David and smacked him with the flat of his hand across the side of his head. He walked away, using his feet to kick all of the toy soldiers around the room.

David sat amongst the ruins, tears running along his cheeks, filled with rage, admonished by his inability to defend himself or his armies and then, once he had calmed down, he patiently reconstructed the day's script.

To his surprise, his mother did allow him to go to the special art classes and offered to take him. He accepted this as a matter of course. He guessed mothers do that sort of thing after all. For once she did not complain or chastise him. He thought that she may even have been proud that he had been selected. He heard her on the phone with her cousin, almost bragging about him, although she never directly told David him what she thought.

On the first day of the special Saturday art classes, his mother parked by the curb of the Museum's main entrance and told David to go up the steps and through the big brass door.

He climbed the grey stone steps but had to wait for an adult to pull open the heavy door. His mother waited in the car, lighting up another cigarette.

As David entered the museum, he stopped dead still and looked up. Slowly he allowed his eyes to take in the immensity of the foyer, the tall, thick marble columns and the gold covered metal work with all of its curls and twists. His eyes were as large as plates and he smiled, almost giggled. He had never seen anything so grand except for the few times he had attended weekend kindergarten religious classes in the huge grey stone Jewish temple in the downtown area - and in the film Ben Hur.

Once all of the children arrived, a man and a woman teacher, who had been speaking with a few interested parents, asked the fifteen kids to sit in a row on the shiny floor.

The chill of the floor made David uncomfortable, but his fingers caressed it. He leaned close to it. Marble, a deep burnt red, crossed with a million fine green and black veins. A whole world. The mysteries of rock and earth, something that had been buried in a mountain, now so finely polished that it reflected every light bulb in the ceiling and every flare of sunshine pouring through the windows high above, glinting off the red surface and into his grey eyes. He touched the floor again and was amazed at how smooth and cool it was and he wondered if it had once been alive.

He suddenly realized that he was being spoken to. "Yes, you", the large lady teacher said, "Please put your arms behind your back".

He was embarrassed. He didn't know the other children and had no idea if they knew each other. He understood that his preoccupation with the intriguing marble floor meant that he missed the instructions. The large lady teacher asked the children to close their eyes and to promise not to peek.

David did so but felt wary, isolated and the cold of the marble floor was seeping through his trousers and bothering him. But he kept his eyes closed and listened. It was a matter of bravery and honour.

There was a shuffling behind him and something pliable but wiry was put into his hands. It was as large as a kitchen sponge, bendable and formed from what seemed like hundreds of separate coils of something he could not identify. It was odd but not unpleasant. He fought the temptation to open his eyes, to jump up and stop this foolish game but he kept still. Games, he hated games and puzzles; a waste of time guessing when he could be learning.

A few moments later the man teacher said that the kids should carefully describe to themselves what they were holding. "Try to understand its shape, how wide and long and thick or thin it is and to think about what it's made of and what colour it might be."

"Even to guess", said the big lady, "what it is".

And then the thing was collected and large pieces of paper and thick crayons were passed to each of the children. What wonderful crayons they were; fat and densely coloured with pointed wax heads. He could almost feel the tip peeling away as he imagined drawing a series of intersecting lines with the wax leaving welts of purple or red trails across the innocent plane.

He stared at the sheet of spotless white paper lying against the deep red floor but was overcome by shafts of sunlight falling though the high arched clerestory windows that ran across the long front of the foyer. The light was magnificent, another mystery. It was like honey pouring from the morning sun. Spoonsful kissed the opposite walls where they met the marble floor. The honey rolled onto it, glowing out of each golden pool. David sat there, cold bottom, scratchy hands, wheezing slightly, wondering about why light was so beautiful.

"Yes you", said the same large lady loudly. David looked up and realized he had wandered again. "Draw what you felt, please."

He glanced around quickly and understood that he had been distracted by the light while the others were seriously attending to the task, some bent double, others on their knees with their faces close to the big sheet of white paper, drawing tiny images in the corners of the lonely white plane.

For his lack of attention or rather his preoccupation with marble and light he was still fascinated by the paper, the coloured crayons and the glimmering golden pools. This correspondence between experiencing something with one sense and understanding it with his feelings opened a world of perception to him. It was as though he had just learned to read the world in another way and especially in terms of darkness and light. He excitedly threw himself forward and drew long orange rectangles across the white sheet, filled the spaces in between with vertical grey rectangles and up near the top he attempted to create the perspective of the arched windows and the sky beyond.

The lady teacher watched for a moment. "What are you doing?"

He looked up at her. "Drawing what I felt."

She was stymied. The man teacher came over and looked at what David was doing. David sensed he was going to be in trouble again.

The man teacher squatted down and studied the drawing more closely. He glanced up, looked at the windows and the pools of light and back at David's drawing, but now a generous smile spread across his face. Gently he asked, "Why are you drawing the foyer?"

David looked up at him. "I'm drawing the light."

The man teacher looked up at the woman who was still perplexed and again looked at David. "Why are you drawing the light?"

David sat back and looked from the man to the woman and back to the man. "Am I doing something wrong again?"

The man teacher smiled. "No, we're interested. It's different from what everyone else is doing and, and a lot bolder too."

David looked to his left and right, seeing those around him were still drawing tiny squares filled with squiggles like a messy plate of spaghetti and still only in the corners of the large pieces of paper. He looked back at the man teacher. "I thought the light and the shadows were pretty. They made me feel something inside and the lady asked us to draw what we felt."

The man teacher could not contain his delight. "That's just great, what you are doing and how you understood Miss Winterton's request. Good for you son and I hope you come back next week. My name is Mr Whipple." Mr Whipple looked up at the smiling Miss Winterton. "You agree, don't you?"

Later the children were taken on a tour of a few galleries. Most of what David saw was overwhelming, alien and incomprehensible to him; redolent with a world of royalty, sallow Mary's holding the baby Jesus with a glow around its head and Christ suffering or maybe dead on a big wooden cross. But then there was a painting of an old man holding a large, leather bound book as though it meant the whole of life to him. David felt the man was staring right at him.

He looked closely at the shadow on the background behind the illuminated side of the old man's face and at the light on the background behind the shadowed side of his face. David sensed that this trick of light made the man appear solid, as if real and David felt an overwhelming sense of sadness in the man. He also thought about how valuable the book seemed to the man. This was not a painting, it was real like a man or maybe like a photograph he might see in Life Magazine. Something was alive as though blood was moving in the veins beneath the paint. He loitered behind the others, in front of this painting, feeling that he knew something about the man, as though he was or could be his unknown grandfather. He looked at the name of the painter. It was a very difficult word but never would he forget the 'Rembrandt'.

When he saw an opportunity, he approached Mr Whipple. "Why does the man hold onto the book as if it's real important to him?"

Mr Whipple squatted down and looked at David, studying something in his face. Mr Whipple looked at David's name badge. "Well David, the book represents knowledge and wisdom, something the man values more than most things and so he holds onto it as if it were his grandson."

David was moved by the explanation and by the patience Mr Whipple showed in so carefully answering him. "Thank you, I think I understand." David turned to walk away but Mr Whipple gently took him by the shoulder and turned David back to face him. "You're Jewish, aren't you?"

"I think so but nobody talks about it in my family."

Mr Whipple was taken aback for a second. David could see the confusion in his eyes. "David, next week when you come back, look at that painting again. You will see it is of an old Jewish scholar. I thought that might interest you."

Excitedly David blurted, "Mr Whipple, I thought he could be my grandfather."

"Almost, David, almost."

"I saw pictures of people burning books. It was bad, I mean I felt that was wrong. Is that why the grandfather holds the book, because others will take it from him and burn it?"

"That's a long history but basically, yes you're right." Mr Whipple rocked slightly away from David and looked at him as though appraising something. "That's really impressive."

The painting evoked in David the feeling that he was a part of some mysterious history and perhaps his isolation from his family and the children in this class and in his school was a sign of his belonging elsewhere. Maybe it was all a mistake that he lived with these people who either hated him or didn't care about him. Maybe he had been mixed up in the hospital or he had been adopted by mistake.

That night he lay in bed and cried silently to himself, certain that his living in this house was a confusion. But it frightened him. Where did he belong, whose child was he, where were his real parents and brothers and sisters and why did he not have a grandfather who loved books?

During the next Saturday class, the children were taken into a high narrow room that had a painted story, which continued from wall to wall. There were pictures of plants growing around the doors, round brown-faced men and women growing glowing vegetables. There were swirling clouds and baskets of fruits, steel beams and a car factory assembly line with black and brown and white men hard at work. Richly dressed tourists gawked at the workers and in front of them all was an evil, thin-faced priest who seemed to be leading his wealthy flock in disdaining the workers, looking at them like monkeys in the zoo.

David thought that the whole world was in that huge mural and the walls were vibrating with life flowing out of the earth and through the winding plants into the fruits and to the farmers and workers. David sensed that everything was connected from the soil to the roots of plants to the weather which nurtured them; from the farmers who harvested the food to the women who pounded the maize to bake the bread; from the women's bread to the miners who dug the minerals hauled to distant ports; from the sailors on the ships that transported the minerals to the mills that coked the iron ore; from the men who pressed and punched the steel into cars that produced the owner's profits; to the priest and the wealthy who owned and disdained the workers. Everything had a meaning and everything was interrelated.

Mr Whipple explained that the famous revolutionary Mexican painter, Diego Rivera, had been commissioned to create the mural but once it was seen by local religious leaders and the powerful factory owner, Henry Ford, they demanded the painting be covered over. Mr Whipple said that the curator of the museum, to his lasting credit, refused to allow that to happen.

Afterwards David asked Mr Whipple what 'revolutionary' meant. Mr Whipple explained, "When bad people create a bad system in which workers are not free to express themselves or when the owners take so much for themselves that the workers can't feed their families, eventually people get so desperate and so angry that they fight against the system. That fight is called a 'revolution'. What the workers and students hope to do is change the bad system for a better one."

"Oh, that's what the American Revolution did?"

"David, do your parents answer your questions?"

David looked away. He bunched his shoulders up and crossed his arms.

"It's okay, you don't need to answer."

David instinctively reached for Mr Whipple's hand and held it. He looked up at him. "They don't like me to ask questions. My mama says I'm a smart-aleck."

"And your father?"

David looked at his feet and spoke quietly. "He never talks to me unless he's angry."

"David, I don't want to contradict you mother but you are not a smart-aleck; what you are, is very smart. You ask me as many questions as you wish. Okay?"

David smiled and said quietly, "Okay".

As David walked down the wide low steps of the museum at the end of that Saturday's class towards his mother's car, he knew his life had changed. His impressionable mind sensed that in his loneliness there was a consolation because he was convinced that somehow he was a part of something wonderful and transformative, something vital and special that he might participate in and this gave him renewed energy to learn and to experience this stuff called art, and it began to offer him an explanation as to why he seemed different to those around him.

CHAPTER 4

The Colonel, an obese man sitting behind a small desk, sucking on a sugar cube, didn't bother to look up when his Sergeant entered. The Colonel slurred, his words struggling around the melting lump held between his thick lips and his heavy tongue. "Another one?"

The Sergeant hesitated to answer.

The Colonel's eyes, ringed with swollen fatty tissue, slowly moved away from the report he was reading on his ancient computer to study the expression of his hesitant subordinate.

The Sergeant knew he must offer an explanation. "It's a foreigner sir, an American."

The Sergeant understood that a 'foreign' case could easily blow up in an officer's face, that handled badly and made public, it could very well have the officer made an example of in the European and American press. The military officer's corps and the higher-ups in the secret services had been mercilessly shredded in the show trials and disappearances of the previous two years. Those who survived were, for the moment, considered indispensable, had powerful allies or had been luckily ignored, as had been the Colonel. But this, a 'foreign' case, made it difficult for him to maintain his low profile. If for any reason it got out of hand, he would be condemned or if he handled it too easily, the political apparatchik would become suspicious. They would speculate that he had foreign contacts – that he was a spy; that the leader's enemies delivered the Colonel a sacrifice to help him up the security ladder. After all, all those years ago, he had been trained by the CIA.

As those fears struck both men like sharp sand in a windstorm, the Colonel realized he must step into the unknown with a tone of authority.

"Do you have political approval?"

The Sergeant dipped his head and held up the warrant with the functionary's pale grey stamp.

The Colonel nodded as he pressed his lips together. He knew it was probable that his office was bugged and that secret service agents, not unlike him but of some squad he knew nothing of, eating halva and drinking coffee in a damp basement not far away, were at the very moment listening to his every word.

"The stamp should be black as black ink can be, as black as night…as black as this spy's soul."

"Yes sir. The political officer's ink pad has had a lot of use in recent weeks."

The Colonel knew the Sergeant understood the weight of every word.

"Well then Sergeant, let us do our duty. When is the warrant active and where is he?"

The Sergeant and the Colonel walked side-by-side down the long sweltering corridor towards the entrance to the armoury. The Colonel held out a pack of Marlborough for the Sergeant.

The Sergeant took one; they stopped as he struck a match to light the Colonel's and his smoke. "Sir."

The Colonel looked into the Sergeant's taut face. "They want us to break him."

The Colonel nodded. "Is the fancy doctor on his way?"

"He'll meet us here but he won't arrive before eleven."

"And the suspect?"

"The political officer told me he's almost crippled from some back or leg problem. He's old. He can't run far but I've sent Private Majid to check his movements out."

By now Muhammad was baking the first of his stuffed flat breads and already the yeast and fennel perfume ribboned into David's French window. Suddenly in his powerful right hand, Muhammad had a long, serrated blade extending from a curved pearl handle. Grabbing a bunch of fresh coriander, he rapidly reduced it to into fine shreds. David mused that for a poor man, the knife must be his pride and joy and maybe his protector. Strange are the unexpected skills that people possess; perhaps no stranger than the unexpected vices they also harbour.

David paced for a moment, knowing time was running out, he hesitated and then reached for the next print. He stared at its soft amber forms, the out-of-focus tree and the jagged edge of the foreground rock.

'By the time I made this picture I was beginning to understand images were not "taken" but created. Framing, focus, filters, exposure, depth of field and printing created a presence, my presence in the image.' He struggled to remember. 'Around then I began to see the print before I released the shutter. Presence was what transformed a tree, a pond and a cloud into something beautiful. It was not a simple recording, it was not a mirror of the world; it was a refraction obtained through the prism of my being and through all I knew and felt about the world.'

David looked more closely at the details. 'Early on, around when I made this picture, I began to realize there's no objectivity, only a relative correlation between what I believed to be true and what was, in some measurable way, actual. Ptolemy's universe was replaced by Galileo's, was replaced by Newton's, was replaced by Einstein's.'

David laughed derisively. "Aren't we fools? Insistent that our relative truth is absolute. Infantile. Scared that the world is not as we define it and too often ready to kill to defend our faulty beliefs."

He nodded several times to himself. 'I knew that what I created under the guise of it being photographically accurate was in fact a distortion. I wondered, didn't I, what right I had to impose myself on the world?'

His eyes moved from the fixed world of the print to the changing world out of the window. 'Now in this foreign country, where I've come to observe a variety of the human plague, which I've not previously witnessed in detail, what have I really understood?'

He whispered, "So much for truth, so much for my ego imposing itself again".

David's eyes concentrated on the pale blue sky blanketed above the city's curved orange roof tiles. He felt the soft air on his face, closed his eyes and incanted.

"And we will remember we have been educated in the shadow of summer trees and once we could hear the footsteps of the wolves and once, we could smell the coming of rain and once we found dreams and sensual suggestions in the popping of golden figs as they ripened to fecundity under the light of the moon. And we will remember that it was when we joined together that we became safe, and when we learned to draw the bison and write a poem of love and sing a praise to our fellows that we became human and discovered that, for all our masculine convictions of a far off heavenly father, the symbol of the erected column meant nothing less than swaggering braggadocio until we crossed it with the horizontal slab, that symbol of the earth's horizon and all that lay beneath it … our soil, our roots, our verdant life-giving mother."

David felt the air on his forehead, smelled the odours of the day and heard the sounds of the street as he held onto the door more firmly. For a moment Mehmet's face intruded his reverie; his temper flared and opening his eyes wide, he looked into the bright southern desert beyond the town to scour the image from his retina.

"Open to me your wound, mother, let me plant my seed mother, give me sustenance mother and wipe away my boyish tears…I no longer want to be a ship upon a bolting ocean or a shipwreck wasting in the waves; I no longer want to be a hunter in the dying forest searching for a lonely prey; I no longer want to walk again and again to my death alone; I no longer want to dominate, to eliminate, to make war upon the other. And yes, you were right, I know now that there is no other but me and again and again I destroy myself, drown and pillage and burn and rape myself. Please mother, do not enfold me in your shroud just yet but show me how to dig my fingers into you, to love and honour you, to nurture you as you have us; please mother, enfold me and teach me that my tears are of joy and celebration and as they feed the earth, we too can, year by year, grow and produce and reproduce without injury to you or ourselves."

With the door against his forehead and the breeze caressing his cheeks, as Mehmet's face intruded yet again, David stirred, his drawn cheeks reddening with anger. He gasped, "I've been set up."

"Please mother, give me peace. When I listen, I hear that we, the men are the sons and daughters, perhaps the apprentices or death's gatekeepers. I will open my eyes and unblock my ears and tell you what I see. That is my job, that is what I promised I'd do."

Distractions. David did open his eyes, shook off these thoughts and wondered how long it would take for him to get to the pictures of her. Perhaps, if he timed it perfectly, he would have her image in his hand as the pills took effect, just as the brutes would break down the door, just as his mother would enfold him, just as his heart would stop.

•••

Eventually the asthma David had been born with got worse and with it he developed severe skin rashes. His mother reluctantly took him to an allergy specialist who prescribed a restricted diet, warned David he must not be tempted to eat the proscribed foods and told his mother he must have two injections a week.

"How long?" she asked.

The doctor was used to Midwestern abruptness. "We'll start off for six months and see how David reacts."

David was sitting on the doctor's bed, shirt off with his weeping inner elbows and neck rashes exposed. He watched his mother's calculating face as he felt the heat building up in his skin and the prickling begin in the open sores.

His mother demanded, "How much?"

"They'll be eight dollars an injection."

His mother blanched. "But that's..."

David watched the two of them.

She repeated, "That's..." She feared to think what her husband would say.

David calculated, waited for his mother's response and then offered, with a shocked quaver, "But mama, that's three hundred and eighty-four dollars." He was overwhelmed by the size of the number.

She threw him a look and retorted, "I know how much it is".

David realized he had embarrassed her. He looked down at his feet.

The doctor and his mother were silent.

David spoke quietly. "Mama, I don't want these shots. I'll stop scratching."

His mother looked at him with an expression he did not understand.

"I promise, I can stop and I won't eat any of the bad food. You won't have to worry. I won't need the shots."

"Davy, you know how you like chocolate and ketchup."

"I can do it, really."

The doctor turned to David and spoke quietly to him. "David, I can see you're a smart boy and I believe you'll do all you can not to break the diet but the injections are needed because they help your body to build an immunity against the things it's sensitive to. The diet stops you from taking in things you shouldn't eat but on its own it won't cure you."

His mother said, "Davy, if the doctor here says you need'em, you need'em. Don't you worry, we'll work it out." She looked up at the long, pockmarked face of the doctor. Memories of the Second World War were written into his flesh. "It never ends does it?" she murmured.

The doctor smiled slightly. "I'll talk with my partners and figure something out. You know, a package deal."

"Oh God," his mother whispered, "We always got one foot in the grave."

Tears ran down David's cheeks.

The doctor looked at him and then turned to his mother. "Is everything okay at home? Does David get on with his brother and you know, are things, well, are they okay?"

"Sure", snapped his mother, "we're a family".

The injections had a minimal affect. The rashes created angry, itching dry skin which, when scratched would weep. All too often not scratching was impossible. The itching drove David to distraction and shortened his already short fuse. Learning self-control for the diet was simple, a matter of responsibility and willpower. But it was too great a challenge for the child to maintain an emotional equilibrium while dealing with the constant itching and pain.

Taunted by his brother who constantly called him a freak, he pictured himself in school as an outcast, a deformed, disease-ridden monster. He thought that he had become on the outside what his brother was on the inside. He felt alone and condemned.

His private hell developed all the more at each dinner when his father sat to his left at the head of the table, his brother to his right next to David, his mother at the opposite end from his father near the entrance to the kitchen, and his grandma, his father's mother, who had recently begun to live with them, sat across from the brothers.

Joel often moved his left hand stealthily under the table and when David least expected it, Joel would suddenly pinch his thigh near the top of his back-of-knee rash or scratch him with a torn fingernail.

That evening, Joel made a particularly deep rip. David startled and turned, glowering at Joel just as his mother placed the platter of dry, long over-cooked chicken on the table.

His father, as usual, in his storm of anger, raised his voice at David. "How many times I told you to behave yourself? If you can't sit still and be quiet, go to your room."

David looked down at the table and murmured "but..." and stopped. He knew that to tell on his brother was useless. No one saw the scratch, no one but his grandma would believe him. He was her favourite among the grandchildren and cousins. He often questioned her about her parents, where they lived, how they supported themselves. What was his long dead grandfather like and how did he treat his sons, including David's father. The story of how his father saw his own father die from a heart attack while witnessing a horse he owned drop dead in a race created tales in David's head about who he, David was, in the long strain of his family going back to darkest Europe...a place of pogroms, pillage and murders; a place he had heard where bad people put Jewish people into gas ovens or chased them down with swords and cut their heads off because the Jews were so hated. These were nightmarish rumours that sat heavily in David.

He suddenly looked from his grandma to his father. He studied his father's fleshy face with its short bristling moustache. 'Papa has grey eyes like mine. Why's he always so mad? Has he been sad since his own papa died? Maybe he's such a bad father because he lost his own papa when he was young.' David weighed this up along with his options.

Joel snuck another poke at David just as his father snarled, "Well?"

David was overcome by anger. He wished to have the strength to turn and slap his brother hard across his nasty face and to tell his father that he knew he didn't love him and that his brother was his favourite and that his father didn't even care that he was ill or that he did well in school.

His mother put some chicken on a plate, stretched across and placed it in front of her husband. "Harry, take your chicken and leave him be, he's probably itching." She turned to David. "You're itching aren't ya Davy?"

Joel chimed in, "He ain't, he's jes bad".

His mother placed some chicken in front of Joel. "You stay outta it. None of your business, wiseacre."

But David's father wasn't satisfied. He looked again at David. "Well"? he demanded, "what's it gonna be"?

His mother insisted, "Leave him alone Harry".

His father, without looking away said sharply, "You always defend him. He costs us all that money and for what? He doesn't get any better and he doesn't behave himself. I gotta work all hours and throw all the money away on this." He grabbed David's left arm, pushed up his long sleeve and exposed the raw rash. He looked up at his wife while shaking David's trapped arm towards her and snapped, "See, all that money and he keeps scratching anyway. It's just good money out the window after bad".

Joel looked up from his plate of food towards his mother, "See, I said, he's bad."

David yanked his arm away from his father with such violence he surprised both of them. He looked across at his grandma whose large dark loving eyes said to him that she knew, she understood but she remained silent. Hers was the silence not of fear but of diplomacy. He looked at his mother who had served his grandma and herself and had sat down. He looked back at his father. He felt guilty for having caused another row. He knew he could not revenge himself against his brother; he knew his father wanted something of David he could not offer. His arms and legs were itching and he felt overwhelmed with a kind of emptiness. The energy to resist, to revolt and protest seemed too great a demand at that moment. He felt weak and small and knew that retreat to within his borders was the best thing for him. His hunger was routed by his desire for the quiet of his room and the idea of a book in his hand filled with promise and splendour.

'I lost papa to a dead horse. None of his fault.'

He glanced at his father and could see only the same disapproval he always saw in his face. David pushed back the big wooden dining chair and stood up. "Okay papa, I'll go to my room." He walked away. He felt utterly satisfied that sacrificing supper for his dignity was right.

He climbed the stairs, went into the bathroom, washed, brushed his teeth, looked at his brother's blue toothbrush dangling next to his swaying red toothbrush, took it from the holder, gently rubbed it along the soap bar and placed it back where it usually hung in the chrome holder.

That night he had the same dream he had been having for months. Numbers flew towards him out of the darkness and rushed at his face. As the dream progressed, the numbers became larger and longer and zoomed with ever increasing speed and colour intensity towards his eyes.

Eventually he fell out of bed with a clunk. He laid on the floor whimpering, chilled, knowing if his mother came in he would be scolded. That night, fortunately his brother, who slept in a matching bed with a matching spread no further from him than four feet away from him, did not wake. David got up from the floor, looked down at his brother's face and wondered if he could actually hurt him. He wanted to slap him over and over across his face, but David could not imagine actually hitting someone. He shuddered with horror and confused, he got back into bed.

Under the sheet and blanket, even on that warm night, his skin crawled and he shivered. When the itching was beyond control, he fantasized that the doctor with the pock marked face would invent a medicine that would allow him to pull the outer layer of his skin off, as he had seen animals do, to cleanse him of all the pits and scratches and sticky weeping.

He lay awake seeing shards of light in the darkness. He tried to distract himself. He remembered walking head down, rain on his hair, looking for fragments of the moon in puddles. Fragments would provide a better view because the pieces would exercise his imagination to grasp the whole. In his deepest being he knew there was something about the way he saw and thought about things that was suspicious to his family and others. He often noticed the glazed look spreading across people's faces when they listened to him talk about a picture he had drawn or a new idea he had unearthed in one of the many books he read.

Eventually he fell into a deep sleep as moonlight crept around the room, as his brother breathed in and out, as people killed each other in Korea, as blond men burnt books and rode large horses over the bodies of dead children.

CHAPTER 5

David knew his life was soon to end. He placed down the golden photograph, glanced at the next one, a black and white of three New York City wide-boy businessmen with the one dressed in a sharp shinny mid-sixties silk suit, spreading his arms wide towards the camera, celebrating his micro moment of fame, ego abounding.

David wondered what was in the little boxes of the American suburbs that gave birth to this overflowing hubris? How could these people, and in particular the men, believe they were so deserving, so much an expression of their God's gift to business, to their women and to the world? The three men in the photograph, multiplied by millions, produce a country sinking in its own consumption, drowning in its contempt of culture and art, blinded by its prurience and pornography, its pride and ignorance, led by other men who, almost universally, utilize personal freedom as an excuse to drain the earth and others of their wealth. Having sold America to a self-aggrandizing material code for short-term profits, David wondered when the people will wake from this long sleep and scream "enough"?

'Why couldn't I embrace a photograph of myself or make such an extrovert's gesture? That man, like so many I encountered, manifested entitlement, whereas I never believed I had a right to assert myself. Perhaps this is what made me a documentarist … an outside observer of other's lives, incapable of believing that my personal existence had meaning or value.'

He looked again at the man's arrogant expression. 'The "entitled" know how to negotiate bureaucrats and officials because they've been trained into it, they feel the society is theirs, whereas I resent all power structures.' He stopped his line of thought for a moment and half smiled. 'My responses are invariably disdain or hostility towards customs officials, the police, judges, politicians or wealthy persons.

'Because I lived up to my principles, I think people thought of me as a troublesome but perhaps honourable professional. When I volunteered for assignments about complicated social struggles, the editors just accepted it.'

Mehmet, the filmmaker, had somehow connected David's name to one of the websites that celebrated his work. That must be how he knew of David. That is why he, David, was now in this fix but he did wonder if there was a link between his registering at the embassies and meeting Mehmet soon afterwards.

David reflected that Mehmet was not to know he would play a significant role in David's destiny unless Mehmet had, in fact, set him up. 'But I knew the risk of intruding into other people's disputes. And for how long have I believed that there is no "other"; their battles are all of our battles. We have no right in claiming a separation; the poor and hungry, the yellow, brown, black, red and white are us, that male and female, the bent grandma and the dying uncle were always me, the peasant and the general were also me.

'Was I too susceptible to Rilke:

Whoever weeps anywhere in the world,

Without cause weeps in the world,

Weeps over me.

'Whenever entering a street, a factory or a home for the first time, I was returning to where I had never been before, but returning because those people, whomsoever, of whatsoever class or colour were a part of me. I made no claim to their love or possessions but believed that through my efforts I was in part, an equal owner of their world as they were of mine. I was, at least in my imagination, a victim, a lover, a rebel in their lives as they were in mine. My intrusion in their lives was an investigation of my and their humanity: their intimacy was my own, their reality was a truth captured at a fraction of a second, and as the light gathered behind my lens, in the circles of confusion, and there behind that piece of glass a chemical process began in which all the swarming silver grains would say: "at that moment, in that place under that illumination, that object reflected light in this way". That was a simple truth I could hold onto.'

The sickness in David's belly came rushing back. There he was, in his late sixties, in pain, ignored by his own culture and country and about to be destroyed by the very forces he has forever resented, a resentment created out of fear.

'What does extinction mean? To not be, to not love or to not eat Muhammad's bread or to not feel the warm air on my skin, to not muse about what is right or wrong, to not learn a new word or see a new film or listen to Beethoven, to not be able to remember her? Was life, no matter how impoverished, not infinitely better than death, if even for a moment in the midst of horror, I could breathe her perfumes or feel cold water splash across my back on a hot and dusty day? For all of the darkness in my soul, I still greet life with an effervescence of joy. I have learned to celebrate the beauty of the particular: the taste of a just picked dew covered apple, the sweet trust of a child, the self-sacrificing act of a street fighter, the pleasure of a woman's warm body or deeply inhaling the sea air.'

He sat down heavily onto the little chair next to the table. Thinking in these ways did him no good in this, his last hour and a bit of life. Another moan crept from his lips and again he felt the anger rising in him, the ancient anger that made his temples pulsate and which had so often driven him to do what he believed he must do, against his best interests and against common sense.

There it was. He had never learned from his English friends how to be pragmatic, how to accommodate himself to what was sensible. His notion of doing the right thing, invariably defined as the morally correct thing, was always more appealing to him although frequently more demanding. He knew he could not live with moral compromise. His sense of intellectual and moral purity was more important than success … but damn, he did regret he never had enough of either wealth or comfort. He dropped his head into his hands and then he smiled for a moment as he remembered an elderly New York Jewish friend who responded to almost every perplexing situation with, "oi, vat a life". David's lips slowly mouthed the line.

Several miles away, Dr Suleiman placed the receiver back on the office phone and left his tinted glass and blond wood surgery in the heart of the wealthy suburb where, for several days a week, he attended to the whims and sensitivities of the kleptocracy's wealthy wives, mistresses and expensive hookers. He knew all the gossip and who was bedding or buggering whom. Often, he smiled to himself as the wife of an officer, politician or judge would leave his surgery, gliding past the unknown mistress of her husband, waiting patiently for her appointment, flicking through an Italian starlet magazine.

His lean well-dressed figure cruised along the steamy street under the chattering palm leaves to where his black Humber was parked. He glanced around to see if there were any obvious security service crows watching. Assured he was on his own, he climbed in and set off, knowing he would need to arrive well within the next hour. It would be better, more certain and secure for him if he did the job rather than allow David to make the 'right choice' or to let other security hacks get their cruel hands on him.

'The leaders want their show trial to reveal the anti-Islamic Western crusaders trying to wreck our country; Mehmet wants a tortured David paraded to the world so that his group can expose the cruelty of the kleptocracy; I want a foreign martyr that our group can claim was murdered by the secret police. David will now understand why I gave him the strong sleeping pills.'

As he guided his heavy car through the steaming streets he murmured, "But better safe than sorry. Better that I should make certain David had made the right choice, and if not, better I should help David along."

He cruised down a side street, turned right into another and then turned back into the flow of traffic along the palm lined avenue leading to the city's main artery. Constantly checking his rear-view mirror, he was certain no one was following him. He was certain that the Sergeant, his one-time childhood friend, had fallen for his plan to stall the Colonel's operation, but the doctor had another game to play as did his friends at the American embassy.

He pulled onto the sea road and there it was, another traffic snarl-up ahead, another of the endless roadblocks. He remembered his father telling him that man's plans make God smile.

'Roadblocks, house searches, interrogations, disappearances, rapes, kidnapping; here none of us can disagree. Disagreement is defined as treason; mistakes are construed as revolutionary acts. Our great leader, the conductor, the captain of our ship, the father of our nation is faultless because he is the people and the people are pure and righteous and the people cannot be wrong.'

Suleiman could have choked on his bile.

Like his hero, Franz Fanon, another man who had lived a double life as a revolutionary informer and as counsellors to the torturers of his own people, Suleiman had to square a circle. This he knew was impossible. The oligarchs, criminals, Sheikhs, bankers and hedge fund bosses had fortunes to invest and fortunes to defend. They were happy enough to consent to whatever their local political and military puppets decided was best to defend their ports, their car dealerships, their airports and the new resorts and casinos. There were so many eastern Europeans in town he often had to remind himself he was not visiting Kiev or Moscow. He was amused to see the old Cold War now being played out between the Eastern European and the Anglo-

American bankers and their economic hit men, but, as in the Cold War, there were so many strange alliances, bedfellows and compromisers that indisputably these capitalists often had complimentary interests in particular ventures and always a profound disregard for local culture, peace and human wellbeing.

It sickened him to think that no regional answer had yet been found to rival the lure of wealth and the American Dream. Pan-Arabism, Communism, Islamic fundamentalism had all failed. He stared into the mirror as he investigated his own moral oblivion. 'Perhaps an Arabic version of social democracy needs to be found and perhaps here, in my country, the incubator of change could be established with courage and cunning.' And of course, the foreign cash he received from his American friends was helpful.

As he inched along the crowded road, behind one of the many cement mixers billowing oil, or the clapped-out bus leaning to one side, overflowing with peasants carrying baskets of ruby tomatoes or bags stuffed with fresh young okra, he wondered if and when the security guys would get wise to his game. Suleiman knew that the Colonel, for all his simpleton fat guy stuff, was a clever and calculating man who was by nature suspicious. And for all of the Colonel's apparent disdain of the Great Satan, Suleiman knew that he too had been CIA trained.

As he crept closer to the irritating and inefficient but always intimidating road-block he considered Mehmet's role in all of this. Suleiman thought of himself as a rational man and, being trained in medicine, a man who understood sacrifice and death.

'I may need to amputate the infected area to preserve the rest. That is a matter of necessity. Ahh, poor Mehmet. If David doesn't play the game according to how I and others have planned it, unknown to him, Mehmet will carry the blame; he will be seen as the liaison while we, the true leaders of change, will survive to plot again. Suleiman was pleased with himself; a dangerous condition in a drowning country.

•••

For many of the years between the ages of seven and seventeen, when David at last left his parents' home, his grandma lived with his family. He was always relieved when she was there. He did not understand why she would be with them for three years and then gone for several, living in California and then in Florida with her daughter, a kindly woman who had been abandoned by her husband. He was known to have been afflicted by a sexual disease; something to do with other men but this was never explained to David.

Wherever his grandma was, she sent him post cards of those places with long, carefully written notes crammed on the back between the stamp and the description of the picture on the opposite side. He loved that the note was especially for him. He loved the cards with their colourful pictures of avenues and palm trees and blue seas and sailing boats. He collected them in a shoebox, keeping them in careful order with the earliest at the far end and the latest facing him at the near end. Unfortunately, neither of his parents ever made him aware how happy it would have made his grandmother had he written back.

When he was with his grandma, she said little, but she cared for him, and to him she seemed to express what he thought was love. He felt a companionship with her unlike with anyone else in his life, save for Mr Whipple.

After school David always went home on his own because his parents didn't like him to have other kids in the house. Although he had found little interest in most of his classmates, he felt alone and had no one to spend time with. Whenever he tried to play catch with his brother it would turn into a competition in which his brother would insist on throwing the ball as fast and hard as he could at rather than to David.

In his bedroom he read more and more books on American history, the Greek myths and biographies of famous people – Simon Bolivar, Abraham Lincoln, Wild Bill Hickok and George Washington among many others. He knew most kids weren't interested in history or art so he was content to be on his own or in the quiet company of his grandma. She would always find a snack for him and a glass of milk when he returned from school and, unlike the rest of his family, she would ask him how he was.

One early autumn day he arrived home, clearly troubled. His grandma looked at him, scooped some egg salad out of a plastic container taken from the fridge, spread it onto a slab of Wonder Bread, added an extra spoonful of Hellman's mayo, cut the sandwich on the triangle, placed it on a plate, poured a glass of cold milk, set it down next to his plate and sat down with him. He was comfortable with her and ate quietly but he knew she wanted an explanation.

He looked into her brown eyes. She accepted all that he was and made no judgements. Maybe he was safe in telling her.

She folded her hands together and slid the glass of milk further towards him. "So?" she said gently.

He risked it. "Today all of the separate homeroom classes were told to assemble on our school lawn around the flagpole. Miss Williams, our principal, made a speech."

Should he go on? He was nervous about what his grandma would think of him. To her he was a good boy and he wanted to be a good boy for her. He knew that to be good was to be honourable, brave ... it was being American or at least like the Americans in the stories he had read of the founding fathers.

He hated the way his parents almost always equally blamed him for fighting with his hateful brother, the tormentor who continually harassed, pushed, pinched and tongue-lashed David. Although David stood up to him, he invariably lost to his older brother's size and unrestrained viciousness. He knew that his grandma saw the truth, that he was not to blame and that he was a good boy.

She waited. She always seemed to have time and seemed to understand that he had, at moments, distracting little reveries.

David found courage in his memory of George Washington and the cherry tree ... to be brave, to speak the truth. He recalled standing in the chill looking from the assembled kid's eager faces up towards Old Glory fluttering above all their heads, framed against the huge blue, Midwestern September sky.

"Grandma, the principal said she was happy because today and from now on we have to include 'under God' in the Pledge of Allegiance."

His grandmother's face closed slightly as she searched to understand her bright grandson's problem.

His voice trembled as he continued. "The principal said that all kids and teachers, as good Americans, have got to say these words 'one nation, under God, indivisible, with liberty and justice for all'."

She saw how upset he was but still did not understand. She touched his arm. "Davy, what's bothering you with this?"

He became more upset and almost cried, "Grandma, I am a good American."

"Of course you are."

"But…", he fiddled with his plate and looked at her again, "But I don't believe those words. They're not right."

She could not hold back her surprise. "Why ever not?"

"I've read a lot about the American Revolution, about how they wrote the constitution and they said we had to keep God separate from, you know, from our country."

His grandmother was confused.

"I mean not from our country but from our government. So this isn't right."

"Well Davy, the politicians know better than us so I'm sure it's okay."

He looked at her. She had made no judgement about him but he had not really said it all. He knew from his experiences with his father that there was something wrong with this God business. The ideas of love and his father, of God and his father did not mesh in his mind, nor did it mesh with his idea of what America was supposed to be.

"Finish your snack now and I think maybe don't mention this to your father or even to Joey."

He looked at his grandma, trying to find a shard of disapproval for Joey, but she was wearing her grandmother mask.

He blurted out, "Joey doesn't understand anything complicated".

He never saw Joel at school but knew he could not rely upon his big brother as a protector like the other kids with older siblings would do. The threat, "I'll get my big brother after you", was pervasive in the playground but not for David.

He had no idea what his brother did after school but he was, to David's relief, rarely around. It was as though they occupied two different planets, coming together only at dinner and in their shared bedroom where his brother would go to sleep and David would read a book using a flashlight under his blanket. For some reason Joel's tease, "I'll tell dad on you", never happened.

David thanked his grandma for his sandwich and went to his room to do his homework. He was disappointed in his inability to tell her what he really felt and he was disappointed that she had ... had what ... had not really taken his problem seriously.

Every Sunday his grandma took him to the movies. In Leah's easy comfort he was exposed to her favourites – Robert Mitchum or John Wayne standing up for America, destroying the savage Indians, that whooping faceless evil that resisted blue eyed good guys from living out their manifest destiny; he became aware of women's breasts being something of desire in those torrid mid-50s films of repressed lust and passion like James A. Mitchner's Hawaii, tossed onto the newly-widened full Todd AO silver screen and he began to sense the terrible underlying psycho drama of people's lives in Three Faces Of Eve and Come Back Little Sheba. The full emotional meaning of these films was beyond his young mind but the atmosphere of dark passions, intense but repressed sensuality and emotional conflict left a lasting impression on him. He was overwhelmed in the warm darkness. Image by image enticed him, comforted and confounded him. He lived a twin reality while in the cinema, being engaged in the film stories and wondering about how the pictures on the screen were made. He loved the light and the colours but especially he loved the black and white films. He thought the shapes and tones were beautiful.

As he walked the half-mile to and from school at eight in the morning and at four in the afternoon, often he imagined the world of bungalows and passing trucks playing a part in the latest film he had seen. He would transform the walk into a journey of chases and thrills, of bars and hangout joints and he would make up stories about people he saw and what went on in the houses or about the valuables only he knew about, being smuggled in the passing trucks.

He liked studying history, geography and English and although he was one of the brightest kids in his class, he was excluded from the group of other bright kids. They went to each other's parties, they gave each other Valentine's cards and they visited each other's houses after school where they were given pieces of cake and glasses of milk. He had been with many of them since kindergarten and had grown up with them through elementary school but he was a stranger to them.

One day, when he was walking home through the warm slush of a late spring snow, he was caught up by Susan Lichtenstein, a pretty, slight, fine looking girl in his class. Secretly he had liked her for the last year but was too shy to say anything nor did he know how to approach her. She had raven hair, large eyes and very definite eyebrows and eyelashes. Her skin was much darker than any of the other kids which David did not consciously think about but found attractive. He did not know about Ashkenazi and Sephardim then.

"Hi", she said, "I didn't ever know you walked home this way".

At first, he was too surprised to answer but he fell in step next to her. She looked at him for a moment not knowing why he had not responded. "I walk over on Littlefield but sometimes I walk this way instead of along Shaffer. I don't like Shaffer with all those bad houses and all the big trucks going by."

"I know", he said and then hesitated and looked at her. He could only think about how pretty she was. She looked at him, her eyes like dark saucers. He thought she must see everything in the world with eyes as big as hers. He smiled faintly at her and offered, "When I go to school in the morning, it's really busy. I don't like the noise of the cars and big trucks. I like to hear the birds and the wind instead. In the winter I like to hear the crunch of my boots on the snow."

"That's just how I feel", she oozed.

The next day Susan approached him between classes. "You were really good in geography today. Mrs Turner was soooo impressed."

He smiled.

She put her hand into her pocket and pulled out a little pale blue square envelope and offered it to him. "Here."

He looked at it with uncertainty. His name was on it, written in a fine fancy scroll. No one had ever offered him a secret envelope. He looked into her eyes and with a quavering voice asked what it was. She pushed it towards him. "Read it later."

He did read it and saw that it was an invitation to her birthday party in two weeks' time. It had a special note saying, "please please come". At the bottom were the letters "RSVP" which he did not understand.

That evening he showed it to his mother. "Mama, what do these letters mean?"

She said it's 'stuck-up stuff' that really means the girl wants you to tell her if you are or not coming.

"Mama, can I go?"

"It means you gotta take a present. We can't afford a present."

He hadn't thought of such a complication. "Are you sure I can't go without one?"

"No you can't! They'll think we're poor. Better you skip it. Tell her you gotta do something with your family."

"Are we poor?"

"What do you think? I mean do we look like we're rolling in it?"

He did not know what to make of this. He had never thought about it and it confused him. "Mama, what do we have to do? I mean where are we going on the day of her party?"

She looked at him with the pinched mouth she often formed in difficult moments, an expression that telegraphed that she was not in the mood for his questions. "Tell her anything. I don't care what you tell her."

He thought about this, wondering if his mother was actually asking him to lie. He didn't want the answer to that question. "Maybe I can make her a drawing."

"Who would want a drawing from you? You're not an artist, you're not famous. She'd be insulted. No, just tell her something." With every answer his mother became more impatient.

He did not know why he felt so offended, so deeply hurt by his mother but he did, and he could feel his temper rising. "You never let me have other kids over, you never take me anywhere, you don't want me to go out alone and now you don't want me to go to a party." He blurted, "And you want me to lie?"

She was startled and spat out in her venomous way, "It's a little white fib, not a lie, a fib."

"But it's not right to cover something up."

"For God's sake, be quiet. Go to your room and don't come down until you can behave nice."

He stood looking at her, believing another piece of his world had fallen away. He tightened his fists and thought of Susan's sweet voice. His face went red. His mother shouted at him, "Stop it". The pressure built in his head; suddenly blood poured from his nose. The blood ran down his upper lip.

He did not go to the party nor did he tell Susan why or provide an excuse. He felt trapped by the necessity to lie and the desire to be truthful with her. Susan, confused by his silence and apparent rejection, did not speak to him afterwards. He knew the girls whispered about him. He sought refuge in learning things and in the books he read.

When he was about eleven or so he began to be embarrassed in front of his school-mates, and in particular amongst the girls and especially Susan, whom he was by then secretly craving in the uncertain miasma of nascent sexuality, that he alone amongst them went on Saturday or Sunday to the movie picture house accompanied by his grandma while the girls, so carefree and mature, went with each other. He longed to be with them, to be able to define himself as an individual rather than a respectful grandson; he did not want to be seen as a dependent child needing to be escorted by his elderly relative.

But there in the darkness of either the Royal or the more fanciful Mercury - its auditorium walls frescoed with glow-in-the-dark images of the Messenger trailing across heaven's skies after the rising sun - he was suffused in celluloid dreams. For those hours, facilitated by his grandma, the everything of dreams seemed so possible. He knew he would grow up to be a peacemaker, a brave man, indeed a hero.

One evening, when his parents had gone out and his brother was off with friends, his grandma was alone, sitting in 'her' chair near the television, quietly reading. David went and sat on the floor near her. Knowing he wanted to talk, she put down the magazine and looked at him. "Davy?"

"Grandma, I ... well, I mean ..."

"What is it?"

"In school, my classmates ... they make fun of me."

She leant forward and lifted his chin up gently so he would look at her. "Why?"

"Cause, well you see, when they go to the movies all together, they see me and then they make fun of me behind my back."

"But why?"

He looked away.

"Davy?"

"I don't know grandma. I guess they're silly, that's all."

She nodded. "Don't you worry, we don't have to go till it all clears up."

That night he lay in bed and repeated over and over, "I'm selfish, I'm selfish…"

He awoke early. Joel was still sleeping. 'Is this what it's like to live? Everything makes me unhappy. Does everyone else understand what happens? Is everything always so complicated?'

CHAPTER 6

David could feel his pulse beating away the seconds against his watchstrap.

He picked up the next photograph. It was an intricate image shot on infrared color film of a derelict he had befriended on the Bowery in New York.

'Acch, what was I doing, what was I thinking?' But it was in the late sixties and so experimentation was the mode of the day. David looked at the man's profile. In this image he was bent forward, pink vomit flowed from his aquamarine face. The infrared film migrated the colours to a space that was at once bizarre and violent.

David had fallen in love with the reductive aesthetics of the Bauhaus and in particular with their idea that 'form follows function'.

He remembered, 'I used the harsh chroma to express the social violence wrought against that guy. But I imposed on his reality rather than simply brought it into relief against an unconcerned world.'

David looked out of the French windows at the warm coloured midmorning light streaming through the dusty rays.

'This picture, what a problem. What was the guy's name?' He paused and dug deep but nothing came. A nameless man lost to his fate, lost to the booze and his misery, a man whose soul died in the Korean War. 'God, what I didn't know. I was only photographing a shell. How arrogant. I thought somehow I'd be able to help the man. Why didn't I get it when he kept hitting on me for money and why didn't I see those impending threats when I could offer only a few bucks? A poor photographer, all I had were pictures and kindness to offer. Neither was enough and neither was what the man needed. What a jerk I was.'

David looked down into the street towards Muhammad.

'I've always been a poor judge of people. But at some point, back then, I decided I preferred to be cheated and emotionally injured by people than to be endlessly suspicious and assume they were out to cheat me. That would have been the road to cynicism and would have eroded my desire to create an art of and for people. What I never accounted for was that often I was simply a device, a tool in other's lives to facilitate their needs. It wasn't evil nor even a calculated opportunism but rather ...'

David dropped the photograph as if it was suddenly burning his fingers.

'Mehmet, Mehmet really is using me. I'm sure of it.' His brow creased as if pushing his inner monologue along. 'I've been set up? Was this all a ploy to bring attention to the nascent rebellion? Have I become his puppet? All the talk about being a fellow artist, being a brother in arms, a comrade; was I simply a cog to be disposed of for Mehmet's imagined greater good? And Suleiman, with his American education, his secretive acquaintance with American Embassy officials; Suleiman, the provider of the strong sleeping pills, the person who introduced me to Mehmet ...'

David had a detailed understanding of the Soviet show trials in the thirties and fifties. He remembered that believers in the Soviet concept of the 'new man', the communists who gave as they could and received as their needs required became convinced that if they were true to Uncle Joe and mother Russia, they would swallow their innocence, admit to the false accusations and go quietly to their own executions knowing that to do so served the revolution. This self-sacrifice to the state's paranoia was an historical imperative.

David tossed this around, glanced at his watch and recalled what he long ago realized while witnessing a man slowly bleeding to death on the white marble steps of a distant courthouse. When history is used as a rationalization, when the 'historical imperative' becomes the explanation for violence and destruction, at that moment, whoever invokes this doggerel, whether the authorities or the rebels, a political leader or a priest, or even Mehmet or Suleiman, they have forgotten their responsibility to their brothers and sisters. Since the advent of hyper globalization, invented terms like 'business sense', 'the free market' and 'consumer's choice' became not too distant relatives of 'historical imperative'. All of these are seemingly sensible explanations to rationalize acts of inhumanity; they explain the West's war on terror, the use of torture, the curtailing of civil and human rights, the promotions of the arms trade, sieges of cities, non-judicial murders, liaisons with brutal dictators, regime change, cutting social services and educational opportunities, refusing to make the poor and elderly more comfortable, the acceptance of hunger and homelessness in the shadow of extraordinary personal wealth. This is rationality in the service of inhumanity; inhumanity as signs of the infectious plague that inhabits us all.

David lurched forward as if dizzy from the whirring ideas. 'What I still don't get is whether the politicians are blinded by ideology, simply ignorant, corrupt or in one way or another, evil. And, which of these describe Mehmet and perhaps Suleiman?'

At his film's desert location, Mehmet turned away from the viewfinder, asked his assistant the time. He knew David well enough to understand that he had a rebellious spirit with a durable personality, and that he would find it difficult to submit to the will of the authorities. He knew that David, even for his back and shoulder pain, was a tough character who would not surrender quietly to an ugly fate. Would David accept his responsibility to the people or would he respond as a self-concerned individualist?

His crew watched Mehmet and paced. They feared falling behind schedule for which they were penalized with more than fines. Every crewmember knew that to not achieve the imposed productivity was seen as an act of rebellion, an assault upon the state. "After all", said the political officer assigned to the unit, "If you let the schedule down, you let the production down, if you let the production down, you let the audience down and that is an injury to your fellow citizens, and when you injure your fellows you injure the state and"… he paused long enough to emphasize, "you assault our leader who is the people".

Mehmet wondered if David would do something foolish: throw himself from his little balcony or overdose on painkillers. 'And who would that serve? The rebellion would not have its obvious foreign martyr; neither the American nor the British press could make a stink out of an apparent suicide of an old, semi-retired photographer in poor health, and the government would not have a foreign spy to parade in front of the TV news cameras, reminding the population how only the dear Leader could protect them from the imperialist intentions of the infidel crusaders. "No", he whispered, "Killing himself would never do".

David sat quietly; the dizziness had passed. 'Fear, its just fear.' Had he lived all of his life to end up in this tortured land, a victim of a venal kleptocracy's madness or worse, a sacrificial goat for his 'friends', or worse yet, a commodity bartered by his own government to its local allies in the struggle for regional domination? This idea struck him forcibly. 'Am I being traded by the Brits or the Americans in some bizarre game of power brokering?'

David's arms had wrapped themselves around his middle and he rocked slowly to and fro. He complained to himself. 'I've spent my whole life preparing to die. I've lived in my own shadow trying to figure out my worth. All I've done is record other people's troubles, thinking I was telling some truth that would change the world, but in fact, all I've done is try to answer my own questions.'

His ceiling fan whirled slowly, struggling with the limpid supply of brown energy. The street sounds, so human and comforting, dimmed.

David remembered the day he first met Kate. He and his reporter Margaret arrived at the scene of a horrendous massacre in the hills above Sarajevo. It was beyond anything he had seen, even in Africa.

Margaret turned towards David. She saw the horror in his face. She liked him but she didn't know him well. She recalled the rumours about his reputation: "too radical", "too political", "too much a moralist", "short tempered", "a know-it-all". Were there real reasons for people's dislike? But she found him good company; she appreciated his need to analyse the things they encountered; she thought his photographs were outstanding and he was polite and sometimes fun. But now, what was happening to him?

Margaret was a middle-aged journalist, experienced and with a strong instinct for survival. She had been sent to cover the developing Bosnian story with David. She was cool, intelligent and although an English pragmatist, she held the left liberal moral high ground. "David?"

He waved off her inquiry.

"We've got to get this done. Please." She scanned the forest. "There's something in the air."

David, pale, stared at Margaret. He didn't respond.

"David! Come on." She looked at him more closely, twisted around, peered into the woods and returned her attention to him. "We've seen insurrections, riots ...this is the same; less forgiving but the same."

David whispered, "This is not random, this is genocide." He grabbed Margaret by the shoulders and pulled her to him. "This is genocide and what're we doing about it?"

Margaret sensed there was not only a threat in the air from the men who did this but also from David suddenly losing it. She spoke with urgency. "Not now David! Use your camera, show people what's here."

David stammered and looked at the bloody ground beneath their boots. Margaret was by then caught between her own temper and fear of the returning murderers. "Shoot, damn it!"

David grew calmer, surrendering to his fate. "I've lost it. You've got to lose it sometime, someplace; I've just lost it."

Margaret took a step towards him and whispered, "Tell the truth, show them what's here!"

He stared into a void.

Margaret shouted, "What the hell are you doing?" She then stomped in a circle around him, fuming, throwing her arms out as if in an argument with herself.

He looked across the forest clearing, across the bodies of men, women and so many children towards the novice photographer, Kate, who had just beaten them to the plateau. There was something about her he had only imagined but had never seen outside of books. Tina Modotti. 'Is this a justification for my indifference? Is this comfort?' It was as though he sensed in those dark eyes of hers there was poetry or knowledge that could soothe him. 'Love comes at odd moments.'

Margaret again shouted, "Telling! It's the job." She turned away and continued to circle. "Think story; it's how we stay sane."

David walked away, holding onto his cameras and more or less babbling to save himself from breaking down completely. "We've each told a hundred stories about a thousand crimes." He turned and shouted, "Nothing changes. Nothing! Our lives are useless. We have no effect. We do not change minds. We only confirm the suspicion that all the bloody foreigners are crazy and somehow different and maybe even deserving of ...." He shot his left arm out, looked around, looked at her and shouted, "Deserving of this."

"David, we're reporters not Gods!"

He shouted again, "You know what we are? We're the damn fillers between the ads!"

Dust motes floated between his eyes and the French window. He glanced again at his watch, and at the pills. He whispered to the light, "Maybe we never escape our childlike nature, staring in bewilderment at our incomprehensible lives upon which we try to impose ourselves until we're old enough to understand that we are powerless in a world of murders, unless we ourselves become the bad guys."

He stopped rocking. He looked at the box of photographs. He heard the sounds of the street hawkers, a motorcycle backfire, a fly somewhere in his room arguing with fate; he heard his watch ticking and looked at his hand. "It's us together, not a single finger but the fingers clinched together, a whole hand that makes the difference. That's how we confront the bad guys, that's how we make a better world."

David walked stiffly to the open windows but as the day warmed up so did his aching body. Below, a toddler was playing on the broken pavement that the nameless woman from the key shop had recently swept clean. The toddler attempted to stand but tumbled unharmed onto her side. She seemed bemused and found a new way to lurch forward, extended a leg and then began again to climb up, clinging to a crate while she uncurled her left leg. She almost stood and, seeming to lose faith in her other leg's support, she crumpled to the ground again. She looked around, appraising her possibilities. The nameless woman came out of the key shop and picked the child up. As she did so, she looked up at David and smiled for a moment.

David was thrilled by the child's joy in being alive and discovering these simple tasks. He glanced from person to person on the street below and wondered if any of them knew how lucky they were to be in possession of what may, for the moment, have seemed an endless life. 'I have ninety minutes; they have an infinity of hours.'

His thoughts returned to Mehmet. He pictured him, heavy set, serious but occasionally jovial. Mehmet the filmmaker with his beautiful girl friend, joking, laughing, toasting, "David, our friend."

'Mehmet.'

Dr. Suleiman was growing impatient and worried that his plan was dissolving away with each moment he sat in the traffic jam. Trained in medicine, he disliked relativism of any sort and in particular the kind of sloppy relativism that allowed people to shift their beliefs based on what was momentarily convenient. He wondered what that meant about his life of lies. Was that relativism too or simply a necessary tactic to serve his unwavering beliefs? He thought that perhaps, in the snail like movement towards the soldiers and police ahead, it was not the time to consider such a delicate matter. Was this intuition or paranoia?

•••

By the time David was twelve he had read enough to know that he did not know who or what he was. With virtually no guidance from his parents and no solidarity from his brother, he needed to figure it out more or less on his own. He had been brought up to think of himself as an American, one of the good guys that helped to save the world from the dread of Hitler and from the Red Menace. And yet he knew from his grandma that he was simply a misplaced European with bits of him from Poland, Russia and Germany.

What did that mean? The first Diaspora sent Jews to the ends of the earth, as far away as to what is now Morocco, southern Spain and Portugal, to Greece and Venice and the entire periphery of the Mediterranean world and there were rumours that the Jews had even fled as far as the south-western coast of India and beyond to parts of China. But some had migrated northwards to what became Constantinople and then across the Black Sea to Odessa or to the grassy mouth of the Danube Delta. Commerce, pogroms and jealousy instigated travel along the great European rivers; Jewish traders travelled settlement by settlement up to what became Kiev and eventually Moscow and otherwise along the Danube to the Rhine and finally to the cold outposts of Poland, Lithuania and the Baltic coast. Great cultural centres were founded and the Jews created dynasties based on trusted family members manning outposts in banking, trading, production and fishing ports. Somewhere in all of that movement, somewhere in the villages or towns, in the temples or cobblers' workshops were his roots.

His America offered him heartache, illness, children around him interested in things he could not relate to like sports, trading marbles and baseball cards. He saw other kids were concerned with their clothes and worse yet, with jewellery. None of this made sense to him. He had seen boys burn butterflies to death under magnifying glasses on a sunny summer's day, he had seen them race toy cars down driveways and then fight over who cheated and who won, he had seen them play baseball together, hostile, bitter, filled with accusations and name calling. Yet they all seemed to have a secret knowledge about what these events meant and all of them seemed to know which ballplayer was a hero and which rules were to be played by. All of them had been taken by their fathers to football and baseball games and had been taught the rules and strategies. Because his father and brother never spoke to him, he knew nothing of these things. But he thought, how many of them know the story of Odysseus or who guided the dead across the River Styx? Who knew about the struggle of Bolivians to free themselves from the cruel Spanish and who even knew about where Spain was and about the terrible war that had been fought there in the 1930s? Who among them knew of the Lincoln Brigade and its American heroes? He may have been on his own, excluded, unpopular with the other kids and unloved by his family, he may have been a physical monster with weeping sores but he knew things they had no idea about. Although ignored by the social world around him, he loved knowledge and of course, given his isolation, he began to wrap his identity into it.

He understood that what John Wayne and the rest of the blue eyes had done to the Apache, the Sioux and the other twenty-five million American 'Indians' was what Hitler had done to the Jews and Roma, homosexuals, the mentally unstable, Communists, trades union leaders, artists and intellectuals. He was uncomfortable with this. He worried about it and he began to believe that the American Negro was still subjected to the same treatment, perhaps not as pervasively severe as the others, but he was beginning to read things that were disturbing. He heard words and phrases like 'segregation', 'whites only', 'lynch mobs', 'commie symp' and 'nigger lover'. He heard, uttered by the more intelligent of the bigots, 'commie symp nigger loving yids'. They seemed always to be spat out by old Jews who had fled Russia and Eastern Europe, boys with blonde hair swept into what was called a 'duck's ass' and by balding, heavyset men who looked like B feature film heavies.

For many years a black woman named Evelyn worked for his family. She was referred to as 'the girl who did' by his mother. David loved her. She was sweet and tender to him; she was gentle and laughed easily and would slap her knee when he did something she thought was funny, throw her head back, laugh aloud and say, "Davy, I sure don't know how you come up with that stuff but it's real great".

Behind her back his father and other relatives referred to her and her people as niggers, nigs, jungle bunnies and his brother snarled they're "all a bunch of spades". David was repulsed by the hostile superiority used by his relatives and others towards Evelyn and could not understand why they pretended to like her when in her presence.

One day, in the company of his relatives he asked his father why Evelyn worked for them. He felt he could safely do this in front of the other family members.

His father, as always, impatient with his younger son, snapped, "Your mother needs help, that's why".

"But papa, you and uncle Marvin call her bad names."

His father and the others were amazed at his effrontery. 'How dare he', was the thought that travelled from squinting eyes to tightened lips. Only his older cousin Barry smiled.

His father fumed and looked at his mother as if to say, 'you deal with him'. His uncle Marvin, a small moustachioed man built like a dumpling who peered owl-like from behind his large, thick glasses, leaned forwards. "Davy, we don't call Evelyn bad names. She's a good one. There are a few good ones and a lot of bad ones. She's special, that's why your parents let her work for you. They help her.

The money gives her security and lets her live a decent life but it's only 'cause she ain't lazy like the rest of 'em."

David looked at his uncle from across the food-laden dining table. His uncle had always been kind to him and David thought he must be clever because he was his smart cousin's father. "Why are they lazy?"

His father abruptly stood up, grabbed David by the arm, pulled him from the room and forced-marched him outside into the backyard. He leaned down from the spreading girth of his waist, still holding David by his arm and spat, "That's enough of your nonsense today. You stay right here and don't move until we go home."

David yanked his arm away, moved back to a safe distance and shouted at his father, "You leave me alone, I wasn't doing anything, just leave me alone. You pick on me all the time. You don't take me to baseball games, you don't teach me anything, just leave me alone like you usually do."

His father, taken aback, returned to the house. David watched him go. In the middle of his anger he saw that his father was turning into a pear-shaped object.

America had fought a war in Korea, had gone through the House Un-American Activities communist witch-hunting paroxysm of the McCarthy era and had settled into the smug TV dinners and big chrome fender era of Eisenhower. But to the horror of parents everywhere, there was a new, fearful apparition to deal with. No longer were the nation's children to be seen and not heard until they became adults in the workforce. A cultural, chronological phenomenon called 'teenager' had arisen along with a trainload of attitudes, which included embracing a depraved music called Rock and Roll. Suddenly there was Elvis and his hips wiggling all the styles, beliefs and manners of the older generation into a sexual jelly.

Unknown to David, he was entering not only that period designated as the 'teen years' but also the historical moment in which the concept raised itself above the safe parapet of cling peaches, mom and America do-or-die apple pie. All that he would do, would be judged not just by class, wealth, religion, colour of skin or street address, but also by being a teen in the age of Elvis Presley. From then on, David's father began to have an authorized newspaper-approved set of standards to judge his wayward, troublesome son's every action.

David came from a house where few of these things were discussed, where there was no question but that one must vote Republican, where silence was the rule and joylessness the general demeanour. It was a house like a nation state whose borders were closed, where outside information entered through controlled filters and censorship. Other than the nightly ABC television news broadcast there was the reactionary Detroit News, a paper that had led the campaign against Diego Rivera's murals, and there was the Readers Digest. This was a monthly magazine offering pre-digested all-American essays and religious stories. He heard his smart cousin refer to it as 'Reader's Disgust'. David liked this humour.

With his sullen father's control of which TV shows to watch and which newspaper to read, with his self-preoccupied mother, his cautious grandma and his vicious brother, there was not much breadth for discussions about history or social concerns.

David, at the age of five, had attended half a year at a weekend Jewish kindergarten. Later he realized he did so because his mother's father was still alive and probably pressured his daughter into it. Once his grandfather died, David was provided no other religious training. He had seen his two older boy cousins study Torah and have their Bar Mitzvahs, he had watched his father study the bible and his father and his grandma go off to the Christian Science church but he had never been invited to go with them nor did either of them ever speak to him about religion. Later, and quite dramatically, he discovered that they assumed his belief in God.

By the age of twelve, having read so many history books including those about the Jewish people, he asked his mother if he could go to the local temple on the following Saturday.

"Why, why would you want to go there?"

He knew he would have to defend his request and that he would have to place no demands on her to get his way. "I just read this book about Jewish history and want to see what it's like." He paused as she appraised his answer. "I mean, it can't hurt and I can walk over there on my own. It's only three blocks away."

"All those old men with tattoos. Why bother?"

He had trouble with the two thoughts together… 'old men and tattoos.' "Mama, why do they have tattoos?"

She darted a look at him. "You wanna go, go. You'll have to wear something respectful, not jes any old school clothes."

He was unsure why the tattoo question seemed to swing the request for him but he let it go. Anyway, if he saw tattoos he might find the courage to ask about them.

On the following Saturday he put on a white button-down shirt, his black dress slacks and his smart jacket and walked to the temple. He was nervous as he approached. He had no idea what he was to do or what would be expected of him.

Middle-aged and elderly men stood around in clumps outside of the small temple, talking loudly with each other, gesticulating, in some cases shouting and pointing at another person. He saw that they appeared poor and that they all had the same style caps on their heads that he had to wear when his cousins had their Bar Mitzvahs. Many of the men had white silky shawls around their shoulders with long threads hanging from them. Was he supposed to be dressed like that? Would they let him in? Did he have to pay? He only had a quarter and two nickels in his pocket.

Soon the crowd began to move through the doors into the cool darkness. He meekly followed as if he did not exist. Just inside the foyer a hand landed solidly on his shoulder. David was startled as he turned to see an old man with sunken eyes holding a white skullcap towards him. David did not know how to react. The old man smiled and placed it on David's head. "Now go in and learn", rasped the old man in a thick accent. David mumbled a thank you, turned and entered the temple interior.

It was all of one colour blonde wood with an area for sitting and another smaller area separated from the congregation by a low wooden balustrade. Behind was what to David looked like a large cupboard with tall, ornately carved wooden doors. As one old man incanted in some language David did not understand, two elderly men went to the cupboard, opened it and took out a very large scroll wrapped in a decorated white and blue silk sleeve. Respectively they brought if forward, removed the sleeve and laid the scroll carefully on the central lectern.

A murmur went thought the crowd as off to the right a solid, middle-aged man with a trimmed beard entered and walked directly to the lectern. He thanked the two elders who sat down nearby. This broad-shouldered man folded his hands and looked at the congregation. David sensed something odd, something defiant in the man. David saw the man's intelligent eyes look at him for a moment. He felt special, proud because such a distinguished person had noticed him.

This man, the Rabbi, began to speak with a deep voice, rolling out beautifully pronounced words with sentences so fascinating that although David was not certain what he was saying, he was certain it meant something to him.

"This week we have seen a startling and disturbing event. In this great country of ours, a country in which some of us were born and to which others were brought as children or as innocents fleeing the recent barbarism of Europe and the Soviet Union, an event reveals that we are heading towards greater intolerance and increased racism. This week we have seen a book of poetry, a book brilliant with the light of passion and invention, confiscated by US customs, a book written by a fellow American Jew, a book he could only get published in England. And why?"

Several men in the crowd murmured. A man near David said loudly, "'Cause he's a commie queer, that's why."

The Rabbi stopped and looked at the man. He looked at him for a long time. There was tension in the hall. "Brother Eli, your reaction is why I am speaking about this. Who amongst us is to say that books should not be published, that authors should be arrested and books burned again? That book Howl is a cry for America by a man who is distressed by the same things that should distress us. Cruelty, the heartlessness of the corporations, the refusal to look at ourselves in the mirror, the refusal to allow criticism and the author's rejection of the bitter racism that divides our land."

Another man with yellow eyes called out, "That Ginsberg's a faggot pervert, he's nothing but filth."

The Rabbi looked at the man as he did Eli. "We are quick to judge and we are too quick to ignore the poet's cry about America because of his sexual preferences. His criticism of America does not make him a communist just as his sexual preference does not void the value of his thought. Have Jews not seen enough intolerance, have we not witnessed enough hatred towards us because the rest of society, the dominant white Christian society, also sees us as a type? Do we really want to sit in judgment of Ginsberg and all homosexuals? And if so, where does our intolerance and hatred stop? With homosexuals and with Negroes, maybe with them and Cubans and Mexicans, and then with Germans and all Catholics and so on until we can say that we will be tolerant only toward whom? A neighbour in need or do we say no, not to her because she is an unwed mother or because her father belongs to another sect?"

David listened and was overwhelmed. He knew that he wanted to be able to speak like this man with passion, clarity and wisdom. He knew he would come back. He longed to hear about justice.

As he walked home he realized that there had been no mention of God. He was confused and wondered what that meant. He was also amazed at the openness of the debate. Suddenly he felt the skullcap on his head. He impulsively grabbed it and hid it in his pocket. For the first time he thought that being alone on the streets, he should not allow strangers to see he was Jewish.

As he encountered the wider world, and as he read more, he began to think that he needed to be cautious of revealing his Jewishness to others. He knew that whatever this Jewish thing was to him, it did not include God. Certainly it was a part of his identity but an identity he needed to disguise in a world hostile to Jews. He did not understand this; he simply felt it.

That night there were more nightmares: numbers flying at him again, books burning in the streets, a yellow eyed man looming in the shadows, his hand reaching slowly for David's neck, the walls leaking with suppurations and running with blood, thugs rushing through the streets breaking windows. He cried out and woke himself. Covered in sweat, freezing cold, his brother looking at him with his strange eyes.

Joel hissed, "Shut up cry baby".

During the following week he visited his older cousin Barry who lived on the next block from him. Barry was a reader of books, the only other reader he knew. Secretly David looked up to him. Barry was remote but friendly towards David. They talked about what they both had been reading. Barry introduced David to Andre Malraux, Jean Paul Sartre and Albert Camus.

David wanted to know if Barry's Bar Mitzvah made any difference to how he felt about things.

"I did it for my parents. They wanted it. They said that even though I thought it was a waste of my learning time, it would mean something to me in the future."

"Does it? I mean has it made a difference?"

"I think they meant in the future when I get older."

"Oh, in that future." David hesitated and then he blurted out, "I went to the temple on Saturday to see ... to see what they did there".

Barry was incredulous. "Why? I mean I did everything I could, not to go and you went on your own?"

David was embarrassed. He did not want to seem the fool to Barry. He did not want Barry to dismiss him, to think he was like his brother, to not want him to come over and discuss books and ideas with him. *"I just finished reading a history of the Jewish people and wanted to see what it was all about."*

Barry considered this. "Davy, that's good, that's real good."

David was not certain what was coming. He knew Barry could be sarcastic. He had seen him run ropes around Joel whom Barry disliked almost as much as David did. He had witnessed the dumb look on his brother's face as he tried to figure out whether he had again been made a jerk of or not.

Barry went on. "'Cause you don't believe in all that God stuff, I guess you went as a matter of seeing our history."

David smiled and nodded. Not only had he escaped condemnation, he may even have gained some points in his favour. "I want you to explain something to me. I listened to the Rabbi talk about why a book of poems was arrested by customs...."

Barry corrected him. "Confiscated. Do you mean Howl by Ginsberg?"

He was surprised Barry knew exactly which book and who the author was. "Yes", he said with some surprise. "Anyway, he talked about that, but he never mentioned God."

Barry blankly stared at his younger cousin.

"I mean, this Rabbi, like priests and all, he's a, he's a man of God so why doesn't he talk about God? I don't think he mentioned him once during his sermon."

"'Cause you went to a reform temple. Had you gone to an orthodox temple, well first they wouldn't let you enter 'cause you haven't got the side curls and all that stuff. You know, beaver hats and stuff but had you snuck in you'd hear them talk only of God and not the world. If you asked them what the world is, they'd say it's a reflection of God and had you asked the reform Rabbi what God is, he'd probably say he's a reflection of man."

David was confused again. "But they're Jews too, the ones with the beaver hats. I mean, is there more than one kind of Jew?"

Barry smiled and messed David's hair with his hand. "Hey, there's you and me to start, right? We're Jews without a God.

There's our parents who pretend to believe but don't practice. There's the reform temple down the street where Jews believe in the commandments and God but not all of the silly stuff that came from Poland after the war, and then there are the Orthodox with their clothes and beliefs stuck in the eighteenth century. Amongst them there's all sorts of different important teachers and rabbis with slightly different interpretations of the historical commentaries on the Talmud."

David was dazed with the information and with his cousin's knowledge. It was one of those door-opening moments onto the bigger world. These distinctions, which separated things within what he thought to be a single category, gave him an insight into how complex the world is. David believed more and more that knowledge was the key, not only to understanding who he and the world are, but more importantly, as he began to define himself, it helped him to distinguish himself from his brother and all those kids from whom he felt separated. He could identify himself as someone who loved and respected knowledge and that by becoming knowledgeable it would be a kind of salvation from the ignorance and savagery around him. The boy needed, as do all kids, an identity that mattered and he was realizing that it was to be forged by him out of what he gained from books as well as from life on the streets.

The following Saturday David chose his clothing more carefully. He felt that on his first visit he had been over dressed and too fancy for the temple. His mother had not asked about what happened nor what he thought about it, so he felt free to go again. He put on his best black trousers, a new red sweater and eagerly went along the road to the temple. He had remembered and clutched the skullcap in his hand. He recalled the Rabbi's words and mingled them with thoughts about injustice, about his brother, about his mother never allowing him to question her and about his silent, uncaring father. He was certain the Rabbi would eventually unravel these things for him, and meanwhile David would not have to worry about God.

As he arrived, the men were entering the temple. An older man, muscular and unshaven looked at David. It was the man who, the week earlier, challenged the Rabbi about the poet. He turned to a fearsome-looking man next to him, mumbled something and he too looked at David. They stopped short of the entrance. The fearsome lanky man reached out and grabbed David by the shoulder. As he did so the left sleeve of his worn jacket slid up along his arm revealing a line of blue numbers tattooed on his inner wrist. David was as shocked about being grabbed as he was witnessing the tattooed numbers. The man's lined face filled David's view. In spite of himself he felt revulsion from the tattoo, the yellowed whites of the man's eyes and the overwhelming odour of garlic on the man's breath, slithering out of his mouth over and through gapping blackened teeth. The man barked at him in that strange language. The other man joined in and then several more men surrounded David. His ears were filled with foreign words. One man picked at his new red sweater as though it was offensive. They shoved him away from the door while continuously yelling at him. David was too shocked to cry and too frightened to talk. He backed away, terrified and confused.

The old man who had given him the skullcap appeared between the other men. David was relieved. During the week, as he relived the events of the previous Saturday, he had thought of the man as being like the one in the special painting at the museum. But the old man darted his hand forward, snatched the skullcap from David's head and shouted at him, "How come you wear red to God's house? This ain't party, this ain't birthday, ain't fancy American drive-in. Go away, get away from temple." He yelled, "Get away, go on, this God's house!"

David was stunned by the hatred and the violence. He slowly walked home wondering what the Rabbi would have said and done had he seen the treatment they gave him. By the time he reached home he decided that religious people were sick and he wanted no part of them. It was a belief that made him even more lonely but more reliant on his own will and his own strengths to face life as a series of coincidences, which until then, at the age of twelve, he was not faring well with.

CHAPTER 7

David worried about the depth of Mehmet's religious convictions. As David never had a god, he knew he could not truly understand the difference between losing belief in one and never having had that belief. He had been told by a practicing Christian who was among his friends, that whatever good David had done in his life was meaningless as it had not been performed in the service of the church. To Muslims like Mehmet, as David was the son of men who knew the Old Testament, David must be an accomplice of the devil, having turned his back on the prophets and the word. A Jew whom he knew said, "David, your atheism is between you and God". He smiled and passed the potato pancakes.

Mehmet was instrumental in David's crisis. Mehmet had sought David out, befriended him, convinced him to help the movement, cajoled him into living up to his political convictions, told him that retirement from life was not an option and that he could not expect to visit Mehmet's country and simply observe for his own needs. "We are not a sociologist's laboratory or an artist's moral problem; we are a people in pain." Was Mehmet a believer or a past believer who was able to rationalize a sacrifice in the name of his current beliefs?

David, the victim. This was an intolerable thought. He would not perform a dance of death to other's choreography.

He turned away from the light and the windows, from the sweet perfume of lamb and fennel, from the shimmering palm trees and the hum of cars and lorries, ancient buses and braying donkeys, towards the sanctum of his memories.

He looked at the next print. The deep black of policemen's uniforms spread horizontally across the middle area of the composition. Each figure was engaged in an act of violence: pushing, punching, smacking with truncheons, twisting men's arms, kicking men in the shins, kneeing them in the groin. Other men, many with wild hair, were almost all in defensive positions: arms raised to block a strike, legs twisted to protect their genitals, hands clasped over their heads to receive the force of the swinging clubs.

Brave men and women, marching for their principles knowing that at some point they would face the weight of the state, but these unemployed men and women continued their journey from Birmingham to London, attempting to show the rest of the country they were not lazy scroungers but people who were strong, industrious and set on claiming that they were workers who wished to work and to be active participants in creating the wealth of the nation; they were not born to be idle and here, on this long uncomfortable march, they would prove their industry. But they were an embarrassment and so the state fomented a riot. They became victims, heroic victims cast out of history except for David's pictures.

David thought these thoughts and remembered his attitude towards the marchers had been condemned as too partisan, too political; 'that I had no business to have an opinion but simply to shoot the shots and let the editors decide the usage, which always meant let the editors define a story they had not witnessed. That was the real political control the owners had over truth ... and over me; a combination of arrogance and ignorance'.

He placed the print face down and felt tears rising. He had rarely cried since childhood. These tears were a surprise: floodwaters of frustration and anger, tides of futility returning again and again.

He gulped air into his mouth. 'I must be level headed. Did I let myself be trapped? Did Mehmet, the director of actors, understand my character flaws and take advantage of them? Did I want to be seduced, to feel useful again, to affirm my belief in internationalism, to prove our ability to overcome prejudice and deep-seated fears of ancient enemies?'

And there it was, radiant before David. 'I, like most of the rest of us, cling to the hope that we are civilized and truly human and that those two states of being encompass an unprejudiced acceptance of religious, class, ethnic and gender differences. In reality though, just beneath the surface of our everyday lives, in a pool of memories written deep into our cultural DNA; suspicion, fear and finally hatred are forever lurking and when tapped into, our good intentions are consumed in the flames of species and race memory … in irrational violence. The crust of civilization is thin and the notion of forgiveness is easily eroded. People who are worried about jobs or bread or their country's honour are too easily led by the reckless demagogues. They use God, the church, patriotism or their daughter's purity to encourage mayhem, rape and slaughter. Suffering a problem? Find a diversion - a war or an enemy within, usually of a different race or some group possessing a shade different skin colour or interpretation of the Holy Scriptures. Eradicate the 'other' and you'll gain salvation. Usually exhausted and traumatized after a war, a rebellion or a civil insurrection, people take a while to notice that the violence has destroyed most of what they held dear while the conflict enriched the ruling elite.'

When David first met the American educated and loquacious Dr Suleiman, they talked for hours. They agreed that to see the terrible truths about humanity was an almost forensic exercise in looking into our hearts of darkness rather than broadcasting a nihilistic cynicism. Suleiman said, "History has an ebb and flow. There is peace, progress and success. This leads to contending factions wishing to have more power, wealth or perhaps fame. Then there is war, violence, disaster and finally exhaustion, trauma and rebuilding. And so on."

Suleiman leaned close to David, across his tall chilled pastis and whispered, "Monsieur David, we are a deeply faulty species which has unfortunately gained the top of the animal kingdom's pyramid, but our time is passing. Our cleverness resides, as in all species, in the shadow of our genitals. Too many for too few resources. Soon we will have full scale food and water wars as we already have oil and territorial wars." He shook his head, sat back, took a sip and laughed. "But hell, we are only capable of planning for tomorrow. Like if a fine actor, or one who is used to delicate discussions, he became grave, slid his drink away from him, leaned forward and spoke in his deepest, quietist voice. "Help us to create social democracy here. For us, as for Europe and the US, it is our last refuge before we allow the cancerous hedge-funds and their ilk ruin all of us as one." He laughed again. "I have a problem, convincing others here, who are, shall I say, less lenient towards the West, that the Anglo-Saxon and Jewish bankers and hedge fund operators are not your current-day version of the ancient Crusaders." He smiled broadly, clapped David on the wrist and added, "They're not, are they?"

David replied quietly, "Putting aside your racism, don't let your ego get in the way either. They, whoever 'they' may be, are not just after you, they're after everyone and everything. The Arab world is not a special target, it's just another target."

David enjoyed Suleiman. When Suleiman suggested that David should meet Mehmet, he had to admit he was intrigued. 'But now, after all the "friendship", I'm certain Mehmet has been playing me. Was he that clever? Suleiman said he was a fine director, an actor's director.'

David the puppet? David the victim? He shook his head to dispel these thoughts.

But now he dwelled on Mehmet. In this life and death maelstrom he felt gutted.

'Mehmet used me. Mehmet is no different from all of the other cynical people I've lived and worked with, whom I trusted, helped and even loved in Europe and in the US. And how long had it taken me to recognize that whatever culture does for people, that even if it really suppresses the beast in us, people, and sadly even cultured people, will nonetheless manipulate others for their own advantage with few defaulting to an emotional or moral position which puts others first. Many people embrace the Dali Lama like a bandage or an anti-depressant.'

David saw his reflection in a pane of the French window. 'I'm looking at a naive man who has tried, throughout life, to impose my belief that others could be good and kind for purposes other than their own advantage. But I knew this was not because I was a saint, but because I needed to believe it for my sanity - a relic of childhood.'

The pain of this left him momentarily without energy, disheartened and feeling that he should simply roll over and expire. 'Could it be, that even at 66, I'm still under the influence of my family? Had I not come to reconcile all of that? Ridiculous, a man of my age, still burdened by a long ago and far away history.'

He looked at his watch and looked at the light shimmering in the glass of water next to Suleiman's pills.

An hour away by car, standing on a dune, looking across the empty zone, Mehmet was worried that the real-life drama he had constructed would not play out like one of his films.

His first assistant director, standing quietly behind him awaiting instructions for the next set-up summoned the courage to speak. "Please sir, we need to know where to set-up."

Mehmet knew he had written a good script for David but perhaps, he thought, he needed understand his character more clearly.

"Sir, the camera crew are waiting. Do you want the equipment up here? Is this an extra set-up?"

'David is not an actor, he is flesh and blood and more, he is a Jew - and Jews survive because they are cunning, suspicious, careful.' Mehmet turned towards his first assistant and looked at him, wondering how long he had been standing behind him, and then he turned away. 'But was this not a set of stereotypes too?' He liked David, admired him. It was rare to meet an older person who is still fired up by injustice and seeks unconventional, if not to say egalitarian answers.

The first assistant pleaded, "I can give the crew an early break."

Mehmet turned towards the questioning man and realized his crew were worrying and waiting, that the political officer would soon ask what the problem was and he knew, even at the best of times with the best of the political apparatchiks, that they were incapable of understanding the creative process and that empathy was not a quality they usually snacked on.

He saw the concern on the first assistant's face. It bothered him. 'Weakness, powerlessness, importuning, begging.'

According to the script the Sergeant had done well, the trap was set to spring. Suleiman was now in play and would convince David to surrender, to become the movement's little chicken, their international martyr. Should he risk borrowing the political officers sat-phone again, just to make sure? But he thought it would be suspicious and, being suspicious, he might trace the call. It'll be okay; David was set up, cornered like a fly in the spider's web.

•••

David looked out of his music classroom window. It was early spring, 1958. The thin lemon-yellow sunlight danced through the young leaves making patterns on the classroom's walls. Unemployment in his city raged at 20 per cent. His father had lost his long-held job selling furniture and was now selling candied apples from the back of his car.

For the last few months his father was even more sullen and removed as though embarrassed by his own presence in a room. His mother, who now had a job as a doctor's receptionist, told David, "Your father's an even-tempered man. He's always angry. It's something I can rely on."

There he was, on the eastern edge of the Great Plains, one-third the way across the American continent, in a city reliant on producing motorcars, tires, military machines and rockets. In what was the seventh richest city in the US and therefore one of the richest in the world, men and women like his father had lost their jobs while the captains of industry continued to make a hash of design, raw materials, production, distribution and in particular, the wellbeing of their past and present employees. All of this filtered into David's young mind and made him uneasy. America, the land of opportunity, seemed anything but.

In his music class, David was supposed to be practicing singing the National Anthem for his coming graduation ceremony.

Because he had done well in the Scholastic Aptitude Tests, he had been invited to attend a special school for gifted children in the downtown area. It would mean two long bus trips a day from the northwest of the city where he lived, via the gutted industrial centre's huge empty factories with their rusted pipes and broken windows, through the black ghetto with its once grand Prairie style houses now tumbling down, then along the front of the stony-faced Museum where he had taken the special art classes, and finally a short walk through the fountains and modern buildings of the university to the school.

His father said, "Extra money for the bus fares when instead he can walk to the local high school ... nothin' doing. The local school's good enough."

"More than that", his mother responded, "he'd have to travel through a rough area of town".

"You bet'cha", agreed his father. "Anyway, he'll jes mess it up and get tossed out or something."

That, they thought, was the final word on the matter.

One Saturday morning David went down to the basement where his mother was clearing up old boxes and stacks of clothes. The washing machine and dryer were vibrating in the far corner. His mother was near the roaring metal furnace. Its mouth agape, ready to receive more tributes of paper and whatever else she had to offer its waggling fiery tongues. He knew this was some kind of cleansing ritual she occasionally went through. As he arrived at the bottom of the stairs, she was bent over, opening and investigating something in a cardboard box that he recognized.

"Oh no." He rushed to her side. "Mama?"

She looked up at him as she picked up his shoebox of postcards sent to him by his grandma. She snapped, "What?"

He reached for the shoebox. She turned slightly away, as if preoccupied with the postcards. He decided that to distract her, it would be safe to try a new argument about the special school. "Mama, you love cousin Barry, don't you?"

"Yea, why ask such a silly question?"

David looked at the shoebox and instinctively reached for it. She paid no attention to his outstretched hands.

"Mama, it's an honour to have been invited to the special school that Barry goes to. You know Auntie Bern is really proud of Barry going there." His hands were still suspended in front of him.

His mother looked at his hands and at the box of cards and said, "Honour, schmoner, you're better off with your own kind".

He did not know for sure what she meant but suspected it implied that if he went to the downtown school he would be around Negroes or Catholics, or someone she and his father did not approve of. "But cousin Barry goes and he's alright and you love him so you wouldn't want him to not be safe."

She held the shoebox of postcards with one hand while the fingers of her other hand ran through them as if they were 3x5 file cards of patient's information he'd seen in her office.

"Mama, I'm old enough to take the bus."

"If you don't like my decision, ask your father again." She looked at the shoebox with his fine collection in it.

He recalled the inky reds, blues and greens, the Buick and Cadillac convertibles in front of space ship looking restaurants and suntanned girls on beaches.

"Waste of space", she said.

He looked at her with total incredulity. "Mama?"

Again he reached for the box and again she ignored him. He mumbled, "Speak to papa?"

"And why not?" She was growing impatient. She needed to continue her cleansing as though this purification ritual would bring her a moment of peace.

He blurted, "Why not?" He was more bemused than angry, quickly trying to calculate whether his mother was unexpectedly toying with him or whether she really had no idea that her husband never communicated with David.

He stuttered, "Mama, papa never talks to me".

To his surprise she all but shouted, "What are you saying? Your father loves you and worries about everything you do." She looked at the box again. "You don't need this; jes collecting dust."

David stared blankly at his mother. He felt he had entered some mad dream and then he lost it.

"What am I saying? He never talks to me except to tell me off. He never asks me about school or my grades or anything. He doesn't love me and you know it."

She leaned towards him with a threatening glare. "No to the bus trips."

She looked at the box of cards and then at him. "You don't need this junk anymore. Baby stuff." She turned abruptly and tossed the whole box into the furnace.

David was horrified. It was as if a death had suddenly occurred without warning. He had no idea what to do. He gapped at the flames licking his treasured pictures. The heat seared his face. He was pierced by his helplessness and felt as though a piece of him, of his history was being devoured by the open jaws of the furnace. All of his care for the wonderful images, all of his imaginings of the faraway places with warm winter suns and palm trees were being eaten by the flames.

The nightmarish glare of shouting storm troopers burning books somewhere in Germany, the same men who would later gas his relatives, pirouetted in his mind; he felt a rage hotter than the devouring flames tormenting his guts. Had this simple act by his mother and his helplessness been an assault on his grandma. Had he let her down?

He glared at his mother, wanting to shout at her that she was the same as his father and that now he knew for certain that she too hated him and that he was probably adopted.

The panting flames and the fizzing of the inks and paper suddenly made him see that his mother hated his grandma. When had she hugged her; when did they kiss each other; when had he seen a smile pass between them? He was convinced it was because his mother worried that his grandma knew and would one day tell David he had secretly been adopted. When there was trouble at home his grandma, whom his mother knew loved him, was sent into exile.

His mother eyed David's strange expression and hissed, "Now go upstairs and don't come down until you apologise."

In his room he was overcome by dread. He could still smell the burning inks. He pressed his forehead against the cool window and looked out across the desolate and uncared for backyard. No palm trees, no summer sun, just an old elm with its unloved dark bark; no flowers, no seats or swings like other kids had. It was empty but for unkempt shrubs and patchy grass. He promised that he would never hurt his grandma again.

He remained in his room all day. His thoughts drifted to his next school and his new future. He wasn't bitter about his parent's decision, or at least not as bitter as he was about the wanton destruction of his postcards, his history. By the age of twelve, his expectations for any support from his parents were pretty low. Anyway, he had been offered to be a part of an experimental advanced courses project in the local high school. Maybe he could make a new start for himself.

This was not the only thing running through his mind. Several years earlier, his mother had abruptly stopped taking him to the museum's special art classes. One week she announced, "I can't spare the time to take you to your art classes anymore. Anyway, you've grown out of 'em."

"But mama, they teach me a lot."

"Nonsense", she said, "that's the end of it".

He held onto his time with Mr Whipple and many of the conversations they had together. One day David had asked, "Is art really special, is it different than other things we do?"

"Art is like love, these are the two most precious things we create as human beings."

With his constant questioning which Mr Whipple enjoyed, David asked, "I understand that people create art but how do they create love?"

"Well David, love arises but I don't know, we don't really understand how ... maybe it is simply chemical attraction, maybe it's because the person we love supplies us the things that our own personalities are short of, so they make us feel whole and we love them for that. But for love to last, every day must involve a creative act or an intervention in the relationship ... we need to imagine how we can please or help or support the person we love." He looked at David's open, engaged face. "You see? I said 'imagine'. There is no art unless the artist can imagine what he is going to make. Imagination is at the centre of art and of love."

Mr Whipple studied David's face for a moment. "You with me?"

David was working through all that his mentor had said. He knew that, unlike with Barry, he could ask questions that might make him appear slow but that Mr Whipple never seemed to mind and never seemed to judge him.

"I think I got it. I just need to figure a few things out from what you said."

David learned that life would offer a continual set of opening and closing doors and each fated, chosen or coincidental step would change his life forever. He was sorry he would no longer see Mr Whipple who had taken a special interest in him and more sorry that he had not been able to say goodbye. Simple kindnesses, polite thankyou letters and social participation were not things taught to him by his parents. He never had contact with Mr Whipple again. He had not been given sufficient belief in his own importance to realize that those with whom he had a relationship would want a sustained contact with him, and he had learned from his family that to survive he had to constantly flee to within his own defended borders. These unfinished endings, the closing down and walking away were becoming habitual.

As he sat in his music lesson surrounded by his classmates singing out of tune, he remembered a day, maybe a year ago, when he opened the pages of a celebratory annual published by Life Magazine. He turned the pages, looking at the ads for cars, cookies and refrigerators and came across a set of photographs that took his breath away. They were in rich black and white, glowing off the smooth semi-glossy pages. Picture after picture showed, in an almost three-dimensional sharpness, the effects of war on American soldiers from the battle for the Pacific in 1945. The young soldier, covered in slime and dirt and ringed with sweat, holding the innocent body of a new born baby amongst the trunks and tendrils of the jungle; soldiers ducking low as an almighty explosion is set off just beyond them; the stunned face of a young shell-shocked soldier. He saw that the photographer was called W. Eugene Smith and that he was born in the Midwest. David's world was once again altered. Diego Rivera's museum murals; David's continual amazement with the look, beauty and effects of light and his dream of throwing off his stultifying background - the tiny world he lived in - to achieve a life of heroic truth-telling all fused in Smith's photographs: Smith from the Midwest.

Afterwards, in the several years between when he no longer went to the museum and the last year of elementary school, he started to read books on aesthetics and magazines about photography. He was proud of the fact that he could even pronounce the word "aesthetics" but it truly intrigued him. The more he read, the more he believed that his salvation from the ugly world of his home and city would be found in beauty and art. There was no question. All the art classes, all his love of Rembrandt and since then his discovery of Raphael and DaVinci, of the Fauves and the Blaue Reiter had been leading him to this moment of realization. He was sure Mr Whipple would have been proud of him.

As the kids around him in the music lesson continued to sing and Mrs Marshall, the teacher was busy at the piano, he thought of the night after he had discovered Smith. For the first time he had a complete vision of his future. He would study photography and he would study history so that he could understand what to photograph. Someone would pay him so he would be free to travel and with his camera as a weapon of truth, he would photograph all of the bad things, the injustices, the brutes and bullies and he would reveal them to the world. He was certain that the photographs would be published and that once they were seen, all the wrongs of the world would be righted. He would not get married but stay free to roam as he wished. That was that.

The piano stopped. David looked up. Mrs Marshall, sometimes a harsh music mistress, was glaring at him. "What's wrong with you David? You haven't sung a note since sitting down."

He glanced around. The other kids, including Susan were looking at him. He felt they were cannibals, waiting for his beaten body to fall in front of them when they would pounce and devour him.

"I...", he hesitated, "I don't like the song."

A ripple went through the class.

Mrs Marshall, a tall woman, stood up and walked a few steps towards him. "You don't like our National Anthem? Why don't you like our National Anthem, young man?"

He decided he had to say what he thought. "I don't like the opening line."

"The opening line, the one that says, 'God bless America, the land that we love'? You don't like it? What don't you like it?"

He looked around from face to face. He was interrupting their singing, their smug little community of gossip, parties and visiting each other, their whispering about clothes and hair and baseball stars. He knew he was heading into troubled waters. "I don't like the God part."

"Why? Don't you think God should bless our great country?"

A wad of paper hit him on the side of the face. He looked around, heat rising in his rashes, feeling he was out of his depth, knowing that confrontations made him uneasy. He looked again from face to face and then up at Mrs Marshall. He said in a soft voice, "The constitution separates God and country. People fought for that."

Miss Marshal could play the piano passably and sang devotedly in her church choir but she had no experience in intellectual debate, even with a twelve year old. She took a moment to decide how to deal with this ... this affront.

In a constrained voice she told David, "The song, our national anthem, asks God to bless our country; it doesn't say that they are joined together."

"Maybe Miss Marshall but I know there's America but I don't think there's a God."

The other kids made various noises and one shouted, "You're a commie". He decided to continue. Somehow he was now perversely stimulated by the adversity. It is as if it defined who he was. He shot out of his chair. "Can someone prove there's a God? Huh, who can prove it?"

Mrs Marshall asked, with a quavering voice, filled with repressed rage, "Do your parents believe in God?"

He darted a look at her. "My father and grandmother read the bible every day."

"Do they know how you feel?"

He shot back, "I don't feel, I think!"

She charged over to him, grabbed him by the arm and dragged him out of class, along the short brown lino-covered hallway floor, around the corner past the drinking fountain down the main hallway and into the Principal's office without so much as knocking. She said nothing to David but delivered him to Miss Williams, condemned him *without a trial and left in a self-righteous huff. There was no inquisition. It was a truth; he was guilty of a heinous sacrilege.*

David felt strangely calm and in fact a little proud of himself. They had been taught that America defended freedom of speech and belief. He had employed both and he thought, 'therefore I'm living up to the Constitution'. But he reminded himself that most adults were pretty contradictory.

His mother arrived at the school, apologized to the Principal and said, "His allergies sometimes cause him to be over emotional. I can tell ya, it'll never happen again. We'll see to that, never you mind". She looked at David. "Your father will have something to say about this."

David thought, 'that'll be a change'.

Miss Williams studied David. "Where did you learn such thoughts?" As she finished her question, she eyed up David's mother, whom she instinctively disliked.

"I read the Greek myths."

His mother felt impending horror overwhelming her. The principal folded her hands and waited.

"The Greeks believed in many Gods."

"Yes", said the principal, "and so"?

"They believed in some Gods but we say they were not real, they were myths. So how do we know this one is the real one?"

"David", his mother scowled, "that's enough".

"But mama, even if I'm wrong, our constitution says God and country shouldn't be mixed together. A lot of people came to America so they could be free of that".

"That's enough, I said."

His mother stood up and demanded he immediately leave with her.

That night he heard nothing from his father and wondered if his mother even told him about the event. He thought of Smith's photographs and how he would have a camera one day soon and be able to make pictures as great as Smiths.

Later he had a dream unlike any other he had ever had. He was at first walking and then bounding as though his feet were made of rubber and on each successive step he jumped higher and higher. Soon he was flying over a valley, seeing below a river and green grass and animals and then groups of people walking together, all wearing brown robes. It was exhilarating, breath taking and joyous but then he could no longer control the bounding and it became threatening. He was soaring out of control. He was frightened and called out for help. He woke in his usual cold sweat; his pillow and sheets around him were soaking and he was chilled but his rashes were on fire. The torment lasted most of the night.

The next day, still shaken from the confrontation and his restless night, he walked to school through the rainy May morning, tired and aimless. He liked the soft green of the new leaves and wondered how the other kids in his class would react towards him.

On his route to school there was one major crossing where the school's safety patrol, composed of older kids, watched over the younger ones as they crossed, making certain that they obeyed the lights. 'Stop, look and listen before you cross the street ... bla bla bla.'

The safety patrol boys wore white canvas belts around their waists with a top strap like the police wore that crossed from their right hip to their left shoulder. David arrived as the lights turned red against his crossing. He waited, thinking about his classmates.

The patrol boy, a large kid, heavily built with a big neck and a fat red face turned around and looked at a younger boy who was standing with him. David vaguely recognized the younger boy as someone in another homeroom class of his own grade. The younger boy nodded. "That's him."

The older boy bent down towards David. "I hear ya take the name of our Lord in vain."

David was startled. He did not know what to say. He noticed the cross around the kid's neck.

The older boy pushed him. "Yer a commie."

David felt fear and hatred rising. 'Like my brother, another bully'.

The violence occurred so quickly David had no idea how it happened. The older boy shoved David again by hitting him with both fists on his chest at the same time. David, thrown backwards, met an obstacle and flipped onto his back landing hard on the pavement. He realized the younger boy had squatted down behind him, which forced the tumble. David's head hit the cement with a thwack that stunned him. His fear and pain were completely overwhelmed by anger. He rolled over to his right and for the first time in his life he struck a person, landing a series of blows on the younger boy just as he tried to scramble to his feet. The older boy grabbed David by his coat collar, dragged him to his knees and punched him blow after blow across his face. His cheeks stung, blood spurted from his nose. He swayed but stayed upright on his knees. The younger kid struck him across the back and the older boy shouted, "That's enough, you can see he's even got red commie blood." He pitched towards David. "You tell anyone 'bout this and it'll be worse next time." They sauntered away towards school leaving David on his knees, stunned, bleeding and dizzy.

It was as if he was stuck to the ground, not knowing what to do. He was dazed, embarrassed and felt all of his dignity and pride had been stolen. His vocabulary was composed of ideas not violence. He vaguely remembered his brother and his cot but the idea slithered away in what was now becoming a pounding headache.

He swayed from side to side. The rain fell harder. He took his handkerchief and blocked the blood running from his noise. He looked around and saw all the passing cars. No one noticed; no one cared. He gathered his schoolbooks and bag and stood up. He was dizzy. He lurched forward onto his knees and vomited.

When the doctor looked at him he said that David needed to rest for at least a week in bed, staying as still as he could and in a darkened room. He was concussed but it was not serious.

His father came into his room only once during the week, looked at David and walked out shaking his head. David knew, as far as his father was concerned, he was now a lost cause.

While he lay alone in the silence for that week, he decided he would learn how to protect himself, that he would somehow earn money and buy weights to make himself strong. He would be silent and gentle but impregnable. No one would ever hurt him or those around him again. He knew he would have no support from his parents to do this, but he would figure it out.

All the stories of the Jews in Europe going passively to the gas chambers joined up in his mind with the need to defend himself from the crude bigots, racists and brute bullies forever. He promised he would not allow himself to be a victim ever again. He must be prepared.

A month later, at his classes' June graduation, he was not permitted to go on stage to receive his diploma. Neither of his parents attended the ceremony, he was not invited to any of the parties and so ended his elementary school career, an all A student, except in his Music class, on his own, alone and in disgrace.

CHAPTER 8

At last Dr Suleiman's four by four reached the roadblock. He was concerned that if he didn't make it through quickly, his plan would be jeopardized and his life endangered.

He observed, as if at the zoo, how the country boys in their ill-fitting uniforms, were ringed with sweat and encrusted with sand, diesel fumes and road dust caked on their faces, a dust poisoned with the heavy metals of oil spewing from poorly timed engines and cracked exhaust pipes. 'Asthma and cancers, more patients for the foreseeable future.' He disdainfully watched as they dumbly looked into each car. Most were waved on but they stopped a bus and forced all the occupants onto the pavement to show their identity cards. These poor peasant boys, drafted into the Leader's army, hastily trained to become the blunt instruments of oppressive state policies, knew how to kill a goat and skin it efficiently within minutes; talents which, when transmuted, were handy tools for the regime.

For centuries they had been the forces of reaction across the world and here, as everywhere, they acted unthinkingly for the state against their own best interests. They were encouraged to be suspicious of all city folk who, their officers shouted, "Are exploiters of the fellaheen". They were taught to hate the educated classes who, the political commandants sneered, "Withheld medical help from their parents and encircled them with laws that dishonoured Allah. City people are evil; they sup on the bile of the devil. They are one and the same as the evil tempters who taunted the holy Muhammad."

Dr Suleiman watched, crept forward and waited but his patience was wearing thin. 'After all, I too am in the service of the Great Leader,' and, he smiled to himself, 'I too am in service to others as well. But, as far as these uneducated boys are concerned, I have a right to be somewhere on time.'

The Doctor pulled up to the soldier who stood in front of his car. He pressed the moulded plastic button. The tinted glass driver's side-window smoothly, silently slid down to reveal the empty face of the dumb looking boy, no more than eighteen, gawking at him, gawking with menace. Even with the air-con at full blast, Dr Suleiman could smell the boy's unwashed body. He thought it reeked of every mountain village he had been in, but without the pungent perfume of the pervasive Billy goats.

The young soldier lifted his hand, flattened it parallel with the sand below and the heavens above and thrust it through the window towards the doctor. His naturally rough country manners were further eroded by the minute power he held for that moment.

Suleiman reached across to the passenger seat, picked up a plastic laminated identity card and laid it on the soldier's palm.

The soldier jerked back his hand, looked at the card, clearly could not read, told the Doctor to stay put and shambled towards an officer.

Suleiman was surprised to be asked for his identity card as most people in the cars ahead had been waved on after a cursory inspection.

When the officer in charge read the card he became animated as though he had just felt the tug of a fish on his rod. His head snapped up and he shouted an order. Immediately a dozen soldiers surrounded Suleiman's car. A captain, with drawn pistol, charged towards the driver's door shouting, "Hands on the wheel, hands on the wheel, let me see your hands."

Dr Suleiman was shocked. This was totally unexpected. Here he was on a secret service mission but suddenly an army suspect. As his hands grasped the wheel he thought, 'They've done it, they blew my cover'.

The captain grasped the handle, threw the door open and grabbed Dr Suleiman by his shirt and jacket and tried to pull him out of the car.

Suleiman shouted, "My seat belt!".

The captain, angered by his own incompetence, smacked the doctor several times across the face and shouted, "Free it, open it".

As Dr Suleiman unlocked it, he was dragged out of the car and forced to his knees by the captain and several of his men. Shoved again, he landed with his face in the sharp sand, and with a knee pressed into his back, he was handcuffed from behind.

Now dazed and bleeding from the scrapes, he was pulled up, pressed against his car and the ranking officer, a dusty Colonel meandered over as if going to buy an ice cream on a holiday beach. His face approached Dr Suleiman's and he whispered, "Couldn't last forever, could it?"

The Doctor gathered himself. He appraised the Colonel. 'Somewhat intelligent, not particularly vicious, high school educated, probably a city boy.'

"Colonel, you know as well as I, that even the innocent are guilty now."

The Colonel smiled. "Well it's your turn."

Suleiman nodded. "Okay, you realize since I can't know about things I haven't done, you are going to have a problem."

The Colonel, taken aback by the captive's coolness, stirred from foot to foot but replied, "I'm following orders, doctor".

Suleiman could tell that he had the Colonel on the run and decided to pursue him. "So am I. I'm on my way to arrest a foreign suspect. My commanders, who, as you will understand, drive around in brown cars, want this kept low key … the guy's an American … and I'm the only one who can keep him under control, to make a silent, invisible arrest in the name of our Leader." Suleiman looked at the Colonel's face carefully. "You sure I'm the guy you're after? You really don't want to cross your wires with my bosses. You really don't want to delay my assignment."

The Colonel took a step away. This was suddenly much more dangerous and complicated than he had bargained for. His was a military, not a secret service authority. He ordered the captain to watch Suleiman and he disappeared into a Land Rover.

The Doctor, calling on his professional knowledge, knew that the Colonel's skin colour indicated that blood had drained from his face … a sure sign of fear. Suleiman, educated in London, thought that in a crumbling kleptocracy, like the one now ruling his country, the inefficiency, the waste of talent, the placing of people in charge whose only merit was party loyalty rather than intelligence or training, meant that the left hand never knew what the left hand was doing. This was all a mistake.

David was certain that he could neither get away through the airport nor across the border by road. That left the impossible journey by foot to the eastern border or somehow an escape by boat; a far more appealing idea in this spring weather, even though he feared the sea and death by drowning.

He looked out of the window again. His eyes searched carefully up and down the street. The only odd thing was that the normally reticent Muhammad seemed to be in conversation with a young man who was clearly not a local. The young man peeked up from under his wraparound sunglasses towards David and quickly looked away. He had another word with Muhammad and ambled off along the street, empty handed, without a purchase, cocky.

David stepped back into his room and wondered. Muhammad's cart had not been there for that long. He remembered that it only appeared after his first meeting with Dr Suleiman?

He was staggered. 'No, it can't be. That's too paranoid, too clever, too long term. This is an Inshallah country; "if God wills it"; men don't have to worry about making it happen. I'm not that important, sadly not important at all … why me? Or is there a bigger game being played here?'

'Muhammad, a crow, the call, Suleiman and his Americans.'

"David, beware", he whispered to himself.

Mehmet paced as he waited for the reflectors and a four-meter square diffusion screen to be secured. He watched the grips set the stands, lock them onto the butterfly and lift it higher and higher as his cameraman shouted and gesticulated to them. Once satisfied, the cameraman approached and asked Mehmet a question that Mehmet did not hear. He turned, walked away to the top of a dune again and looked across the Empty Quarter. His cameraman, a Lebanese Christian, found the Moslem Maghreb professionals rude and arrogant. He was ill prepared to see that Mehmet was entering an emotional meltdown.

Mehmet scanned the undulating dunes with their sandy hillocks and stony moraines. 'Empty like our morality, our bravery, our world. We are all traitors to something – our loved ones, our country, our workmates, our comrades, our friends, our own loyalties, our own beliefs.' He sank to his knees. 'What I do, I do for the best reasons but the best reasons require sacrifices.'

The previous day his girlfriend argued with him about means and ends. 'And here again is the problem, destroying innocents for my own beliefs. Is there a difference between those who believe their one way to God is the only way and those of us who believe our one way to politics is the only true way? Even black and white film has tones of grey, imperceptible graduations from black to white but I only accept that something is right if it agrees with me without deviation, that it is 100% white. If not, then it is impure, completely wrong, unacceptable and needs to be destroyed. What of my friend David in this? He is a man I honour although a Jew but none the less, talented and a man on the right side of things.'

The fat Colonel and his thin Sergeant were waiting, smoking again, wanting to know why Suleiman was off the radar. Three of the Colonel's most trusted men were leaning against the battered, threatening cars, also smoking, impatient.

The young crow Private Majid, whom the Sergeant sent out to scout David's street, reported back to the Colonel with his words nervously tumbling out. "I spotted the American on his balcony and the old bread-maker who has a stall across the street told me the spy usually stays in his apartment except for a midday wander around the neighbourhood and then he stops in the café under his apartment for an afternoon meal."

The Colonel flicked his ash, closed his eyes as if thinking about the information and dismissed the young man with a wave of his cigarette. He looked at the Sergeant and nodded approval. "Good thinking. Thorough. If we're not all dead by the end of the day you may go far."

The Sergeant smiled. He had plans to go far.

David, no longer willing to wait, dug though the prints and found one of her. He pulled it out carefully so as not to scratch its surface. "Oooohhhh", escaped from his lips. "She was ..." he closed his eyes and remembered. 'Peeling an orange, juice splashed on her belly; the shadow of her breast against a cotton robe; she moved across their room like velvet in a breeze; twined with still rivers, an orchard in spring.'

He looked at the water glass shimmering in the light. The glass and the pills - suicide, a quiet death in a tin pot country.

'Would I have loved her as much had she been plain looking, ugly or deformed? I want to say "yes" but I knew her beauty had within it, qualities of nobility, dignity and distinction that informed who she was. There was also charm that crept from the corners of her lips and eyes. Her beauty was complex and inseparable from the woman within. There must have been a profound relationship between who she was and how her inner life occupied the contours of her face that portrayed her beauty. She was not pretty, not petite, not a little trophy woman; she was tall and elegant and moved lightly with a straight spine. Something between a dancer and a diplomat.'

He placed the print down. He could barely move his eyes away from it. He was tired, disappointed with life and with his failures. He could feel the blood leaving his head. He became dizzy. He grasped the table to steady himself. He looked again at her face. When animated by her wonderful intelligence and her powerful presence, it was a gift in his life.

'Could I not have found a way, a word to convince her not to go up the hill that day?'

He slumped onto the chair and was overwhelmed with self-loathing. Irritated with himself he grabbed the pills in one hand and the glass of water in the other. "Screw them all", he seethed and then her name escaped his lips as though the mere sound of it would recreate life. He moaned, "Kate, my Kate".

•••

It was burning hot as David walked along the pavement carrying his portfolio. The late June sun scorched the Great Plains and all of its towns and cities that summer.

As he left his street, he saw a local joker frying an egg on the roof of a black '58 Chevy. There was an election brewing between the inspiring young Senator from Massachusetts and Eisenhower's malevolent vice president, 'Tricky Dicky' Nixon.

David's cousin Barry introduced him to thinking about politics. This was new to him but he liked it; it tied some things together for him - his father's unemployment, the fact that Negroes had never been allowed to register to vote in the South, that America was doing some bad things in faraway places like the Belgian Congo and Vietnam, places he hardly knew of until Barry talked about them.

"You know Davy, we need to keep this between us; my parents don't like me talking about this stuff."

"Okay but Barry, Negroes are Americans; why wouldn't our parents want them to have the right to vote?"

Barry smiled at his younger cousin's naiveté. "'Cause they're racists."

Another new word; another big concept; another introduction to a wider world.

"You know the Founding Fathers, as great as they were, just didn't bother to free the slaves and to give women the vote. Boy did they screw up."

"But these days ... I mean ...." David's memory strayed to the day his father dragged him into the garden at Barry's house in front of the whole family.

Barry smiled. "You remember, don't you?"

David walked along Wyoming Avenue thinking about what Barry had said. By now David was perspiring, dripping sweat and worried that the wedding photographer he was about to ask for a job would think him too unkempt to work with him. Before he left home, he had neatened up, put his white long-sleeved dress shirt on to make certain his arm and neck rashes were covered but the scorching sun had ruined his best-laid plans as he ploughed through the late morning heat.

Within his portfolio there was a set of pictures he had been shooting over the last two years. Among them was a low angle photograph of a boy on a bike against a summer sky with huge puffy clouds behind his head; there was a picture of a pot of flowers sitting on a glistening cement driveway during a rain storm; there was a portrait of his grandmother lit by the broad soft light of a window. He was nervous. What would the professional photographer think? Would he be worthy of the job as an assistant?

David found himself in front of the photographer's shop. He studied the pictures behind the big plate glass window. They were of brides and children in painterly looking backgrounds, all with flawless skin and perfect smiles and teeth. There were a few black and white images of weddings and Bar Mitzvah parties and a portrait of an old man with a hooked nose wearing a skullcap and a tallis around his shoulders. It was a pale reminder of the Rembrandt in the Museum and it irked David that such a cheap copy of a wonderful work of art would wind up staring at him from a shop window on Wyoming Avenue. There was nothing interesting or exciting. David's heart fell.

He had for the last several years read about and discovered the pictures and stories of the great photographers. The articles and books helped David to make sense of how they lived their lives and what photography meant to them. He looked at their pictures in the photo magazines and he tried to copy their style to learn how they did what they did. He thought he should know every technique and out of that would grow his own style.

During his research he had come across Edward Weston's portraits of revolutionary artists from Mexico. He learned about Orozco, Sequeiros and then came across a name that rang many bells in his memory, Diego Rivera, the mural painter who had created the hall of steel and workers and cars and the ogling tourists in the museum he had attended for a time as a child. He remembered the wonderful teacher who expressed such kindness to him and who answered his questions without making him feel that he was an idiot.

Amongst Weston's portraits were photographs of his lover, Tina Modotti, a beautiful Italian-American actress who became a photographer and a radical, a brave woman who followed her beliefs and died from exhaustion, having sacrificed her passions to the great, tragic and insane ideologies of the twentieth century. In her prime, Tina was a dark haired, full bodied beauty photographed in the nude many times by Weston in exotic locations like his tiled, plant strewn terrace in Mexico. 'Terra cotta', 'cacti', 'revolution': words that held poetic and erotic tension and mystery, words that drew him away from the cold, flat plains and crumbling factories of his city. And Tina, full of passion, beautiful.

David peered at Weston's landscapes and portraits and certainly at the pictures of Tina but as well he was amazed by the still-life images of nautilus shells and cabbage leaves. He wondered how could he be so moved by a picture of a brassicas or a twisted green pepper?

He discovered that Weston had written and had published what he called his Daybooks. David read them from cover to cover, studying the associated images. He began to understand that the life of a photographer could be the life of an artist, that within Weston's images there was something vital, attractive, necessary to him. He discovered one can live life for beauty, that this was real and that Weston had done it. What he also saw in Weston's deep focused images of people and things was a respect for and a love of each element in the frame. He was reminded of what Mr Whipple had told him about love and beauty.

Later David began to call this "presence"- a way of creating a situation, of composing, printing and revealing a powerful concentration on the person or object in the frame. Presence. He saw that the camera can reveal clarity and expressiveness. Constantly Weston's images brought him to think of love. With this vague stirring, David believed he too could express his love of things and people, of the very fact of living and even of feeling the pain of life through his pictures.

Perhaps his brutish brother, his distant parents and the emotional and physical pain he lived with day by day would lead him to need love more than to want revenge. He was certain that evil was blind and goodness possessed open-eyed clarity.

For now, under the hot summer sun, he knew that if he could get a job with this wedding photographer it would be a stepping stone to a larger world of terraces and exotic plants and far-away places and to something Barry had referred to and Weston and Tina were involved in: revolution.

David met Norman Day, the wedding and Bar Mitzvah photographer, a short oily haired and oily mannered man who seemed to take a liking to him. Although he did not bother to even turn the cover of David's portfolio, he hired him.

For the next four years, while in high school, David worked for Norman as an assistant, schlepping cases, loading film holders and holding the hair light just at the right angle and just out of shot, always behind the group. He lived each occasion in the shadows; he didn't learn much about photography but, for his age, he made a substantial amount of money. He did learn how to eat quickly, to not draw attention to himself, to hold the backlight and to listen to the mindless chatter amongst Norman's older employees about football, hunting, sex and the rest of men's vulgar stuff without making comment. David remained apart but faultlessly polite and a conscientious worker. He learned that these attributes made it difficult to fire him and that he was considered an acceptable oddball, a dreamer but none the less he was trusted. For the first time he was a team member. For all of his disdain, as they jabbered about sports and girls, he liked the sense of this community of men united by a professional goal.

One day, in the second year of working with Norman Day, David asked him if any painters had influenced him.

Day looked at David for a long moment. David was now taller, square shouldered but still gangly. David grew uncomfortable in the suspended moment; Day was regarding him differently than he had previously.

"Well," he slowly intoned, "it's like this; the people who come to me for their portraits want to look perfect, to be caught in the mirror of their dreams. And part of that is to make them seem to be a guy or gal with old country traditions. You see, I make them look like they're in an oil painting and then, in forty years' time, they will be one of the relatives on the library wall of the baronial den in a rich suburb. So my little allusion to Mr Rembrandt or DaVinci or whoever you think I'm aping is to make them feel good about themselves."

David struggled to take this all in but he realized that Day knew more than David had previously thought and he promised himself he would not underestimate him or others again. David knew instinctively that he had insulted Mr Day by the way he almost spat on the word "aping".

Day smiled at David's concentration. "You get it, don't ya?"

David spoke before he thought. "And it makes you rich ... I mean you make money doing this ... flattering them?"

"Sure Dave, I guess you could put it that way but I don't know about rich." He walked away talking more to himself then to David. "We get by, by and by, we get by." He stopped, froze for a moment and then turned towards David. "It's better here than there." Mr Day lifted his left arm and slid back the sleeve of his immaculate white shirt and suit jacket revealing another of those tattoos. "You know what this is?"

David nodded slowly as if in a grieving trance. Quietly he said, "Yes sir."

"Remember one thing. No matter how many hours we work, no matter how many insults we take from the rich, it's better than driving a cart in the old country or seeing your father chased down by a mob of Polish peasants." He paused and then thrust his wrist forward again. "And the rest of it."

"I'm sorry."

"Don't be, you had nothing to do with it."

For the first time David realized that he has never before heard the foreign inflection in Mr Day's otherwise perfect nasal American Midwestern English.

Day turned to go and then stopped again. "David, it's easy to become guilty through silence. Make sure you don't join the other side through silence."

He stood still for a moment and then spoke quietly. "Most people live a rough life. I give them a little kindness. Pictures taken by professionals have different qualities than snaps. They have emphasis, power and they can have a kind of perfection." He looked closely at David and then the ceiling. "A perfection we don't often get in life." He turned away again and added, "But you know Dave, if I can create it, then it's real, and I like that."

David watched Mr Day disappear into the darkroom. He stood still, breathing lightly as if not present. He left the shop and stopped in front of the window display. He looked at the pictures carefully, more carefully than earlier. He noticed how the superficial smiles were belied by what was show in the sitter's eyes. There he discovered what had previously been in front of him: a depth of humanity; woe and pain he had ignored.

David was thrilled but admonished. 'Maybe Mr Day, like many other people, maybe even like papa and like those men in front of the temple, quiet men, sad men have seen a lot, maybe too much and while rich in their souls they were silent in the face of an overwhelming sense of uselessness; they had become confused by the onslaught of life.'

"No", he whispered, "I must never underestimate people".

That evening, David sat on the back steps of his home. The old elm shimmied in the warm air currents. There were a few June bugs lazing around, teasing the dusk with their illuminated bodies. The air smelled sweet and all was quiet but for a distant barking dog. David felt the earth spinning towards the night.

Forever this has been as now: Mr Day's tattoo, Day's father chased by Polish peasants; what they both experienced in the camps.

People live within their history, which is an active part of who they are. World events, like the rise of Nazism, become personal. The importance of history is to appraise it in order to understand the present but also to recognize it as real part of our daily lives. Americans may be the people who defeated the bad guys but we are also the people who enslaved some and performed our own genocide against others.

Softly, so as not to disturb the evening, he whispered, "Who are we?"

During the rest of the summer, between David's disgraced graduation from elementary school and his entrance to high school, he began to work for Day on most weekends. He suddenly had more money than he could imagine.

His parents had aroused enough interest to be suspicious and his brother was jealous but they left him more or less alone and alone he was.

PART II

CHAPTER 9

'When you sleep next to me, and I, restless, murmur, "it's four o'clock, only four o'clock", my nostrils caress your warm body, your honey-brushed skin danced upon by glints of city light and your freckles worn by my thousand kisses. When you sleep next to me, and I, restless, know it's sunny somewhere east, I remember headlines, I see their stricken mouths, I divert to watch the tree of your dreams growing through the hours. When you sleep next to me, and I, restless, know that I secretly celebrate what has happened to those east or south of us has not approached your secret jewelled reverie. I remain between stricken and suspended, waiting for the belly of dawn to be tickled by your leaves at four in the morning.'

The news throughout Europe reported: "Sarajevo, a war is brewing. Mladic's Bosnian Serb army, supplied and shored up by the Serbian forces invading with Yugoslav artillery and armour from across the Bosnia-Serbia border, surrounded the city. Bombardments hour-by-hour. Hundreds terribly wounded and killed. No one is safe. The assaults are random, meant to break the spirit of the town rather than to conquer it. Vicious, horrific, the worst manifestation of state backed inhumanity on the European continent since the demise of the Nazis and the Communist Gulags. NATO sits on its hands; the EU watches like gormless spectators as savagery plays itself out in its garden. Today the Serbs purposely targeted cultural places. They destroyed the national library and its fine collection. True barbarism."

David was there to cover the civil disruption but as it turned out, he unexpectedly got caught at the beginning of the war. Early in his career he decided to dedicate himself to political manifestations and people's rebellions rather than inter-state conflicts. To survive in the chaos of opposing marches, riots and street battles, he became an expert in reading crowds and learning how to duck and dive on the streets between and behind the lines.

The evening of the day they had witnessed the horrific massacre in the hills, he walked into the Hotel Europa's bar, or what remained of it, for a much-needed drink and saw her struggling to buy a glass of wine. With his bad French and mediocre German he was able to intervene successfully.

They sat together and drank and drank, fleeing from the horror into the momentary relief of alcohol, a shared language and a surprising attraction.

The ragtag band played Sevdalinka, a heart-breaking music at the happiest of times but during the siege, it was heart rending. Love, loss, regret, death, home, family, turbulent rivers which move like women, the moon over tear dripping meadows. The old singer croaked these tunes as if he had a special communication with Pan and the accordion and clarinet, the fiddle and the tambour players layered the laments into thick emotional clouds.

David studied her. A delicate nose, high, sculpted cheekbones, warm coloured fine textured skin, an elegant long neck. 'She must be married but there's no ring; well, she must be loved and in love. A woman like this cannot be on her own and alone ... but most men have no common sense.'

They met earlier in the day when both arrived at the scene of the massacre. Bodies of old men, women and children mown down by heavy machine guns, coups de grace at close quarters, pools of blood, flies, possessions strewn by the killers pillaging for money and jewellery, and a herd of wild white horses racing through the woods, constantly circling like tormented souls needing to find rest.

David heard she was new to war photography and was assured of it when she turned white and vomited. One wag in the press corps said he had heard that the new arrival was wanted by Interpol. "For what," asked David? The wag bunched up his shoulders, lit a cigarette and said, "Homicide ... in Spain.

She, David and his reporter Margaret, were first on the scene and left when Serb irregulars returned and opened fire on them. In between, David had his altercation with Margaret and had pulled Kate to safety.

Here in the crumbling Europa, with many of its gold tinted wall mirrors blown out, the band played and Kate and David finished a bottle of wine. She took his hand. "Do you dance?" She was leaning close and imploring rather than requesting. He stood up and lightly pulled her away from the table. They danced slowly. She responded easily to his less then elegant moves.

Their bodies, tightly joined, swayed slowly against the rhythm of the next, up-tempo song.

"Are you staying?"

She nodded 'yes'. "They're going to need us here." She stopped in her tracks and looked into his eyes. "You're not, are you?"

David was confused but delighted by her directness. "Until a few minutes ago I thought I'd be leaving on a UN flight in a few days."

"Where to?"

"LA."

"Sarajevo to LA.?"

He nodded. "There's a trial deliberation about some white policemen caught on Video who badly beat a black guy. If they walk, all hell will break lose."

"And?"

"Life changes."

She tugged him gently towards her and began to move again. He felt her body against his.

Quietly she asked, "What are you doing tomorrow?"

"There's a Serbian Orthodox church on the hill to the south of town above the brewery. A concert is planned by the Bosnian Muslims and Serbs to celebrate their unity in the face of the siege." He paused and considered for a moment. "It'll be another blood bath."

She stopped moving and pushed herself slightly out of his enfolding hold. "Why?"

With the wine and the emotions of the day, David felt his energy drain away. He staggered and sat down.

She followed and sat across from him. "You okay?"

He nodded.

"Why another blood bath?"

"Mladic, the Bosnian Serb general, won't let it pass off without an attack. He's a mad dog."

"Are you going?"

"If it bleeds it leads."

She thought for a long moment and looked at him. The light from the broken chandelier illuminated her face as if in a Hollywood film.

He realized what she was thinking and shook his head from side to side.

She smiled. "I once went to cooking school." She smiled again. "Would you believe it? They taught us that if we could not kill, gut, skin and cook our food, we had no right to eat it." She studied his face. He smiled faintly. "How will I tell the truth unless I see what they see and know what they're going through?"

He gently took her hand. "Today was bad enough. You don't want to be traumatized so early in the game."

"And you?"

"I've seen a lot of street violence, terrible beatings and wounds, people run down by jeeps and horses. That's all bad enough, but this …this is my first war. I'm here by mistake. My editors didn't expect this. They want me out and the war guys in."

"So why risk your life tomorrow?"

"I'm here. I'm a witness. In between the ads, I show the world what it's up to."

She nodded. "Are you cynical?"

"No, not cynical. Never sure if I'm a realist or a romantic, but not cynical. It's just that when I was young, I thought I could make a difference with my camera - that I'd turn over the stones and shine a light on evil; that people would see it and help to change it." He paused and played with her hand. "It hasn't worked out that way."

He picked up his empty wine glass and watched the reflections scatter the light. He looked at her radiant face and then swung his Leica forward from under his jacket, grabbed it, tapped the lens barrel and pointed. "That wine glass has probably brought more truth into people's lives than this piece of glass in front of my camera."

"Sorry for yourself?"

He smiled and shook his head from side to side. "No. I'm tired of the meaningless violence, of our capacity to hate, of our foolishness, of our holding onto false prophets and being bombarded by millionaire's munitions and shape shifting words. I'm tired of the brutes, the irrationality, the racism, the religious beliefs that lead people to kill each other."

His eyes followed down her long neck to the top of her sweater and then down to the outline of her breasts. He closed his eyes, had a fervent image of her nude and then looked up at her again.

She asked, "What time are you going tomorrow?"

David's head was dancing with memories. He looked again at the pills in his hand and the shimmering water glass. He was overwhelmed by anger. 'These bastards, Mehmet and the rest of his cronies, the cops and secret service, maybe even Suleiman have found political, personal or judicial reasons to destroy me: the outsider, the American, the Jew, the man who asks questions.' He closed his eyes.

The hard stone of her reveries was always contained, a noble gift. Burnt sienna skin, Etruscan nose, but eyes those eyes, midnight eyes, like carbon fields glinting the moon's smoothly tinny rays.

He thought of her and then he remembered the remarkable Annie, his cousin's delicious, passionate, politically committed friend.

Innocence destroyed because of people's beliefs in their right to impose themselves on others.

He was overwhelmed by revulsion. He swept the pills from his hand and flung them across the room.

•••

As he had not cultivated friends at his elementary school, he was on his own with the long summer before him. Barry could only occasionally be visited because he had his own circle of friends who were older then David. He was careful not to intrude but one day Barry told him he wanted to introduce him to a friend named Annie Gross. Barry told him that her parents were great people and her father was a hero.

"They run a book club with really interesting books and magazines and they need someone to help wrap bundles to be mailed all around the country and even to Mexico and Canada."

Barry was usually cool but he now spoke with enthusiasm. "I told Annie about you and she said if you meet and she likes you, you could maybe work for them a few days a week through the summer."

David felt shy and a little irked that he had to pass a sort of personality test to get a job wrapping books. "What's Annie like?"

"Amazing. She's soooo bright and knows so much."

"About what?"

"Politics, and racism, the Spanish Civil War, the Lincoln Brigade and Trotskyism."

David blinked. He was being overwhelmed by these names and words. "What's that? I mean I don't know much about any of it. The Lincoln Brigade yes, but the rest, well, she'll laugh at me."

Barry put his hand on his younger cousin's shoulder. "You'll see, she's great. I know she'll like you."

"But why?"

Almost casually Barry said, "She'll respect you like I do 'cause you're intellectually hungry."

David stared at his cousin. He had never thought of himself in that way but realized, as the words left Barry's lips, that it was true.

He was hungry and more, he wanted to be hungry and he cared about what he asked about. He felt he wanted to know everything and that somehow his salvation and identity were to be found not in beauty alone but in knowledge and ideas. 'Intellectual, I'm intellectual.'

David was nervous about the meeting but told himself that if he failed the personality test at least he'd have work from the photographer to make a little money.

He met Annie several days later at Barry's house. To David she was breath-taking. Not a beauty but totally unlike anyone he had ever met. Her long straight nose was big but somehow okay for her face and perfectly projected from between her very green eyes with their thick guardian eyelashes and slashes of long glossy eyebrows. Her lips were not full but she had a very large mouth that was constantly in motion when she spoke and also as she listened and thought about what was being said she seemed to chew the ideas. Her pale skin was framed by shoulder length dark brown hair with a long full fringe, which was as mobile as her mouth. David was mesmerized as much by her looks as by her intelligence and her attacking way of expressing her beliefs. And what beliefs.

"My father was in the Lincoln Brigade. What amazing experiences he had and fortunately he came back in okay shape."

"Okay?"

"You'll see", she said. "When I think about what happened to other people, he was lucky." She looked up into David's eager face. Her eyes burned through him with passion, with determination and what he would learn later, with a tragic madness.

Annie leant towards David and asked quietly, "Have you heard of Isodora Dolores Ibarruri Gomez?"

David looked at her animated mouth. He realized she was sharing rather than teasing. He shook his head 'no'. David felt humiliated; he was failing the test on the first trial.

"La Pasonaria who helped defend Madrid…you know?"

David breathed deeply with relief and nodded yes.

Annie pulled away. "You do?"

David had looked up the Lincoln Brigade and the Spanish Civil War before meeting Annie. He remembered a photograph by a famous photographer called Robert Capa, of a Republican soldier, arms flung wide, at the moment he was struck by a fascist's bullet. In the same article, La Pasonaria had been mentioned and David had been gripped by what she said in a speech. This brave woman insisted that the fascists would not gain victory in Madrid by shouting "they will not pass". Impossible for David to forget that. He looked at Annie's moving lips, pursing and withdrawing, stretching and pursing again. He all but whispered, "They will not pass".

Barry was dumbstruck by his young cousin's knowledge and felt very proud. Annie sat back on her legs folded under her and smiled. She straightened her black and green plaid skirt over her knees, reached forward, tenderly took David's left hand in her two hands and looked at Barry. "Well, I guess he's your cousin alright."

David looked at her bare knees. His eyes trailed slowly up along her thighs, across the swelling of her breasts, past her neck and her still animated mouth and settled back on her sparking eyes. He had never been affected this way before. He felt a warm stirring between his legs and a painful moan welling in his chest as though a deep sense of loss was about to overwhelm him. He gulped and suppressed his misery and his blossoming joy, knowing he needed to keep those powerful emotions private. It pained him, yet he was proud that he could at last control himself.

Several days later, during an overcast clammy morning, David met Izzy, Annie's father. David extended his had to shake Izzy's while simultaneously realizing that Izzy's right shirtsleeve was empty. David froze, feeling he had transgressed sense and manners in some terrible way, as if he had thrown all the pain in Izzy's eyes back into his face, as though David was now somehow complicit in Izzy's injury.

Izzy grabbed David's right hand with his hard, powerful left hand, whose strength seemed to make up for the loss of the other one.

Izzy pulled David's hand gently to his own broad chest and held it firmly.

"There's no reason for you to know. It's okay son. What I can't do with my hands I do with my mind?" He pulled David further towards him. David smelled garlic on his breath. "And anyway, it's always better to be stronger on the left."

David looked at Izzy quizzically.

Izzy smiled. "You'll do well here. Annie told me all about you and if you come recommended by Barry, you gotta be okay by me."

All the rest of the summer, every Tuesday and Thursday, he worked at Annie's house filling orders, finding books, checking them off, wrapping them and taking them to the post office.

He saw names like Marx, Engels, Trotsky, the League of this and the Party of that, Joe Hill, the Wobbles and on and on with more names and ideas than he had ever heard of. It frightened and intrigued him. 'The world is so big, filled with so many events and people and I know so little.' He wished he could read as quickly as his fingers could rub across the covers of the books.

He watched Izzy from the corner of his eyes whenever he was nearby. David was enthralled by the man's determination and energy.

And Izzy, as his daughter, used words like hot ingots. Izzy had a view about everything. He articulated ideas using bushels of facts that piled into the room as if witnesses to his truths. For the first time in David's life he heard things about the 'Commies' and Red China that sounded positive. Izzy railed against US imperialism, US warmongering, US racism and on and on. He fumed but spoke with such passion that David believed Izzy might be onto something, the something that had always made David wary of God, religion, closed minded kids and adults, about the hypocrisy of his racist family, the confusion between God and the state and about his deepest suspicions that Americans really were contemptuous of ideas and full of hatred towards bright people.

For now, David was content to listen and to try to understand without showing too much of his ignorance. He began to feel he had been allowed entry to a private club with its own rules and language, but he had been admitted because of knowing someone and some things. Knowledge and Connections.

After the first few weeks of working there, he began to think that on every trip to the post office, a walk of four blocks, he was being followed. It was always two men, usually in overcoats, even on the warmest of days. At first, he hoped it was an odd coincidence but later he grew more suspicious as the men entered the post office behind him, lurked in a corner and then followed him back to Annie's house but stopped at the furthest corner of the street.

He mentioned it to Izzy who unexpectedly laughed uproariously and said, "David, don't worry. Its classic FBI intimidation. They're only interested in me. If they follow you it's 'cause they're bored silly, 'cause in fact there's nothing bad or illegal we're doing here. Most of the ex-Lincoln Brigade members are spied on ... the Feds got nutin' better to do."

One day Annie quietly approached and sat next to David as he was wrapping books. She watched for a few moments in silence and then bent forward and stopped him by taking his hand in hers. David was surprised and thrilled. "Barry tells me you like to photograph."

"Yes, I love it." He turned towards her. Annie's face was close to his, so close and intimate that he involuntarily pulled away with embarrassment.

"Why?"

"Why do I take pictures or why do I love it?"

She giggled and sat back. "You know, you talk like you wrap packages. Everything very exact, very defined."

David was on shifting ground, not certain what she meant, where the conversation was going and if he was under attack and yet she had been so close to his face. "Is that good or bad?"

"It's good and special to you. When you ask Barry something he just talks, tells you everything he knows all in a few sentences; when

you ask my father you get a full lecture with all the data, facts, references and his entire political philosophy; but you are very exact, wanting the questioner to be precise about what they are asking. I think that's good, and it makes me think and it gives you room."

" 'I think it's just natural. I'm never certain what people mean."

"Anyway, why do you take pictures?"

Could he really tell her what he thought?

"Come on, give."

David smiled. "You really want to know?"

Annie bit her bottom lip and shook her head up and down, her fringe bobbing and her hair bouncing on her shoulders. "Yes, really really."

David hesitated, quickly thinking about how he could explain what was still to him a mystery. "I had a dream once that I could make peace between people. And then I saw pictures by a photographer who showed me how crazy war is. These two things made me think that if I could travel around and show the truth to people with my pictures, I could help change things."

Annie listened carefully and thought about what he said. "You free on Saturday?"

"During the day."

"Ahhh, gotta hot date Saturday night?"

Embarrassed, he smiled. "No, I'm working as an assistant to a photographer in the evening."

"Wedding?"

"Bar Mitzvah."

"Okay, have your camera ready and we'll go down near the river along Gratiot Avenue. There are a lot of really groovy old joints along there; real old Detroit. You'll love it."

David did not understand her offer or what any of this meant, he did not understand why she had leant so close to his neck and why she was being interested and kind to him. 'She's seventeen and I'm thirteen. Doesn't make sense.'

They went on that Saturday. It was a strange and intriguing voyage into an old world. It seemed everyone they encountered had either a foreign name and accent or a thick American regional accent. Annie was forceful, unstoppable and ballsy. She could ask anyone anything and get them to agree to let David into their shop, workplace or restaurant to photograph while she charmed them with questions about who they were and where they came from. She was young but so forceful and people loved her attention. Meanwhile David was exposed to an old world of dusty clocks, ancient mechanical table games, bottles filled with candies, liquids and preserved fruits. All too soon he ran out of film.

Annie dropped him home and never mentioned the event again. David could not figure it and thought that life was too complicated for him. 'Do others understand these things? Will I ever be a man of the world? Did I upset her?'

CHAPTER 10

David carefully screwed the base of his laptop back on, slid the hard disk into a protective case and placed it inside his box of prints.

His eyes scanned his apartment for the last time, closed the door behind him, tuned the large old key to lock it, paused in the cool hallway and leant against the door's solid olive wood panel. With its long straps over his shoulder and the body of the straw shopping bag under his arm, the box of photographs was securely held within it. Out of sight beneath the box he had placed a compass, a small pair of binoculars, a plastic raincoat wrapped in its carrying sack, a bottle of vodka, his Leica and a few other possessions. He paused, listening to the calming domestic sounds, which, like passing daydreams, delicately floated from under doors, down the stairwell and through the hallway's open windows. Normal sounds, contented sounds of rugs being beaten on balconies, infants gurgling, the soft dull strike of a knife chopping onions on a wooden board. David had never been attached to a place, an apartment, a city, but now, as he prepared to flee for his life, he felt his resolve might easily dissipate, even as he knew he had a long day ahead.

He pushed himself away from the door, descended the stairs and noticed the now more prominent odours of simmering lamb, onions, garlic and thyme as they toyed with his nostrils.

'This is the right course of action. By the time I exit from this darkness into the street I must appear casual, a man going on an errand. Above all, I will have to convince Muhammad that I'll be back soon.'

Step by echoing step he moved through the cool cement ground floor hallway towards the front door.

'Is the exit being watched? Will I safely step into the burning white rectangle of light? Are the secret police already posted on the street? Those raptors with their tell-tale sunglasses, their expensive black Coeur-sauvage jackets and the bulge under the left arm. They're like teenagers in the States or in Britain; projecting themselves as exceptional and distinctive while conforming to the appearance, actions and slang of every other kid on the block. These local secret service guys are no different from their murderous cousins in the Ivory Coast, Libya, Mexico, wherever; they all look the same.'

As David emerged from the dark corridor, he saw Muhammad look up at him with an interest usually reserved for his baking breads.

'Inescapable, no hesitation, bull by the horns time.'

He walked across the street, greeted Muhammad in his usual friendly way and asked for a bread with chopped tomatoes and dill leaves; no lamb today. He paid Muhammad, took a big bite, chewed, swallowed and made admiring sounds.

Muhammad smiled as David turned to leave but he stopped and turned back. In English mixed with halting Arabic and slightly better French, he asked, "Muhammad, are you planning to be here all day as usual?"

Muhammad nodded yes but looked inquisitively at David.

"Good. I'll be back in about two hours. If you see a heavyset man looking for someone and if you get his attention, will you ask him if he's looking for me and if so, let him know I'll be back around 12:30?" He watched Muhammad to see if he could spot a twitch that would give something away, a secret, a fear.

Muhammad turned towards his baking breads and said gruffly over his shoulder, "No problem Monsieur David. There was a man earlier." He twisted and eyed David.

They looked at each other, neither knowing what the other knew, neither knowing how to judge what foreignness can often disguise or misrepresent.

'Monsieur David, are these the best breads you've tasted in all your life?"

David smiled. "Better than anywhere."

"I will give the son of dye makers your message." He paused as if considering his next words carefully. "Please remember a poor man's bread. Ach," he intoned, "but a poor man better than the dye maker who works in foul water and slime all day."

David understood Muhammad had guessed what the young man who had questioned him earlier was and he knew that he, David was now a target.

Muhammad handed David two more wrapped shawarma. "Here, they are good on journeys."

The two old men stared at each other for a long moment. "It's for you, no money; now go."

As David walked along the sweltering dusty street he wondered if the old baker had turned away because he feared he would reveal his emotions. David was now sure he was right about Muhammad, that he was, if not an agent, one of the many reluctant thousands in the pay of the secret police, what the Israelis call 'a handle'.

As David wove amongst the passers-by, appreciating that his muscles had loosened and that he felt strong for his age, he scanned a part of history he knew well.

'It never changes. The bad guys learn from the other bad guys. The East German Stasi, who bribed, cajoled, intimidated so many in the population of that ill-fated puppet state to become informers on their wives, work associates and even on their parents, that they corrupted the whole society. Castro had done the same in Cuba and on and on back to Samarkand under Tamerlane in the fourteenth century. Murder and mayhem is our default condition. Uncertainty, fear, aggression, regret and pretence weave our political systems together, stitch our lives into the cloaks of the wealthy and powerful. We are tailor's threads, never seeing sufficiently clearly that together it is we who create the mantle that wraps us in the material of our own lives and keeps us bound in their power. Complicity and silence may be morally different but the consequences are the same.'

So, thought David, 'Muhammad may be in their pay but he helped me'.

David walked along the street through the heat, taking in the oily odours of the fish shop and then of the spice emporium with its tangy smoked paprika, warm and comforting perfumes drifting from the conical piles of fennel and mustard seeds, the sweet tingle of ground cinnamon, allspice, cloves and nutmeg, and the awakening tang of preserved lemons in brine and the pickled chillies in vinegar.

The distant breeze of cumin that rose from her armpits, the rich but evasive whisper of Coco Chanel mingled with the sweet sea spray - an allusion to the purest oyster. His nose against her, he was delirious in the perfumes of her body, that first night in Sarajevo. His lips against the side of her breast, his left hand gently sliding over her soft warm belly and sweeping over the rise of her hip and then plunging to smooth his palm around her inner thigh.

From the helter-skelter of Arabic script, signs, piles of food, boxes and crates of goods, he imagined a painting he had seen. It was no wonder Picasso painted the breasts of women so close to their eyes. These are the places men call home and their unity is what men imagine brings a calm death even while it ignites them.

David crossed back to the sunny side of the street and turned left into the busy avenue. He was certain Muhammad had watched him until the turn. Halfway along the street he dropped into the tobacco-stationary-newspaper-everything else shop where he sometimes found the previous week's Herald Tribune often with whole articles blacked out by thick felt markers. He purchased a letter sized single brown envelope, a map of the Mediterranean basin and a popular local newspaper. The tall but bent thin young man who owned the shop knew David did not speak more than a few words of Arabic. He looked curiously at the paper and up at David who smiled, folded the map, slid it into the envelope, pushed them safely down into his straw bag, paid the young man, turned to the window and fiddled with the newspaper, all the time carefully watching the street. No one following but he smiled as he remembered that they are, after all, secret police.

The young man glided up next to David as he prepared to leave. He gently took David's arm in his strong grip. David, surprised, looked at him and was again captivated by the tight curly steel hair; a man prematurely grey. David had always thought he must be part sheep or a man who suffered a terrible shock. The man's face was serious but not threatening.

"English or American?" Before David could answer he continued. "Once I had to hide from the authorities. I got a burnoose, a cane and walked like an ancient beggar. No one noticed me." He peered at David for a moment and then out of the sand scratched window onto the street. "Walked through a police line, unsteady, head down, complaining to myself. No one stopped me, no one touched me."

David looked at the man's profile. "I've been coming in here for five months. Why tell me this now?"

The man did not answer but walked to the back of the shop, grasped something from a lower shelf and returned to David's side.

He dropped several apples into the straw bag. He gently pushed David towards the door and all but whispered, "People don't always deserve the government they have."

David exited, turned to look at this generous, bent, prematurely grey young man but he had already disappeared into the cool shadows of his shop. David walked to the next corner. He tuned left into the street that ran behind his apartment building. He wondered if he now carried a stricken appearance, the look of a hunted man and that every local could see it. He smiled. 'At this rate, by the time I arrive at my destination, I'll be loaded down with fruits, cheeses, beers and all manner of supplies and advice.'

He knew if he carried straight on, passed the rear of his building and continued for about a mile or so, he would arrive at the sea road that leads to the cliff stairs above the fishermen's harbour. And Muhammad would, in the meantime either delay the secret police for two hours or send them off in the direction he had seen David go; the wrong direction.

'But what of Mehmet? I've got no categories that work, no rules that generally apply, no ideas that are solid and universally applicable. Sure, there are moralists, immoralists and a-moralists. But what does this tell me other than we are all frail, perhaps not able to feel empathy, but we are all human and therefore all human actions are within the ambit of who I am and also of what I may do. If others are capable of love and self-sacrifice, am I capable of hatred and murder? Am I different than my swaggering brother whose main vocabulary was violence?'

After passing by the rear of his building and having walked for several more blocks, David suddenly wondered if Muhammad would be accused of having been complicit with him in his so-called spying escapade. 'Can I live other people's fate? Am I responsible for their lives? They made choices over the course of years that bring them to where they are. Is this a rationalization? Am I finding an excuse to throw someone to the dogs? Have I become the rich man who rationalizes the destruction of other's lives based on business principals? Have I become the demagogue who rationalizes state terror with the principals of historical necessity? Have I become a Mehmet, excusing immorality based on fundamentalist beliefs?'

The day became hotter; the neighbourhood became poorer. He was nearing the port area with its dives, brothels, and cheap restaurants selling plates of food by their weight. Here and there were metal-working and engine repair shops, small breezeblock warehouses filled with Chinese dolls, Korean TVs, smuggled cigarettes, a handful of rocket launchers in transit from an arms dealer to a corrupt state or to some ideological or criminal group, and shedloads of other contraband from around the world. Worse, there were probably children or at least poor young trafficked girls hidden in filthy basements, waiting to be sold as cheap labour or sex slaves.

A miasma of petrol exhaust, slicks of spilled oil, the stench of piss and unwashed bodies filled his nostrils, the nostrils of the foreigner who seemed, even for his average height, tall amongst these continuously underfed brown skinned people.

He walked through the heat and stench with the Arabic newspaper under his arm, hoping that if he appeared determined, others, and in particular the young bravos with their hidden knives, might think that he was a man with sufficient contacts not to tangle with. The drunken Filipino and Russian sailors would also hesitate long enough to give him safe passage as they wondered if he was important. David would be able to move on inexorably towards the sea road, the fishermen's port and if lucky, to the Sergeant's father's boat.

A couple of upper-class boys, looking for hookers to take on a joy ride, stumbled out of a bar across the busy street. They sneered at those around them and laughed, high on cocaine or some other rich man's drug, as they leered at the girls on the game, standing in a pathetic clutch near the kofta shop.

David ploughed on. He remembered how, when first watching the scions of the upper middleclass in his Midwestern university, he was continually amazed at their loud, vulgar, self-assured sense of ownership and of their certainty of being unquestionably right in any of their often, ignorant utterances. What astonished him was their unabated self-regard, so contemptibly manifested in their anti-intellectualism. He understood that their educations were meant to sculpt them into leadership roles as lawyers, judges, and politicians whose need for culture was only to decorate their projection of innate superiority. They employed what to them were 'effeminate Jews and arty faggots' to create supportive canons in art and culture … and if artists adhered to the code, celebrated their paymaster's values and sucked up like leeches on the skin of an ulcerous whale, they were rewarded with money, honours and fame. Challenge them, refuse to play the game and the artist is written out of history or perhaps never into it.

David glanced around and almost smelled the oppression and consequent debasement of the population.

'There's some solace for contrarian artists like me in the Western democracies, unlike in many other places in the world. At least, when we object, we are ignored rather than arrested or worse. Culture was not something to challenge the Western elites with, to question their status quo, to encourage self-doubt. Thus, the uncultured establishment's inability to experience empathy or to conceive of other's suffering … their hollow souls, bereft of the benefits of art, at last make sense to me. They maintain a selective understanding, which excludes sensibilities that could undermine their grasp of power and wealth. Better for security that the scions of the wealthy should be sociopaths rather than humanists.'

Across town, in the armoury, the Sergeant stamped out another cigarette, looked at his watch and then at his Colonel. He saw anxiety creeping, like the beads of sweat on his forehead, into the Colonel's fat-ringed eyes.

"Sir, would you like me to check on the doctor again?"

The Colonel was digging an ever-deeper pit of despair for himself, calculating how he was being trapped between the political cadre, his superior officer, the politician's desire to throw ranking men to the press dogs and his own junior officers, who were always conniving to displace their betters. He looked at his Sergeant with a sense of relief. He thought, 'This is a man I can count on, a man grateful for my gifts to his child, a man delighted to serve the likes of me. He is a good and loyal dog.'

He nodded to his underling as though his cool unaffected speechlessness gave him a macho authority. He loved and often imagined he was in a Clint Eastwood Western or cop film: Once Upon A Time in The Maghreb, Dirty Ziad.

The Sergeant dipped his head quickly and projected clearly, "Sir", and briskly walked back through the corridor that led to the offices.

Mehmet gazed at The Empty Quarter from the top of the hill above the set. He knew that unless he had been seen with David, no one could connect them, although torture could extract some convincing evidence, true or not. But unless David disregarded the telephone signal, he would have prepared himself for arrest. He is a man who understands the need to commit to the greater good.

A hawk soared by. Mehmet remembered that they can spot a rabbit a mile away. And then it struck him. 'Old men have enough discomfort; they do not need to hold onto a few more days of life that might include torture. David is a rational man, a man who could well calculate his chances and is brave enough to sacrifice himself for democracy. He's old, he's unhappy, why not?'

Mehmet watched the hawk as it swooped towards a hapless victim. David is his rabbit and he is the hawk. He watched the bird of prey circle their film set, carrying something in its beak.

Mehmet looked across the landscape. Glaring white rocks, no trees or grasses, withering heat shimmering in the distance creating a tangled mirage. There, behind the rippling wall of air was a hell with burning pyres, black vultures feeding on the flesh of children and on screaming women. Mehmet, the director, the creator was susceptible to portents.

•••

The high school was immense. On David's first day, he entered with trepidation. He would know a few of the other kids from his elementary school but as he had no friends amongst them there would be no natural allies. He was surprised at how few Negroes were in the school and more shocked that there was only one in the advanced classes that he was enrolled in. David had no idea how bright the others in his classes would be but it worried him that he might appear dull or dumb.

He entered his English classroom and sat in the front row slightly to the left of the teacher, a young middle-aged woman with dyed blond hair named Miss Mahler. He thought she had a kind face.

Outside the school window there were still tragic unemployment levels; the steel union's long strike was rattling on, defying the government and the powerful corporations; the Russians had landed a probe on the moon spraying pebbles for a thirty five mile perimeter while kicking dust in the eyes of the Americans; the bullish Russian premier, Khrushchev was petulant about not being allowed to visit Disneyland in California during his state visit; the Cold War, which surrounded all the kids, was still frigid and threatened their existence every day of their lives, or so they were told. And the young senator from Massachusetts was making a good run to become president. David admired him. He was a bright man. He was a scholar; Nixon, his opponent, was a used ideas salesman.

Inside the classroom, Miss Mahler spoke quietly. Her soft tones calmed David's nerves.

"This year in my class you will read Shakespeare to discover the beauty of our common language, you will read Cervantes to discover the moment of the first modern man, you will read some of the great American writers' essays, poetry, plays and novels and you will read Albert Camus." She looked around, studying the mixture of eager,

frightened, worried, open and not so open faces. This was one of the honour's courses and she knew she had the cream of the entering students in front of her.

"Who do you think will be amongst the American writers?" She waited. "A guess? Anyone?" She scanned the faces and stopped at someone behind David to his left. She looked down at her class roster and then up again. "Helen, take a guess."

David turned. He flushed. There sat a girl with huge dark eyes, a head of thick black hair and, as he quickly noticed, full breasts, a narrow waist and rounded hips. She was beautiful ... she was sexy. He became troubled; Annie slipped from his mind, the unobtainable Annie and this instantaneous response, this new awareness rushed over and through him.

Helen seemed confused by the question. Her eyes darted around seeking help. They landed on David who was clearly staring at her. She became distracted from the question. She smiled.

Miss Mahler interrupted, "Helen, this is an English class and although Romeo and Juliet will be read this term and we may even listen to Bernstein's West Side Story, perhaps we need not act it out just at the moment."

Helen flushed and quickly looked away from David. A few classmates giggled.

Miss Mahler looked at David, Helen's chosen focus. David realized she was about to question him. He tore himself away and quickly said, "Thomas Wolfe, Ernest Hemingway, Thornton Wilder, Henry David Thoreau ... maybe O'Neill."

There was a murmur somewhere in the bowels of the class. Miss Mahler said, "Not all of them but excellent choices Daniel."

"David, miss, my name is David. Can I ask something?"

She smiled and dipped her head as if to apologies and to grant him permission with the same gesture. "I don't know if you can, but you may."

David shrugged off the correction. "Why's Camus on the list?"

"Do you know him?"

He nodded his head 'yes'.

"What do you know of his work?"

"The collected short stories, The Plague, The Stranger."

Miss Mahler looked up at the class.

As she did, David realized that perhaps he had seemed like a show-off. People always disliked him for that. His mother would not answer his questions, his brother would smack him, in elementary school the other kids ignored him, said he was a smarty-pants or that he wanted to be teacher's pet. He felt embarrassed and was overwhelmed by thinking that within so few hours of starting to build a new life, of trying to create a new persona, he had already reverted to how he had always been and had already screwed himself. He was certain there was something wrong with him.

Miss Mahler said, "David has asked the key question concerning the whole of this first year of your study. It is a good question and a question, when answered, which will allow you to see many more things about the need for art and literature in our lives and why, without their meanings and messages about our existence, we are so much reduced."

David turned towards Helen. She smiled at him. He was definitely in love.

At the end of class David's heart was pounding. He was uncertain what to do. He horsed around with his books at his desk allowing the others to pass him. He stalled to see if she would say anything. She slipped on her cardigan, gathered her books and walked directly up to him. As she approached, he could tell that she was wearing a warm scented perfume.

"You know a lot."

He looked up, surprised by her comment. He nodded as if to say, 'yes I am in love with you'. What he did say was "I like to read."

"How do you know about what's his name, the French writer?"

"Someone said I should read him. He's really different, intriguing. It's another world, filled with things I'd never come across before. And he's not difficult to read."

She stepped slightly away. "You mean because I didn't answer her question you think I'm not very smart."

David was taken by surprise. "Oh God no. All I meant was that even being translated from the French somehow the English is really straightforward. It's almost like Hemingway or Raymond Chandler."

She looked into his eyes; he was spellbound. Quietly she murmured "Oh, like Hemingway. Okay." She paused, still looking into his eyes as no one had ever done before. "Chandler, okay', she murmured. "Well, I'll see you."

David had not known what to do but he was disappointed. What could he expect? A teacher's pet, smarty pants, smart aleck, his brother's punching bag. He finally gathered his books and realised she had stopped near the door. He slowed to walk past her. She quietly spoke, "I'm really glad we're in the same class."

David's heart leapt.

As he threaded through the crowded corridor to his locker on the next floor up, he thought about Helen. He tried to separate his rising lust from his other emotions. Yes, he knew he wanted to experience something sexual with her but he was not sure those thoughts were acceptable. Did it mean that he was somehow 'dirty', that he was demeaning her because he was so sexually attracted to her? And what was this instant sense of love? Was it only a kind of lust, a sort of chemical expression, or was it something else? And what did 'doing something sexual' mean? He could not, at this tender age, imagine all of those things that his brother and his friends talked about: 'fucking', 'screwing', 'banging', 'ramming his big truck into her tunnel' or otherwise, as he had heard – 'making love', 'sleeping with her'. And he knew that whenever they referred to girls who 'did it' they were always described as 'whores', 'sluts', 'skags'. It was all made so filthy, so demeaning and instinctively he knew it was also hateful towards the girls. He thought that boys and men mostly were afraid of girls and because of that they had a kind of hatred towards them.

He arrived at his locker to drop off some books and to get a new notebook for his next and most important class of the day. While sorting his things, an older kid, two lockers away, big and broad, looked menacingly at David. He slid his eyes sidelong to see what was happening, to appraise if there was a threat. He had grown so used to this kind of presence with his brother it was by now second nature to prepare himself for violence.

The big kid leered and said, "Plaid pants huh".

David was confused. He glanced down at the muted green squares with the mud brown outlines around them. 'Plaid yea', he thought for the first time, 'so'? He looked up at the big guy not certain what the offence was.

"Coon pants. You should ought'a go down back where the jungle bunnies are, you wanna wear pants like that." He slammed his locker with disgust and looked at David. "You should hear 'em. They can't even talk 'merican." He stomped away.

David was shaking both from the intimidation and from the guy's violent way of speaking. And he wondered what 'down back' meant.

Later he would see that was where the shop classes were. Woodworking, plumbing, car mechanics and some cooking courses were taught in big hall like rooms filled with machinery. Almost all the kids there were Negroes and mostly they entered the school by the back door. Seeing this would continue to change David's idea about what America really was and what 'equal opportunity' meant.

Now in a storm of confusion about sexual love and anger about race and fairness he entered the photography class, an option he had nominated. A group of fifteen other kids, all boys, waited patiently. David looked around and sat alone near the front of the room. After several minutes a tall, unassuming middle-aged man entered. He walked directly to the blackboard and wrote 'Busby' with big sweeps of the chalk. He turned. "That's my name. I'll try to remember yours. By the end of term, if you do well, I'll know who you are. If you don't, I probably won't remember to give you a grade."

He looked around, scanning the faces as had Miss Mahler. "Who knows anything about cameras or film or what photography is?"

A tall boy named Ed raised his hand. "I know what 'photography' means." Ed spoke in an entirely distinctive manner David had not heard before. He pronounced his words slowly, carefully, giving them weight, announcing in his delivery that he knew they were important and meaningful.

Mr Busby waited. Ed waited. Mr Busby finally asked, "Are you going to share your knowledge or just tell us that you have it?"

"I am sorry sir. You asked what photography is, not what it meant so I was not certain you wanted my contribution."

Mr Busby revealed his tolerant nature to David and the rest of the class. "Correct, you got me there, but do tell us."

Ed stood up, very formally and said, "Photography comes from the ancient Greek; 'photo' means light and 'graphy' means writing so together it means writing with light." Ed sat down.

'Smart', thought David. 'I've been studying photography for the last two years and never asked what the meaning of the word was. Smart.' He was pleased with this and wanted to know who Ed was.

Mr Busby asked Ed if he had ever printed a photograph. Ed shook his head 'no'. "Anyone", asked Busby?

David looked around and then raised his hand. "I have sir."

"Why," asked Mr Busby?

David felt no aggression from his new teacher but was confused as to how to answer. His mind raced. 'What can I say without seeming a show-off?' He hesitated.

Mr Busby, clearly a patient man, waited.

"I want to make stories; I want to do what W. Eugene Smith does. I know to do that, I have to be able to print so I taught myself, as best I could, to print. And it's really exciting."

"Eugene Smith?" Mr Busby looked at the rest of the class. He looked back at David, he looked down at this class list. "Your name?"

"David."

Mr Busby looked at Ed and asked him his name.

"Edward."

Mr Busby looked at the rest of the class. "You see, it's easy. You make a contribution, I ask and remember your name and that way I can grade you because you've let me know who you are." He paused and looked at David again. "What camera do you use David?"

"At the moment I use a Kodak Pony Four but I want to get something more controllable."

"Such as?"

"A Rollei twin lens reflex."

"Because?"

"I think I would like the square format and because the larger format will give me a more grainless blow-up."

"And why do you want a more grainless enlargement?"

David hesitated. He realized all eyes were on him and especially Ed who seemed mesmerized by David's knowledge.

"Because sir, if I can reduce the grain, people looking at my prints can see more clearly the things in the pictures, so I think it will seem more real."

Mr Busby almost gasped, "More real?"

"Yes sir, because then the photo is less about being a photo and more about the things in it, the people and stuff."

"You've read that man, Marshal McLuhan, who talks about 'the medium is the message'?"

"No sir, sounds interesting."

"David, when you say more real, do you mean more truthful?"

David felt a wave of pleasure pass through him. He instantly knew that was exactly what he meant. "Yes sir, more truthful. The clearer the picture the more truthful it will seem to be."

Mr Busby slowly sat on the edge of his desk and thought for a long silent moment. He looked up at the class, past David and spoke quietly. "While you learn about exposure, cameras, printing and so on this term, I want you to remember this discussion. David is talking about truth, and if there is one wonder of photography, it's truthfulness."

CHAPTER 11

"Thank you, captain, I'll tell the Colonel." The Sergeant quietly placed the receiver back on the hook of the ancient phone, looked up at the fly spattered Japanese clock on the wall, smiled to himself and rose from the desk. He hovered for a moment pondering if he'd covered all options.

As the lean Sergeant walked back towards the armoury, he was compelled to ask himself whether the series of seeming coincidences he had helped construct would lead the American to the father's boat. He only knew of David through the short meeting he had when he loaned the boat, on that sweltering summer's day last August, to his childhood friend.

On that day, the Sergeant was affected by David's warmth and interest in who he, the Sergeant was. It was neither the inquisition of a condescending foreign tourist nor a fiendish spy - an enemy of his leader - but of a man who cared for others. So many questions he had asked, so polite, so respectful, and he did send me the snap he had shot of me on that day. He smiled again as he remembered how proud his father was when he, the Sergeant, showed the photo of the old American gentleman standing on their boat with the Sergeant's childhood friend, Dr Suleiman, and with himself, a fisherman's son. He tried to remember if it was then that he hatched his plan within a plan.

As he neared the armoury, he recalled the tricky conversation with his father.

"You have to destroy the snap. If anyone finds it and connects the American to us, we've had it."

His father gently slapped his son's cheek. "Is this right, what you have arranged? He is an innocent man."

"Father, who is innocent?"

"I've worked hard all my life but I am still a poor man; is God paying me back for my faults and failures?"

"God gave me to you and now I can bring you a gift of wealth. The American is rich. We can take his money, and no one will know or care. Father, this is a gift. God wills it."

His father looked uncertain although intrigued.

"He is an American and I think a Jew … how innocent can he be? But even if I sacrifice an innocent man's life, we will take from him enough to make us secure for many years to come. This will bless your grandchildren and their grandchildren."

His father bent forward and squeezed his son's leg, nodded several times and smiled broadly. "Family and tribe first, and one must honour one's father."

As the Sergeant emerged from his daydream and entered the fume filled armoury, he peered through the haze of cigarette smoke, dust and engine exhaust. He saw the Colonel and his special squad across this vast underground mausoleum, impatiently waiting for him to deliver news.

'How long it had taken to arrive at a position of trust and responsibility; the Colonel accepts me; I show him loyalty; he thinks I am a just another dumb fisherman's son.'

Sergeant Ali had always tried not to hurt their victims. He never took part in the rapes; he never tortured others. He knew the team were wary of him but his protestations that he was a devout Muslim and being the Colonel's firm favourite, sufficiently defused further inquiries. Besides, he was always willing to be the one who put the bullet in the back of the head of those awaiting execution. He would do it quickly and without warning so the victims would not suffer.

As he neared the Colonel and the others, he thought it strange that he was anything but a devout believer and yet he did wish to do good in the world. As he arrived, he thought, 'I am still the innocent child watching my father's dying tuna catch on the small deck of his boat. Ahh, was it not a blessing that I had shown the kind foreigner where my clever father hides the key to the engines on his small boat?'

He arrived next to his profusely sweating Colonel. "Sir, the doctor had been released and should be on his way here."

Suleiman drove like a man on a mission, too fast, too careless. He took corners at speed but felt confident that he knew the roads and the limitations of his car well enough to be safe. Now that the army had released him, he presumed because someone in one of the endless corridors of the secret state had told the soldiers to do so, he felt sure of himself, sure that his cover had not been blown. It had been an administrative mistake: the left hand not knowing what the left hand was doing.

Having grown up in the city, he knew it well, even with all the recent changes to the road system, the new flyovers, underpasses and the sprouting shiny government and corporate buildings that had swept away large sections of the beautiful old town.

Down the coast road, up to the top of the cliff above the fishermen's port, right into the old warehouse road and along for a mile until behind David's flat where he knew he could easily park, get into David's flat quickly, administer the injection and be out within moments with no one the wiser.

Suleiman knew that a locally performed autopsy would never find a trace of the drug and if it did, it would conclude that it came from the sleeping pills. Dr Suleiman smiled, pleased with himself that he had given David the bottle with no markings on it. He thought, 'Untraceable, like me'.

'He's an old man, no real battle; my plan will have the advantage of surprise, youth and strength. If Mehmet's plan works, even with David as a corpse, Mehmet will be boosted into a position of authority amongst the oppositionists and I will have my puppet in place and if doesn't work, then Mehmet is the fall guy. Perfect.'

What Suleiman did not know was that he had just passed a used clothing shop in which David was involved in a ritualistic bargaining for a burnoose and a beaten-up wooden cane. A cup of coffee - short, thick with finely powdered grounds at the bottom, a white cardamom floating in it and then another cup between stories of the owner's poor children and his sick old mother, about how hard his life was, followed with exclamations of joy in knowing the generosity of others and then another cup. To refuse the coffee was to prove oneself an ingrate, uncivilized and unworthy of any consideration, let alone a fair price; but to not engage in the bargaining, the constant degrading of the garment's poor condition, observance of the nasty stain and the occasional hole was equally ungracious. One cannot be passive or neutral in the transaction. David smiled, drank and spoke in his halting French, thinking that the endless cups of coffee are the personal equivalent of the authority's roadblocks.

With Suleiman's car parked out of sight on the narrow backstreet, he placed the slim injection kit into his front trouser pocket, slid out of the car more easily then when assisted by the army captain just forty-five minutes earlier, removed his ripped and dusty jacket, threw it onto the rear seat, locked the doors and moved quickly along the pavement. Scraped face, dirty shoes, blaring white shirt in the spring sun, he was not as anonymous as he would have wished to be.

He reached the main street, turned left and approached the now closed and locked front door of David's apartment building. He remembered it was the second unmarked bell from the top; he rang it, waited and rang again. He cursed himself for not having brought his spare, untraceable mobile phone. He took a few steps back and looked up towards David's first floor balcony. He saw that the French windows were ajar. He rang again, more insistently.

'Has David done my work for me? Was he now unconscious, lying on his old divan with his heart slowing and his blood pressure dropping towards extinction?'

Suleiman startled. A firm knuckle poked his right shoulder. He turned, momentarily angered by the surprise as well as by the firmness of the knock. Muhammad looked Suleiman up and down as though evaluating something odd, suspicious. Certainly, this slim man was not … what had Monsieur David said … 'heavy'. Suleiman was in no mood to be panhandled by this old bum covered in flour and dough. "Leave me."

Muhammad, a proud man who had bent his knee once too often in his younger life to the likes of this city popinjay, lifted his chin, silently turned and walked back across the street without a word.

As Suleiman saw the old man return to his stall, he realized he had misapprehended him and further, realized that now, having been seen and therefore probably identifiable, he needed to act decisively. There were only two possibilities: that he leave immediately, hoping that David was expiring on his old divan or that when he joins the others and he convinces the Colonel to let him, Suleiman, into the apartment first and alone on the grounds of being able to make a discreet arrest.

Suleiman walked across the street to the old baker. He smiled his professional smile and politely asked him what he wanted to say. Muhammad looked at him blankly.

"Really, I'm sorry. I was in a road accident earlier."

"Learn to drive better."

"Yes, good advice, I'll work on it. What did you want to tell me when I was so rude?"

"He's gone, about an hour ago."

Suleiman appraised the man and his information. He unintentionally snapped, "Why tell me this?"

"He said a man would come for him." Muhammad looked Suleiman up and down; his contempt showed in his eyes if not in his tone. "He asked me to tell the man he'd return in a while."

Suleiman, not insensitive to Muhammad's sixteenth century tribal macho myths, snapped, "What's awhile?"

"What's an accident?"

Suleiman, never long on patience or manners for those he considered beneath him, wondered if this historic vestige knew any more, or could he now show his utter contempt for this poor old baker. Suleiman barked, "He definitely said he was returning?"

Muhammad looked up at the doctor. Generations of enmity, years of contrition poured through him like heretical fires. "Inshallah."

David, walked towards the coast road, dressed from head to toe in his newly purchased but used and muddy brown burnoose, limping slightly and using the cane to carry his weight. "Not bad; the cane actually helps my poor hip.' He was concerned that the storeowner had seen the wedge of dollars he was carrying. He looked behind to be assured that no one was following him, neither a crow nor a mugger. All seemed clear.

As he walked, he remembered the next picture in his box of memories. It was a stoutly composed black and white shot made on his beloved Hasselblad, a camera he had replaced the earlier Rollieflex with. A man with swept back greasy hair, bent from the waste, picking shards of shiny coal from the rail line where the trains passed on their way from the mine to the power station. Behind the bent man, the glinting tracks span out to infinity, a shed disappears into the gloom and the silvery grey, low clouds trap this man between the unforgiving sky and the hard, black earth. He appears ill dressed, cold, uncomfortable, perhaps in pain. There is a story, redolent with injustice, inequality and a tattered pride.

'I photographed him; he allowed me to. He said it made no difference to him and no, he did not want to see what he already knew he looked like on every one of the long cold days of his unemployment.

"Life's like that, bitter, empty, unfair. Me only regret's I ain't brave enough to end it meself. But if the transit police catch me taking these wasted lumps a' coal I used to mine meself, I'll do it."

David remembered that was the only moment the man looked up and as he did, David saw that this ex-miner, probably forty-five, appeared to be sixty.

"I will an' all, do it meself. The bairns 'ill hav'ta find a better life on their own. I'm jes a waste a space, extra mouth, no value to the missus if ya knows me meaning, nor to the little'uns."

This heavy-hearted photograph, while tonally rich, was sombre and austere. David had seen many people silenced in front of it and he knew that it inexplicably touched people even before they invariably looked at the title.

Between his first viewing W. Eugene Smith's images in Life Magazine and making that photograph of the ex-miner, David had travelled a long creative journey. 'Odd how disillusionment, in one's religion, country and people, matures one sufficiently to be able to see and make pictures which encompass anger, hope and love in the same frame.

'What is this creativity I have so admired and hold onto as an identity? Surely I'm part craftsman, but I'm also a messenger and what I bring is not craft alone but a cry from the heart, an invitation to see who and what is responsible, and an invocation to respond. Craftsman, messenger and what? Visionary, teacher, philosopher, activist? What tags do I deserve?'

As he moved along the broken pavement, concerned that he still might be spotted, he remembered a quote from the linguist George Steiner, who wrote, 'the best teachers lead their students to the doorstep of their own imagination'. He smiled to himself at this pleasing thought.

David mentally returned the print to the pile in his box and recalled that he never got the man's name nor knew his fate. But thereafter, when the right-wing press referred to the unemployed as 'scroungers', David felt his fury as he remembered that unemployed miner.

He mused, 'Have I become the unemployed miner? The same pained body, the same sense of uselessness and now, hiding from myself in this getup as the miner had wrapped himself in his world-weariness?'

David, whose nose was always sensitive, became aware of the sea. He reached the coast road, crossed over through the heavy, late morning traffic and walked to the railings that offered some safety or at least a warning that there was a precipitous drop just a few meters beyond.

There it was, the Mediterranean, sparkling in the late morning sunshine. He never knew why but from the moment he first saw it, he felt it was a kind of home for him as it was to the ancients. For the first time that morning he felt calmness overcome him. Now warm blood rather than anxiety-inducing chemicals coursed through his veins. He smiled and remembered his short-lived friend, Ed who, on that September afternoon, so long ago, in Mr Busby's first photography class, had alerted him to the origin of words: the 'Mediterranean', 'the middle of the earth'.

David looked to his right along the precipice and saw the long stairs, with cracked and broken cement steps leading down to the fishermen's quay.

'If I can arrive there without being spotted and get down them in one piece, I'll be another beat closer to safety. I just need to avoid the officials, the customs collectors and the few harbour police who sometimes appear and harass the fishermen. This will be a bit of luck.'

•••

Within the first few months of going to high school, David's world grew more complex. There were the beginnings of connections between his interior world filled with teenage angst and the exterior world of others. The others were not only the kids in his classes, his new friend Ed and his girlfriend Helen but also the others he was made aware of by Izzy's constant verbal bombardment. Workers and peasants of the world, dockers, miners, farmers, assembly-line workers and always and forever in Izzy's reckoning, the brown, black, yellow and red people who were overseen, stolen from and beaten down by the white Americans and their European pals. There were more new words entering David's intellectual constructs: 'exploitation', 'imperialism', 'capitalism', 'the opiate of the people' and 'the comprador class'; all of which were vague but seemed to carry, in Izzy's world, mythologies that embodied evil.

David was too preoccupied with trying to understand who he was in the larger, more complex world now less centred on home and family, to fully absorb Izzy's themes. He could not negotiate the immensity of the ideas and unfortunately Izzy's hectoring forced David into a protective shell. He could not ask Izzy questions nor enter a dialogue without having to submit to one of his rants. But David became aware of a vocabulary of ideas that would help him to understand the world more clearly in later life.

Meanwhile David's use of his camera was training him to see more clearly the lives of others'. He practiced watching events in his classes and on the streets while walking to and from school. As he observed he began to define what the events might mean and how they could truthfully be pictured and understood as images without sound or even captions. His eyes were becoming a camera.

In a book about Russian Constructivism he came across an early Polish documentary filmmaker named David Kaufman, who, once in the midst of the Russian Revolution in Moscow, changed his name to Dziga Vertov. He claimed, "I am a camera". David understood this. He began to question why so much interesting work, work that he admired or which excited him, emerged from social upheaval and in particular from revolutionary ferment.

On the streets and in class he saw that the way people held and used their bodies, that their breathing patterns, the nature of their clothing and how it sat across their fat or muscles, that the shape of their bodies and their relative fitness expressed their inner lives. Making conscious the relationship between people's exterior and interior worlds was a revelation; it helped him to become more aware of the presence of others.

His constant reading about photographers led him to Henri Cartier-Bresson, whose work gave expression to a fascinating visual idea. He learned that within each action there is a single moment that is the most revealing of the subject's intentions. That moment is as much about capturing the action as it is about the form of the action in the frame and its relationship to all the other compositional elements. Clarity of composition leads to clarity of form leads to clarity of idea. Cartier-Bresson called this split second 'the decisive moment'. The very name excited David. Concepts were beginning to cross-fertilize each other.

The 'decisive moment' had to be realized before it occurred so that the photographer could set the exposure, frame, focus, and release the shutter at the moment when the event rose to its climax rather than at the moment when the photographer realized it had occurred ... which would be that fraction of a second too late. For David there was something precious and muscular about these ideas. Once absorbed and well-practised he knew they would give him a command over picture making.

He continued to work at the bookshop through his first month at high school. While Izzy's rants were sometimes oppressive, David could see that Izzy ate his own pain by feasting on others' struggles. But David also understood that Izzy's constant flow of words was as much a form of aggression as was his own father's silence.

His fleeting meetings with Annie were sufficient to keep him loyally employed and tolerant of Izzy until the end of September. Annie went off to university and David was told that he would no longer be needed. Annie lived in his heart for years to come. He had fallen in love with her passion and her strength, the very things that led to her tragic end.

David, like all the first- year students, was called into his advisor's office. Mr Mullen, with dull grey hair and dull in speech, seemed more bored than anything; not like the stern principal of his elementary school. His skin shone with perspiration; his eyes were watery.

"So David, a nice little talk, eh?"

"Yes sir."

"Are you liking it here?"

"Yes sir."

"Good, that's one box I can tick."

"Not disappointed then, eh?"

"Sir?"

Mr Mullen shuffled through papers in a manila file and finally plucked one, lowered his glasses from his forehead and scanned the document. "Mmmm, ahhh, aha. I thought so." He looked up at David. "Seems like you were chosen for the Arts High School downtown. Didn't want to go, eh?"

Could David spill the beans about his parents not wanting him to go? He flushed and became confused; he remembered how he had suppressed his feelings about Annie when he first met her; he remembered how life was always difficult. But by then he was learning to cope with life inside the high walls of the school, filled with tough, strutting older boys and men like Mr Mullen rather than Mr Whipple from the Art Institute.

David ramped up his nerve. "Is this like the rest of the world?"

The mild Mr Mullen's face folded in on itself. He wanted a simple answer. He needed clear, concise responses.

"Young man, you will learn to be respectful. Now then, you didn't want to go there ahh?"

"My parents didn't want me to."

His nights were still filled with dread and nightmares now compounded by his fantasies of Helen. What to do, how far to go, what does she want and need, would his desires made real be acceptable to her, would she think he was a degenerate, a sex fiend ... was he really dirty like his brother and his friends? Did his thoughts of her flesh tarnish her?

During the long nights, with his brother always somewhere else, his bedroom was almost silent but for his breathing and his pounding heart. Without the drone of the constant daytime TV, cooking clatter and the steady hum of local traffic, he could hear, across the broad distance of the sleeping city, freight trains clattering over the flat plains. Their horns bellowed like wounded animals as they made their way from the iron ore pits of the cold north and the coal mines of Pennsylvania to the huge factories on the lakes to the east of where he lived. These crying sounds belonged to him, the only one in the neighbourhood still lying awake. They were America calling, telling him that a life was out there and that he would one day need to begin the journey away from this city sitting on its flat plain, away from his disapproving, disinterested and silent family. He knew he was destined to find the bullied and the poor and to tell their stories, to become a voice or maybe a representative for them. He knew he had noble intentions like Odysseus, like Eugene Smith.

These crying sounds of the distant locomotives were like siren songs in the mythologies he had read, filled with enchantment and buried desires with a delicious loneliness, a loneliness in which generations before him trekked across the vast continent. It was a country that had planted itself and had grown on roots fed with the blood of the native red people, the sweat of the black man and the embittered bile of Germans, Irish, Scots, English, a handful of Dutch and French men and women whose determination to establish a life free of religious intolerance, indentured servitude and poverty was their singular aim whatever that meant to those who got in their way. As it turned out, tragically they wanted freedoms for themselves but not for others. Seventy-four years after the signing of the constitution, the United States would pay the consequences in the Civil War.

As he was making money working for Mr Day, he could afford to take Helen to restaurants, the theatre and the movies. He enjoyed taking her to the art cinema in the downtown area of the city. They saw foreign films with daring content. His parents simply ignored that he was travelling through 'those areas' of town.

Helen's parents approved of David. He was good looking and well presented, he had some money to spend on their daughter, he was obviously bright and industrious, and he was immaculately polite.

Polite from a house like his? At around the age of eight, he was with his grandmother as they entered a department store through its heavy revolving brass door. A man, whom David could only describe to himself as a high-class gentleman, stood aside to let David and his grandmother pass though first. David, like all children, had learned artificially and mechanically to say 'please' and 'thank you' but the elderly gentleman's gesture seemed charmed, elegant and something else. David sensed there was within it a piece of civilization and heroism. The man stood back as in 'women and children first'. He had made a sacrifice. This appealed to David. At the moment he decided politeness was a sign of maturity, selflessness, nobility and kindness. He would forever pursue politeness; it would prove he had value.

One late winter's evening after a date, standing in Helen's parent's living room, with her little brother and her parents upstairs in bed, Helen asked, "David, what do you want from me?"

David felt secure with her in that he knew they were of equal intelligence and by then he had stopped being intimidated by her beauty. He was nonetheless surprised by her directness. He stalled. "I don't get what you mean."

She put her arms over his shoulders and clasped her hands around his neck. She looked closely at him. She drew him to her. His chest encountered her breasts. David knew that soon he would be embarrassed by his ever-bulging stiffness if she pulled him closer. Saliva gathered in his mouth.

"I ...", he could not resist this. He pulled her slowly towards him, letting her feel his excitement but also tugging on her back so gently that at any moment she could pull away. But she didn't and for the first time, he kissed her on the mouth. It was intoxication. Thrilling.

She moved her head slightly away. "Did you close your eyes?"

"I don't know."

"I did."

She drew close to him, pushed her hips forward to feel him all the more and whispered, "But what do you want with me?"

He drew his arms tighter around her. "I think you're beautiful." He hesitated. Would his world fall in? "I want to be naked with you."

She didn't move even as he bulged more. He didn't move. She kissed his cheek, nibbled his ear and whispered, "maybe", and then found his lips again.

A few days later, on the Sunday before the end of the Christmas vacation of 1960, David and Ed met at Ed's house with one of the school's ancient large format Speed Graphics cameras and a flash unit that David had borrowed over the holiday period. They were going to 'paint with light', a trick Mr Busby thought his two best students were capable of accomplishing. David was soon to understand that in those days, long before digital photography, Photoshop manipulations and instant imaging, the conceptualization of a photograph was based on hard-won technique and the ability to conceive of an image before it was made.

He had discovered Ansel Adams, the great landscape photographer of the American west. He thought of Adams as the Bach of American photographers because of the grandeur of his images. But there was more. David discovered in Adams' writings the notion of previsualization. He realized to be truly creative he needed to 'see' his final print before he released the shutter and to do so meant he needed to completely control technique.

He tumbled this out to Ed who, in his dry manner responded with a slight smile, "That's interesting".

Disappointed with Ed's droll response, David sat back in the dinning chair and collapsed as though all the energy had been drained from him. His normal exhaustion from lack of sleep stirred him to idly scratch the dry band of skin on his neck. He popped his eyes back up at Ed. "You know, when I first heard you define the word 'photography', I was amazed I'd never asked what the word meant and there I was, after two years of photographing, still not knowing. But I've got to ask something, something I've not said aloud before."

Ed looked at David blankly as he so often looked at the world. But David knew it was a cover up, a kind of protective immutability that gave Ed some distance, a place to hide while he acquired his carefully chosen words to respond with.

Ed blinked and waited as he had that first day in class.

David asked, "You see photography as a kind of interesting technology?"

For the first time since they got to know each other, Ed appeared defensive. "Well yes, how do you see it?" Ed wondered if there was something he had missed, some way of understanding that was not a part of his intellectual equipment.

David groped and then announced, "I feel it." He looked away into the backyard of Ed's house. He saw the naked winter trees scratching the bellies of the low pregnant clouds.

Ed said quietly, "That's not really clear."

"I know." David toyed with the camera.

Ed saw that David had come to a conclusion. "Tell me."

"It's two things. It refracts the world back to itself."

"So it's a mirror which, like I said, is purely technical."

"No," David shot at Ed. "It's more like a prism. A prism refracts light, it separates and bends it."

Ed protested. "But that's not what a lens does."

"Well it does, a lens does bend light but that's not what I mean. I mean I'm the prism. It's what I allow in the frame, what I choose to show with what amount of depth of focus, with frozen or blurred movement, distorted by a wide-angle lens or flattened with a long lens, clear or fuzzy from grain. These are all my choices. I'm the prism. All of it pours though me. That's not just technique or pure science. I'm in the middle of all that."

Ed was surprised at David's impassioned dedication as well as filled with admiration for his articulate description. He folded his arms across his stomach and rocked slowly as do old Jews in temple. He was churning these thoughts, finding a way to absorb them and carefully position them in his body. He stopped rocking and as if emerging from a trance asked, "You said two things. That was one."

"Okay, I'm not really clear about this yet but the second is related to the first. There's the objective function of recording and even with all of the personal decisions at the centre of the process, it's still a recording of light bouncing off the world and making an image. But that's separate from where I take my camera, why I take it there and what my intentions are. That's the subjective part, that's the part, which is about how I show what my point of view is. It is in the telling."

Ed calculated this. "Do you mean that photographs are not necessarily true?"

"Well, if I position my camera badly, shoot up Helen's nostrils using a wide-angle lens, light her with cross shadows so she looks ugly in the picture yet to our eyes, in real life, she's pretty, is the picture telling the truth?"

"It's telling a truth and again it's purely technical."

David dropped his head into his hands and sighed. 'Okay, that's my point. In any situation there may be a lot of different truths, many different realities. I choose one of them and refract it through who and what I am."

Ed, almost apologetic, went on. "Both my parents are doctors. They've taught me to see the world through science. It's all about understanding things rationally. Emotions and subjectivity get in the way for me. They muddy things, they create too many unaccountable problems." He pressed his lips together and jutted his head forward. "Like this discussion."

David nodded. He wondered if Ed possessed a better way to understand the world? Was his insistence on the importance of the subjective too un-intellectual, too vague? What he knew was that he had not uttered the word that swirled around in his head, which was really at the centre of his explanation. He was not certain enough to say to Ed, "Photography can be visual poetry". This was what he had been bequeathed by the photographers he admired as mentors, especially Weston, Smith and Strand - men who had given him a cause to live for and a model to follow.

These disputations with Ed were exciting and always respectful. Neither Ed nor David needed to be better than other, needed to get in the final word. They both sought understanding without having to enter a conflict of egos. They both appreciated the other for this.

He smiled at his friend. "Let's try to paint with light."

That night their conversation didn't let David rest because it seemed so wrapped up with his life after high school. When he thought of his future it was filled with loneliness and terrors. He had glimpses of it: he would have to leave Helen – there was no room for marriage and certainly none for children; he would be on his own, travelling, filling himself with the pain of others; he was certain that he would be dead by the age of 36, dying in the line of duty as had one of his photographer heroes, a compassionate young Swiss named Werner Bischof. David knew he would forget his past, his parents and all the petty attitudes of people around him. But could he take the loneliness? And who was he really? David the American, the Jew, was he his parents' child, or was he really a misplaced European? And would he ever find a community of like minds and hearts, would they be poets and painters or workers and farmers or would they be the wretched and the dispossessed? Would he be equal to the job of proclaiming and revealing? And what did he really have to do to be able to accomplish his dreams?

'I need to know all, to see all, to understand and to be impassioned, yet I need to be tolerant. I need to learn how to entice the light through the lens onto the film and out into the world as ... as reality suspended in an elixir of poetic truth within a monochrome container of exquisite beauty. I need to be certain that what I believe comes as close as possible to the truth and therefore I must, for now, study to understand what lies within and behind the actions and power of people. I need to know that I can translate the loud and agitated three-dimensional world of others into the whispering two-

dimensional world of the photograph and that it will communicate, not only the facts, but the emotional reality. I need to know that my pictures can be as emotionally powerfully as Smith's essays, as grand as Adams' landscapes, as sensitive as Bishof's delicate silvery greys, as poetic as Weston's and as filled with as much love as Weston had for women and especially the dark-haired Tina Modotti.'

The next day, Monday the fourth of January 1960, the first day after the Christmas school vacation, David entered the English class early and recognized that something was wrong. Helen was already in her seat and staring like a rabbit in headlights at Miss Mahler. Sitting behind her desk she was very still, studying a hardback book of maps that lay open in front of her.

David, following Helen's stare, looked closely at Miss Mahler. He saw that her eye rims were red and her cheeks looked as if tears had run through the thin makeup base.

Slowly, quietly David sat down, watching carefully each of Miss Mahler's tiny moves. He thought she was trying to suppress some inner agitation, that her stillness was being enforced by her will. He glanced around towards Helen who silently indicated she had no idea what was going on. As several other classmates entered, David looked again at Miss Mahler.

Always he felt he should act, fill the void, reach out a helping hand, but he knew he had no training in such things. He felt anger flare towards his uncaring parents. This was more intense than usual because of Ed's revelation the day before, that his parents had trained him to think about and analyse the world. David had never experienced nor thought that was what 'normal' parents do. The first time he had witnessed such a mentoring was with crazy Izzy and Annie, but for David that had been a peculiarity created in extreme circumstances.

When the whole of the class was finally sitting, anxious and uncomfortable witnesses to Miss Mahler's upset, at last she looked up, scanned their faces and spoke quietly. "I am an adult and your teacher but I feel pain as you do. When tragedy strikes, it is only within a community of like minds and spirits that we can find comfort." She paused and looked around again. Her voice quavered. "Has anyone heard the news this morning?"

David knew some big European powwow was happening but doubted that could be what had driven her to tears.

No one responded.

Her eyes settled on David. He felt on the spot, anxious but he had no idea why she was looking at him.

"Remember our first day of class last September? Remember we spoke about a list of authors and you asked me, 'Why Camus?'"

David nodded.

"You told me that you had read two of his wonderful novels." She paused and wiped away a gathering tear. "What did you like about them?"

David knew his answer was important to her, that this was more than a classroom quiz. He swallowed his anxious saliva. "He touched me. It was almost spiritual. He made me think more about life and death ... I mean the value of life more than anyone else I've read."

A soft smile touched the edges of her lips. She cocked her head slightly. "Go on if you want to and if you can."

He blinked several times. He thought what he had said was part of a ritual being played out and that it had comforted her. "In all the American writers I've read and even in the Greek plays, life is always held up as something ... something precious. They all assume life is valuable and worth living. For them that's not a question. But Camus makes me think about life differently. I mean, maybe with all the pain we live through, maybe it isn't all that it's supposed to be."

A ripple went through the classroom, a ripple he had heard before. He half expected to be hit on the side of the face with a wad of paper. He half expected to be frog marched out of the classroom.

She twisted a curl of blond hair with her fingers and waited.

"He makes me think about what freedom, I mean what personal freedom really means to us and particularly in relation to political freedom."

David glanced around for a moment at Helen, who was staring at him with her 'wondering' expression. He looked back at Miss Mahler. "He makes me feel that there are adult things I don't yet know about but I feel they're rich and ... and ... and mature in a European way." Another ripple in the class. "And he makes me feel very alone but also a part of him or people like him."

He stopped and looked beyond his eyelashes at his teacher's pale face. "And he makes me wonder if human beings are really plagued by a cruel heart, and all of my wishes to believe we are good are ..." he searched for the words, "are undermined by how Camus shows us a different way to view human activity and to see history." He stopped; he knew he had said enough.

The classroom was quiet. His teacher looked slowly down at her desk.

Suddenly he realized and spoke almost in a whisper, as if his words were a transgression. "He's died hasn't he?"

Tears welled in her eyes and ran down her cheeks. She nodded, tapped a spot on the map, and spoke quietly. "Early this morning, in a car accident near a small village in France. His publisher's car skidded off the road and smashed into a tree. They both died."

She went silent. David heard a sniffle from Helen. He wondered why. As far as he knew, she still had not read Camus.

Miss Mahler spoke from the tree lined roadside in France as she watched her intellectual hero become a part of the earth. "He was a very brave man, a principled man. He believed in peace and in deep human values and he believed that there were very few reasons why we should make war and kill each other. Some called him a fascist and others said he was a dog barking for us against the Russians. And yet during the Second World War he was a selfless member of the resistance, fighting against the brutal inhumanity of the Nazis. More importantly, as David has shown so well, he was a man who could make us think about what it means to be human and to survive in a difficult world of conflicting interests."

David felt honoured by her comments but saddened by his death. 'The world is poorer for this.'

She continued, "In his essays, Camus presents us with dualisms: happiness and sadness, darkness and light, life and death. His aim was to emphasize the fact that happiness is fleeting and that the human condition is one of mortality. He was not morbid, but to him this reflected a greater appreciation for life and happiness. She looked down at the open book and read: "We value our lives and existence so greatly, but at the same time we know we will eventually die, and ultimately our endeavours are meaningless. While we can live with the dualisms of happiness and sadness we cannot live with the paradox." She looked up at the class and finally her eyes settled on David.

"Our endeavours are not meaningless if we create beauty, if we love and we create ease and happiness for others as we love."

She scanned the class and continued. "Thank you all for being so kind. A few months ago, we spoke about how the ancient Greek theatre forged solidarity in their community through their creation of a wonderful culture that helped everyone understand their lives and the lives of others. Today we have shared an hour in which a man of culture has helped to create, maybe for only a moment, a sense of community among us."

David turned towards Helen. She was beautiful even with the stain of tragedy across her face. He loved her all the more because, whether she had or had not read Camus, she cared about a man of nobility who wrote of human values. Maybe she was more like Annie than he had thought. Maybe she would understand his photographs.

CHAPTER 12

Mehmet and his crew broke early for lunch. They had been on location since five in the morning and by eleven they were exhausted, hungry and irritated by the sand gathering in their shoes and in their armpits, groins and elsewhere.

Mehmet was beside himself with anxiety. He had slowly come to an awareness that he must do something to change the world he lived in. The Prophet Muhammad had become progressively unhappier with the world around him, and like the Prophet, Mehmet knew that the answer to his people's unhappiness lay neither with the empires that surrounded them, within tribalism, fundamentalism nor socialism; he knew there needed to be a new way and perhaps Mehmet had found that path with Suleiman and the others.

He remembered the difficult conversation he first had with Dr Suleiman as he tried to enlist Mehmet in the cause of change. Suleiman was convinced that social democratic principles, adapted to local needs, were the only way ahead for their region.

Mehmet had resisted. "But it too has failed; it's allowed the bankers to gather huge amounts of wealth for themselves. They have bled their countries and the people of their rightful wealth and forced them to support the bank's excesses out of their own tax money instead of paying for social care. That's madness. Greed is inherent to their system."

Suleiman knew the argument. "Of course but that doesn't condemn social democracy, it condemns the current politicians. They are aimless, frightened and weak in the face of the wealthy. They're problem is not political but rather anatomical."

Mehmet was confused.

Suleiman laughed at Mehmet's quizzical expression and said, "It's not that they lack analysis but rather backbone."

Mehmet remembered this complex conversation and how much he admired the Doctor's conviction although not his jokes.

He toyed with the succulent slices of pastourma and butter beans in their oily sauce. He idly shoved the thin slivers of red pepper around with his plastic fork and tried to appear involved in his work. He opened the inane murder mystery script to the scene they were working on and stared at it as though being diligent. In the final scene the cops would become the heroes and the great Leader would be honoured for providing strength and wisdom. 'All hail the captain of our ship, our great conductor, our Fuhrer.'

Nervous and on the edge of keeping himself together, he glanced around and was satisfied that the crew, and especially the political officer, were preoccupied with feeding their hunger for food, gossip and a much-needed rest from the burning sun and stinging sand.

He asked himself, what was the big story to tell? It was not, nor would it ever be found in a third-rate TV script like the one now splattered with olive oil from his lunch.

He remembered stories from childhood - of great caravans traversing the deserts, the hum of God he then thought inside a huge airy mosque, the sublime poetry of Jalal ad-Din Rumi and the adventurous sciences of the twelfth century; he thought about the institutionalization of belief and the oppressiveness of the mullahs and imams, about the peasants who become rulers and how they only possess a vocabulary of brutality and murder. He marvelled to know that the Jews of Israel register more patents per year than the entire Arab world. 'Is that the real story? Shouldn't I be filming our fall from grace? What has happened to the once learned Arab world? That should be my story.'

He studied filmmaking in London and knew that the Western world views itself through the tragic memory of the two World Wars and with the guilt of allowing the Bosnian and Rwandan tragedies to happen and all of that through the prism of 9/11. He knew that militarism ran deep in the Anglo-Saxon world, which was one reason for its hegemony. He believed that the West holds a mirror up to itself in Afghanistan and Iraq and that it is in denial about the horror it has caused. He knew some intellectuals and artists saw their societies had become venal and self-consumed and that many citizens, and especially the young, realized their governments were incapable of bringing wellbeing, health, education, prosperity and spiritual and actual peace to them. He knew that all-in-all the politicians had shown a despairing lack of care if not to say lack of empathy for their own poorly educated, drug taking, sex preoccupied children of the underclass it fostered when it eradicated the industrial working class. He saw how those poor kids, from unemployed parents, manifested a powerful sense of entitlement with little sense of responsibility. On top of that, he had seen the West behave as though the world is godless but yet collectively had not found how to fill their empty souls ... so they allowed the financial and moral corruption of the corporations, the banks and the politicians to define them. He was certain the West had sown the seeds of its own destruction and that soon China would grasp world hegemony. This he did not want for his own country and people.

He pushed the peppers around again. The thick green olive oil reflected the yellow tent glowing with the ever-brighter, hotter sun.

'If that is the story of their fall from grace, where is redemption for my own people to be found? Surely most of us know it's not in the consumption of things, drugs and sex. It must be something more inspiring, something in the energy of the people or in my country's soil or, as a last resort, in the heavens.' He stirred himself. 'We're social animals and need to find grace and redemption in each other's company.'

Mehmet glanced up, his gaze falling on the political officer who was listening intently to someone on his cumbersome Sat/Nav. The man's thin pinched features were concentrated, concerned. Was he listening to a report that would suddenly overtake Mehmet's life? The officer looked up and caught Mehmet watching him. He nodded, giving nothing away and carried on his listening and finally mumbled, "Sure, he's an experienced sailor. Time to give the guy a break." He looked back at Mehmet, perhaps to be assured he had not been overheard or perhaps to hope he had been overheard.

Mehmet looked down at his plate of food. Is the story he's searching for to be found in creation or redemption?

The sun was now burning the oxygen. The tent was becoming an oven.

The Colonel listened to someone on the other end of his mobile phone. He seemed concerned and grave. He mumbled a "Sir", hit the disconnect button, came around from the other side of a brown Land Rover, looked uneasily at the Sergeant and lit a cigarette.

The Sergeant, waiting with the others, wondered for a moment and then remembered Suleiman from their childhood. Both born of fishermen's families, both poor but free because, as kids of poor urban workers, the state couldn't care less if they were educated, fed or treated well; the state's interest was to see them grow into semi-literate labourers, soldiers and blunt unquestioning tools of the regime. Both kids were different than the neighbourhood boys of their age, which is why they forged a friendship. Suleiman was acquisitive, quick-witted and would stop at nothing to get his way. Ali was watchful, kind and had learned from his father to help others but always with a crafty eye for self-preservation. In their late teens they parted ways. Suleiman read books and went to study medicine while the academically disappointing but street-wise boy who would be the Sergeant had no choice but to join the army. He was rewarded for bravery in bloody skirmishes with religious fundamentalists. After his experiences in battle he found that death meant little to him. It was not that he had lost his interest in living or that he had reached a religious conversion but that the passage between life and non-life seemed diminished, unimportant. He had worked his way up through the ranks, he had survived in battle, he had been toughened and eventually he was asked to join the Colonel's unit of hardened secret service paramilitaries.

Suddenly Suleiman's car skidded to a halt on the armoury's oil slicked cement floor. He climbed out, immediately shook the Colonel's podgy hand, apologized for being late, scolded the army for its incompetence and embraced the Sergeant. "Long time my brother."

With professional gravity he turned again to the Colonel. "Is it still all right? Shall we go?"

"What do you know about this?"

Suleiman heard suspicion in the Colonel's reedy voice. "Just what I was told this morning; there's a foreigner who needs breaking. Nothing more."

"Do you know the man?"

"I can't say, sir, I was not told his name or nationality."

The Colonel looked closely at Suleiman. "How do you know my Sergeant?"

The doctor, knowing the Colonel was fishing, beamed a broad professional smile and turned to the Sergeant. "Ahh, Ali and I grew up together."

"And this American, did you grow up with him?"

Suleiman feigned confusion. "Sir?"

"I've been told you know him, you've been seen in his company."

"Is this why the army stopped me?"

The Colonel barked in his high thin voice, "Answer my question!"

"The only American I know is an elderly photographer called David something. I've bumped into him …" He hesitated and thought for a moment. "Maybe three times." He looked at the Colonel. "Is he the suspect?"

The Colonel, suspicious of his own liver, watched the doctor as if studying the habits of an insect. He nodded yes.

Suleiman smiled. "I've got to say, they come in all varieties. The man is in his late sixties, he's ill and slow." He looked around at the Colonel's men. They were bored, seen it all before.

"What's he accused of?"

"Spying. We catch spies. He was spying."

"But of what? I just can't imagine …"

"Are you up to arresting and breaking your friend?"

"Colonel, he is not my friend and hardly an acquaintance. And am I up to it?" He nodded. "I'm a doctor. It's a matter of science."

As they climbed into the brown cars and vans, Suleiman sat just behind the Colonel. 'This', thought Suleiman, 'has played into my hands'. He leaned forward and spoke quietly to the Colonel.

"If I'm right, we need to do three things: discreetly apprehend this man, break him for the information and do it all so efficiently that there is no chance for spies, foreigners, enemies of the regime nor, let us say, others who could be jealous of your success, of being able to share your credit once we've done what we need to do."

Suleiman could see the Colonel's shoulders tighten and his fleshy cheek draw across his jawbone. The doctor waited and thought that backing off is better than pressing. He relaxed into the seat next to the Sergeant and waited as the brown entourage struggled through the busy streets.

He turned to Ali, clapped his manicured hand onto Ali's knee and said, "How enjoyable to see you. You look more, how should I say, filled out. Healthy. Is life good?"

Just as Ali turned to reply, the Colonel spoke quietly. "Doctor, what's your suggestion?"

David looked down the long flight of broken cement and stone steps that terminate on the quay just behind the tin-roofed icehouse. Could he make it? He knew that by a third of the way down, his right knee, shattered by a horse's hoof in Alabama all those years ago, and his left thigh, shredded by Serbian shrapnel, would both begin to ache, then rub and become painful, making each movement down onto the next uneven surface more difficult. There could be no haste although he hoped his new cane might ease the pressure. Caught between possible safety below and the security services above, he would be a sitting duck. And then what to do? 'Well', he thought, 'Standing here will not help; hesitation is no answer'.

The few fishermen still on the quay were mending their blue nylon nets and rusting outboard engines. Emptied by their poverty, worn by the long hours and hard manual labour and preoccupied with their tasks, they would pay little attention to an old bum searching for herrings dropped from the dock worker's fish-filled trays as they pushed their laden carts from the landings to the ice house.

David looked at his watch. He thought that unless he was spotted by chance, he probably had forty-five minutes to an hour to reach the bottom and to find a place to hide until the quay was empty and unguarded. Perhaps, he though, at the longest it will take twenty minutes to get to the bottom.

He considered the cliff on either side of the stairs. Wild thyme grew in abundance along the top shelves of the wind-sculpted rocks but as the almost sheer wall below fell away to the sea, there was only a scattering of wildflowers and precariously balanced bird's nests. He smiled. 'The Mediterranean is the provider of all that man could want: fish and sea foods, fowl, herbs and rain for the olive, lemons and oranges trees, wine and onions, peppers, tomatoes, pulses and wheat for pasta. What else could man ask for except a place to hide from his enemies or at least to rest?'

As he limped slowly but steadily down, he thought there were other things which the world of the Mediterranean could offer: 'Comradeship, good neighbours, a life-long partner, culture to feed my soul, ideas to discuss and the freedom to discuss them, a sense of place in the community and a sense of home, a fear from want and the right to believe what I would wish to believe; a panoply of ancient traditions and customs and a heritage of the Renaissance.'

But was it not true, as he remembered Walt Whitman writing: "what binds people together is what binds the nation together in a democracy - a love and comradeship between citizens". Perhaps he was asking too much of an inland sea.

'Step by step, safety or death? This is like my journey away from "doing" to "being". This is my passage from caring about reputation, accomplishment, fame, and income - moving towards acceptance. Only now can I admit, step-by-step in this descent, how I disdained the publishers' political agenda to keep their audience blinded from the underlying truths; step-by-step how I detested the puppet like editors - men and women who stood at truth's door protesting that they were only following orders and if the job was not done by them, someone less caring would be in their place; step-by-step how I wished to love and respect my fellow citizens but ultimately become disillusioned, seeing them as an inchoate pack, bought off by credit, possessions and simplistic ideas, slowly guided into alienation, bigotry, and emotional dumbness, barking to every irrational, morally dubious instigation of the media, accepting opinion as news, and absurdity as fact. Step-by-step it has become, for me, a descent towards capitulating to the plague or an ascent towards truth.'

Step-by-step he accepted that without her, his life had become an entirely private matter. 'What was the line in that poem? 'Each of us walks alone to his grave'.'

As he moved carefully down, step-by-step, now a third of the way, he remembered the next photograph in the box clamped under his arm.

A gangly man, wearing a flat cap, a threadbare suit jacket over a thick woolly sweater and a pair of dungarees, semi-silhouetted against a clear high winter sky, was photographed with a heavy sledgehammer captured at the apogee of its swing. Near the base of the photograph, just beneath the man's hobnailed boots, lay silvery railroad rails on a diagonal across the frame. An image of labour and of a particular man, seen by others as a type, a navvy, a post war Irish migrant labourer searching for a better life and a better wage in England; a type, not an individual – he fitted others' categories like 'worker', 'foreigner', 'peasant' and eventually, when unemployment took root, he and his fellows would become, in the baiting headlines of the right-wing press, 'scroungers' living off the welfare state. David remembered that cold day, years ago, as he knelt and looked down onto the ground glass of his Hasselblad. There in the frame was a man, a flesh and blood statue, but also a metaphor of labour, an image of the industrial age just as it was passing into the age of technology and globalization and with it the deportation of industrial jobs from the once upon a time workshop of the world.

David began to limp as his knee surrendered to pain and as he wondered what had always attracted him to photograph labour. 'Okay, I was driven to hard work, believing that a life in repose was time wasted. A moment of life gone, lost forever. Never did I accept that simply 'being' was a worthwhile state. I have to admit my intolerance of Buddhist crystal gazing middleclass dropouts.'

Step-by-step. 'Has that fisherman next to the shed taken note of me?'

'My psyche was a battleground of historical tendencies. Protestant "doing" in the name of God was for me a way of grasping shards of self-fulfilling creativity. This was in conflict with the persistently underlying and emotionally eviscerating thought that life was a phenomenon without meaning at best and futile at worse.'

Step by painful step. 'Will the fisherman report me?'

'And to boot, I'm an atheist; so no comfort in the fairy-tale of an afterlife. At the same time, I'd reach for comforts – delicious food, warm nights, sunshine, a quiet room and sexual fulfilment. But out of those, inevitably arose the corrosive American Puritanical streak which professes that frills, luxury and comfort-seeking were wasteful and somehow a claim for a kind of pervasive exceptionalism … very un-egalitarian, very undemocratic.

'Only a handful of steps left; I'm okay. The fisherman couldn't give a damn. He's disappeared.

'I think I was strangely old-school before the fall from grace, before the American century rotted on the apple tree, before its monetary value rather than its human value became its most important thing. Politics and personality traits mingled constantly, presenting endless conflicts and rattling any sense of living a just life, of being consistent and true to a particular beacon. What I was certain of was that we all live inside history and all the conflicting forces create the world we live within. They forge our relations, they bear causes and events that determine our lives and choices. Kate's fate and my unhappiness were both consequences of history.

'I know that I rarely sense what I call peace – a suspended moment when neither my body nor mind make demands on me. Maybe my constant craving for sex was really a need for the moments of tranquillity that followed making love.

Not many more steps now. Nearly to her pictures, nearly safe.'

The Colonel's cars reached the sea road and headed uphill towards the steps on their right leading down to the quay and the street on the left leading up behind David's flat.

She stroked his chest. She stroked his ear. She asked, "Are you okay?"

He smiled or rather twitched his lip into what he thought was a smile. The smile faded, he turned to look at her.

He was convinced that life was inconstant as were her looks and body shape. And yet. And yet her warm toned skin, her fine, almost noble bone structure, her freckles and black shining hair, her deep brown eyes were, morning after evening, beautiful to him. Looking at her was his favourite pastime. During the few months they were together, as the steel sleet fell upon Sarajevo, this was the only constant in his life.

He rolled his body towards Kate and wrapping his arms gently around her shoulders, he eased her towards him so that her breasts pressed against his chest. He whispered, "I can taste and remember, I can smell and remember, smile and remember, close my eyes and remember, and so I think of you and love my love for you and you."

He paused before he spoke because he wished her to know that he deeply loved who she was but he also loved her beauty. As he held her he remembered he loved her before he met her, before he knew her. He loved what he knew to be love and she materialized it in a way he previously could only dream of. Tina Modotti actually appeared in his life.

He hoped that he would be able to proceed further down the stack of photographs in the box, to view again her beauty, which was inscribed so deep within his being. But he had only twenty steps to go. His knee and thigh were aching, he was perspiring and his leg muscles were trembling from the effort but he had nearly succeeded and luckily, there were no apparent guards or customs officers around and the handful of fishermen were preoccupied with their nets and engines. Twenty steps away. Nineteen.

Just then the Colonel's convoy swept by above the stairs. Sergeant Ali - the Colonel's servant, the doctor's childhood friend, the other men's immediate superior, staring out of the window calculating his next move, noticed the old woman, or was it a man, in the brown burnoose just nearing the bottom of the long flight of stairs. His eyes moved from that distant figure to the driver's bull neck, to the Colonel's fat cheek, to Suleiman's sharp nose and he smiled; he smiled deep within his body and his being was lighter for a moment.

•••

All of David's life was now in motion.

Nothing had been said to David but his house was filled with rumour and innuendo. They moved like smoke through the rooms, occasionally filling them with the odour of a recently doused fire, fumes of dead emotions.

David overheard his mother and father arguing. Nothing unusual but for a change it was not about the cost of David's medical care. Fragments of phrases and words described the events.

"Joey broke into a used car dealer's locked lot last night", "picked up, for God's sakes, by the police". "Our son; the police" ... "how has this happened" ... "gave him everything" ... "ungrateful" ... "him and the other one, two peas in a pod" ... "should disown both of 'em."'

"Nothing missing, but caught red-handed, flat-footed, on the lot" ... *"hauled to the police station"*... *"our son"*.

"Of course they changed the charge from breaking and entering to trespassing. He's not bad, jes confused."

David's father stormed and fumed at his wife and at Joel who was now eighteen and out of high school with hardly passable grades and dim prospects. Joel was not in the mood to listen to his father. One morning after another shouting match, Joel shoved his father and left the house.

Several days later, David was told by his mother that Joel had joined the army to be trained as a radio specialist and would be stationed in Germany.

"Soon?" David asked with too much eagerness.

His mother scowled. "After his basic training."

"Where's he going to do that?"

His mother looked blankly at him and for that one moment, emptied of venom. "I don't think I've ever said one single solitary thing to you since you were little that I didn't get back a thousand questions."

"I know mama, you never like me asking."

She looked at him. Something in his tone of voice touched her. She smiled and to David's shock, tears appeared in the corners of her eyes.

He felt all of his breath leave him. "Mama?"

She looked down at her hands in her lap, pulled a cigarette from her apron pocket and for a moment struggled to compose herself. "It's just, he's always been trouble in school with bad grades and always misbehaving and now, well, now he's going off to Georgia or Alabama or wherever the hell it is and ...; can you imagine our Joey with all those southern crackers?" She was at a loss. She scrabbled for a match and lit her cigarette.

David wanted to comfort her but had no idea how to do it.

She pulled the smoke deep into her lungs and exhaled. "He's unformed. He's not really fit to go into the world like he is. He needs help but God knows what and how." She looked up at David. "You take care of yourself, you're so ... so, so talented ... you'll be a success in something ... but him ... God only knows."

David felt proud that his mother possessed this view, previously unknown to him, but he felt sad for her. He felt almost nothing for his brother but a huge sense of relief that he would no longer have to put up with him. It was as if he had been given a new freedom. The air seemed lighter and fresher. He could not wait for his brother to go.

'This means I'll be out of high school before he returns. I'll be in college and no longer, from the day he leaves for boot camp, will I ever have to see him again.'

His mother said, "He'll be all right; I know he will. But think of it. The army's no place for a Jew."

The day his brother left, David was at school. Joel had said nothing to David. There were no goodbyes, no "see yas", no "good luck buddy" given or received. Joel, the tormentor of his life just left as though they had had nothing to do with each other. Strangers with no connection.

When David arrived home from school that day he felt the house had a new peace. The malignant spirit of his brother had vanished. He never mentioned it nor did his parents mention it to him. They did not think that maybe he missed his brother or maybe he was delighted. They did not ask and David knew they did not care. He thought they believed that Joel's fate was none of David's business. Only in that one moment of tears in all of David's childhood had his mother revealed warmth and concern.

David wondered if he had discovered the key to his parents. 'They're sort of existentialists, believing that living life has no shape or meaning, that nothing much matters one way or another in relationship to their inevitable destiny. That was why nothing was discussed, society was not engaged and there were no celebrations because in the end, in the face of death, nothing had a sustainable meaning. One simply exists and then doesn't. Life was some curse to be tolerated, and papa in particular had capitulated to exist in a defeated and joyless life, comforted only by his daily dose of scriptures.'

David had classes to be getting on with, things to learn, a girlfriend to understand, a future to plan, pictures to make, a whole world to figure out. At night he was on the verge of discovering his own mythology in a borderland of dreams and schemes separated from the real world by colours and tones, by the memory of golden pools of glistening light, by the face of an old Jew with his hands clutching a book, by large blonde men in military uniforms trying to wrest the book from the man to throw it into the raging bonfire of all books, all knowledge. He saw a tree on a road and a skidding car, a ticky-tacky suburban house filled with dying spirits and there was David hiding under blankets, no, he was being suffocated by the blonde boys, egged on by his uniformed brother. As he showed them his pictures, he was taunted by hysterically laughing people.

David needed to understand what was possible in a world that seemed everyday more venal and more tragic.

'Is this it? Is life this sad passage?' He knew there was an upland out there, a place of red wine and poets and his beautiful Tina Modotti, there was a place where people dreamed wild ideas and talked of love, art and politics. His life would fly to it and in the dark, with the trains crying in the distance and his brother down in some southern town no doubt proving what a man he was by spewing his filth about slags and niggers, with his parents in their bedroom dreaming of empty lands and hollowed out souls, he knew this time would be remembered and become a part of who he would be but he also knew that time, like all the human detritus that surrounded him, was an invention.

Time was measured first by the sun and moon, then by the seasons and afterwards, as men in long brown sackcloth took it upon themselves to define time's passage and our temporal destinies as their responsibility in life, we began to mark time by their vespers - paeans to their imagination, their leap of faith on our behalf. And so the day of light and the night of darkness began to be segmented, foisted upon us by these controlling men. Humans, such as we are, discontented and questioning, needed more refined definitions, distinctions, demarcations to help us explore, to discover and, we hoped, to gather gold onto ourselves. Spices, silks and untold treasures lay beyond the reach of measure. Longitude and latitude needed quantifying so our voyages could be accountable and repeatable and so we no longer sailed headlong into rocky shores or fell off the edge of the ocean. Metallurgy, mathematics, mechanics matriculated even against the voodoo of the men in sackcloth. Their chanting became sailor's work songs, hymns to the unfurling of sails and the caulking of timbers. Cogs and clocks, sea spray and chimeras, the imagined and the unimaginable, monsters and madness, tarpaulin and tar served our lusts for riches and power and for an infinity of future prospects.

Within these men, desires mingled with dreams of departures from the beloved and trusted land to cast a vaporous image of a the future filled with contentment, refinement, sufficiency; a world in the uplands splashed in sunshine, bathed in warmth, a world of loves and lust and sexual fulfilment, of gormandizing and glutted pleasures which contained a house of good health; in short, a world without culture but for that of material development and sufficiency, a soulless world carved from the hollows of other people's bones and mines somewhere, they hoped, beyond the reach of measure.

David's imagination marched him across time and space, his ravings and nightmares growled at him in the darkness, but he knew there was something out there for him.

Towards the end of that first winter in high school, Mr Busby asked David if he knew about the Scholastic Awards.

"Sure, all the girls are entering poems, paintings and short stories."

"David, have you looked at the entry forms?"

David, surprised, squinted against the late afternoon sun shafts pouring into the third-floor classroom. Mr Busby was in silhouette. David saw that if he exposed for the sky there would be no detail to distinguish his teacher's shape from the horizontal window frames. The picture would be inelegant.

"David, have you?"

David snapped into the three-dimensional world of human affairs. "No sir, should I have?"

"There's a photography section. Your shots of the boy on the bike, the flowers in the vase, the fountain and that one of the woman in the farmer's market should be entered. Print them and some of the others, print them large. I'll get them sent."

As Mr Busby walked away, David realized the enormity of what just happened. His photography teacher was recommending that he enter this nationwide competition. This meant he believed his pictures were worthy of being seen, of being judged by famous photographers and not only that, but Mr Busby seemed to have remembered David's best pictures. He was stunned but not quite as much as he would be that evening.

His father entered the house as usual, went to this bedroom, changed from his brown suit to his pale blue trousers and short-sleeved shirt, entered the living room, took his bible and lessons from the drawer next to his red upholstered chair, sat down, opened the bible and then paused just as David had gathered his books to go up to his room to study.

"You're gonna be fifteen soon. At sixteen you can get a driver's license. You gotta begin to learn how."

David was dumbstruck. He could not remember a moment when his father had addressed him in such a way. There was no anger, no recrimination, no demand. He stared at his father, a pear in a chair. He thought he would never allow himself to end up looking like that.' Where's the self-control, the pride?' After all, his father had been an amateur boxer in college, won some fights, he'd been slim and fit then.

"Starting this summer, I'll take you to the big parking lot on Sundays when I'm not working. You'll learn there."

David had no language to respond to his father. He was at a complete loss. He wanted to tell him about his photographs and his girlfriend and working with Mr Day and about Mr Day's accent and tattoo, about the good grades he was getting and how his essays got top marks and how much he had learned about a French philosopher and how he had died young like David was also going to but not before he had done some wonderful things that would finally make his father proud of him.

But he understood that his father had lost interest and was now thumbing the pages of his lessons.

"Thank you, papa," he quietly murmured and escaped upstairs to his homework and dreams.

"Ich bin, do bist, sie sind," tailed off as he became distracted by thoughts of his father.

'Have I been wrong about him all these years? Has papa's silence been intentional rather than uncaring? Has he been teaching me how to be self-reliant, to be a man like John Wayne or Gary Cooper in High Noon – strong, silent, self-sacrificing, always acting on behalf of the community? Was that it; was that his intention? And now papa knows he's needed, that he has to teach me the essential American skill of driving a car, a way to truly join the ranks of adulthood which I can only do with papa's help.

'Have I been too self-reliant and not shown papa that I needed him? Or is papa trying to correct the mistakes he's made with Joey? Is papa feeling guilty? Had his bible lessons taught him that in the world beyond his red chair people actually felt things, responded to his father's silence, may even have needed his father's embrace?'

David looked towards the neighbour's lit windows.

'Or maybe papa was going to teach me to drive so I too can leave home and no longer be a burden to him, so he no longer has to pay my doctor's bills?'

He returned his attention to his German book with its odd 's' and 'f' and wondered why he had decided to pursue this language, the language of his people's nemesis.

But he remembered that one day, when he was six or seven, his father had, for the only time in his life, gathered David in his arms and rolled down a grassy slope with David protectively held against his father's chest, held close and in safety as the green and blue of that summer's day revolved around the nest of his father's enfolding flesh. Never again was that to happen. David wondered why that day and why never again.

Did David embrace German as his father had embraced him, a peculiarity, a threat to embrace, only to find the limits of its meaning? David swallowed hard and realized that for the first time in years he felt tears welling up. Unmanly, un-American, un-heroic. He was glad Helen could not see him then.

CHAPTER 13

Suleiman got his way. He left the Colonel's car with his soft leather needle-wallet in his pocket, thinking no one would discover it. He made his way to the street door and rang David's bell. Again, no answer. He leaned on the bell and became aware that he could hear it ringing from above through the still-open French windows. He waited. His needles in his pocket, the Colonel watching, the dumb Ali waiting, a lowly sergeant probably jealous and hoping he, his intellectual superior, would fail.

'Here I am, waiting for the American, again in thrall to the red, white and blue. Was there no end to their hegemony? Even now, after I've worked so hard to free myself from the colonization of my imagination by the power of the shoddy, un-spiritual, acquisitive American dream and its aspirations for wealth over truth or freedom,

I am standing in the state's security searchlight, dependent on an American to play a role in my own life and death.'

He pounded on the door, leaned back and looked up towards the narrow balcony hoping, imagining that David would step out from the open French windows and wave down to him with his naïve American smile.

Nothing. No David peeking from behind the curtain. Frustrated and with a growing fury, realizing that if David is arrested elsewhere by others and expresses friendship or familiarity towards him, through chance or malicious intent, his own life would be in jeopardy. He snapped his head around towards the old baker. 'He may know what he does not know he knows.'

In the car, twenty meters down the street, the Colonel turned to the Sergeant. "Did you tell the doctor which bell to ring?"

The Sergeant, seeing the trap, pushed himself forward from the rear seat. "No sir, maybe the man's name is on the bell."

Suleiman marched across the dusty street ignoring the honking clapped-out Mercedes taxi and the woman's complaint whom he bumped into and, arriving in front of Muhammad's cart, ordered him to stop what he was doing and answer his questions.

Muhammad looked impassively from behind his now hooded eyes through the charcoal smoke at Suleiman's pursed, accusing lips. Suleiman saw a flicker, a warning of deep discontent if not danger in the baker's eyes. To his cost, he ignored it.

An overwhelming desire licked at Muhammad's now fevered brain - to smash the hot bread he was just lifting into the doctor's taut flesh. Instead, he removed the bread from his humped iron pan, grabbed another ball of dough, flattened it as he spun it between his experienced palms and smacked it down with such force onto the pan that it sizzled and rattled with complaints.

Suleiman knew he was being observed critically from the Colonel's car and by the other agents now spread along the street like a kill of crows. Testosterone, ego, power, command, position, status teased the doctor like mosquitoes.

"Look at me when I speak to you; you know what I am; look at me."

"My ears are good. I can hear you without the curse of seeing you."

"Curse? Curse! Are you stupid, old man?"

"Only God and my wife know the answer to that."

Suleiman darted around the cart and violently grabbed the shoulder straps of the old man's apron.

Testosterone has a power to blind an otherwise cautious man.

"This is no game, old man."

Muhammad seethed between hardly moving lips "My tribe does not play games."

The baker slid his hand into his apron pocket and grasped something cool and smooth.

"I don't give a damn about you, your tribe, your pride or whatever else you need drag out of your miserable history."

Muhammad was old but strong. He was still respected by his family and his clan. He was a man and not a city popinjay like this thing now grasping him by his apron. His thumb found the release on his beautiful switchblade with its long curving serrated edge. Did this fancy little bird not know what pride is, did he not know the old town warrens behind this main street, did he not know that Muhammad had a thousand friends and a thousand places to hide and that his friends would be silent in the face of the authorities?

In the car, the Sergeant spoke quickly to his Colonel. "Sir, would you like me to stop this?"

"He's your old friend; do you trust him to not make more of a scene?"

"He's always had a short temper; he does not like to be challenged and he wants things his own way." The Sergeant wondered if this was too harsh, too personal. To defuse what he had said, he added, "When he was a kid, he was the same."

The Colonel turned towards his Sergeant. "Answer the question."

Ali, the son of a fisherman, asked himself why he had just lied. Suleiman had been a bright, lonely, gentle child taken under Ali's protection. Ali had just described who he, Ali had been as a child. Caring, yes, but angry. What instinct had driven him? For a moment, Ali saw before his eyes, as though flickering like an old film on the windscreen, his whole childhood, with its street fights, its shoplifting and witnessing his father's endless struggle to survive, to outwit the customs officials and the fish buyers. He whispered, "I think this can get out of hand."

The Colonel nodded, balancing Suleiman's probability of success against the noisy, violent scene that will inevitably occur if he, the Colonel, unleashes his crows. He reached into his pocket and pulled out the pack of Marlborough. Instinctively he knew that inaction was his best plan for survival. It was a condition of his office and also one of his nation's known truths. He lit his cigarette and spoke quietly. "How to get into the spy's apartment without making an already bigger scene?"

Ali perked up. "Sir, I can climb up the rear of the building. I'm good at that and at least I can get into the hallway. If the suspect is not there or does not answer, I can pick the lock."

"Hidden talents?"

"In my academy year we were all taught … it's just that I took to it. It's like untangling my father's fishing nets."

The Colonel thought about Ali's offer. Loyal, always understated, humble, a lapdog to the powerful. He looked at Ali through the haze of his exhaled cigarette in the rear-view mirror and smiled.

As the Sergeant reached for the door handle, both he and the Colonel realized that Suleiman and the old man had disappeared. The Sergeant, sensing trouble, darted from the car while the Colonel slowly swung his short legs out. He nodded to one of his leather jacketed sunglass-wearing crows who quickly followed the swiftly running, long-legged Sergeant.

Ali worried, as he bore down on the baker's cart, that Suleiman must have dragged the poor old man down the alleyway immediately behind where he parked it. Ali ran, weaving through the crowd like a footballer, leaping boxes of lemons and spring fennel. 'Odd though', he thought. 'When had Suleiman become strong and cruel?'

Ali gained the corner and grasping the wall, spun himself at full throttle down the narrow alley. In front of him, to his horror, was a ghastly sight.

There was no sign of the old man. Suleiman was sprawled over several crates of tomatoes, his pockets turned out and, with half his body on the ground and his head thrown back, his neck was spewing a fountain of blood from a ragged gash. His face was a pincushion of syringe needles.

Suleiman would die; there was no doubt. All the days of his childhood, all the times they had spent together and although he had come to secretly detest Suleiman for his arrogance and his own suspicion that Suleiman was a double agent, he still regretted that a man of talent should end this way, brutally butchered by an irate old peasant over a petty affront. 'This was the waste of a man, of education, of our people and our country'.

The Colonel arrived, puffing. He surveyed the crime scene and placed his hand on Ali's shoulder. "You were right. Trouble."

Ali weakly nodded and whispered, "Our plans make God smile."

"Go, get into the flat."

As the Sergeant turned to leave, the Colonel grabbed him by the arm to stop him. He whispered, "There was no name on the bell."

The loyal Sergeant nodded, impassively, deferentially.

David reached the bottom of the stairs, somewhat the worse for wear but relieved that his plan had thus far worked. Zakkir's boat was moored where he expected it to be. What a fine, clockwork description the helpful Sergeant had given of his father Zakkir's humble life.

Now, besides eluding human beings and in particular anyone wearing a uniform, he could only hope that Zakkir had kept to his usual pattern of fishing from midnight, returning to harbour by midmorning, offloading, sorting his nets, cleaning the deck, preparing his engines for the next day, loading up the extra fuel cans, hiding the key and going to the bar with his comrades. Once the other fishermen, who were still working on the quay, sailed away or finished their repairs and went to the bars or home, David would have a chance to take the boat.

He hoped that there was fuel on board and that he could remember how to pilot it. An old friend of his, a man he considered a brother, was a Caribbean fisherman who taught him how to read the surface of the sea for signs of shoals and depth and how to ride up the side of waves rather than into them. David thought for a moment how all that one encounters and is taught in life, perhaps seemingly unimportant or even trivial at the time, may become a life-saving piece of information. It gives one hope, if not in people, at least in their knowledge.

If all of Zakkir's habits had been followed without exception, David needed to worry only about being caught by the coast guard's speedboats, being hit by a freighter as he crossed the major sea lanes, surviving whatever the weather threw at him and finding his way by relying on skills he had read about in books. Simple really; just a matter of a little ability and a freighter full of luck.

He heard voices through the corrugated metal wall of the icehouse. They were probably from the men who oversaw the sorting and storage of fish awaiting collection by the buyer's refrigerated vans. David hid at the corner of the building, listening, watching carefully. He thought he'd be ignored from the road, now high above him or maybe, hunkered down as he was, he'd go unnoticed in his dull brown burnoose against the piles of nets and ropes. David will have become a part of the oil, dust and grit. He knew he'd have to risk being on the quay until he was certain whether any fishermen were still working, certain that no officials were nosing around at the far end near the main entrance gate and whether the guards had settled into the somnambulance of the unseasonable midday heat.

David was, after all, a trained observer. He had learned in street battles, demonstrations, riots and revolutions that by carefully observing, a world of menace and ill intent would eventually reveal itself in a reflection here, a wave of a curtain there. But all was quiet, so quiet and still that he could not help but remember another fluttering curtain in another time and place.

The warm breeze rolled down the mountains around Sarajevo and filled his room with a lazy swirl and heat. David held her close to him. Two months of living a dream like life, even in the middle of the siege that surrounded them, even as tens of people were buried every day and as the random sniper's bullet or cascade of mortar, tank and artillery shells destroyed the beautiful city and tore people apart. He held onto her as if her blood pumped through his veins. He thought the fourteen layers of skin that divided them seemed too many, that they held him at too great a distance from her heart.

She gently pushed herself away.

'David,' she whispered in a tone he had never before heard from her.

He studied the cat like eyes in close detail, he breathed in the perfumed heat rising from her neck and arms… cardamom and something earthy.

Inexplicably to him, he felt a dread spreading through him like a rigidifying poison; something that he vaguely knew was a part of his own chemistry.

He moved further from her, waiting for her to continue. Now nothing else mattered; it was as if she had given him the life he never had, she had revealed to him what it meant to be alive, to overcome the constant duality that had imposed upon his life an unending stream like a crazed hillbilly radio commentary.

"You pick 'em, we play 'em, you choose 'em, we spin 'em until the music of God's good time stops and you hicks and Ree-publicans and firemen and cops, until all you school kids and mums out there stand naked before the laws of God, repenting for your evil ways, and you Jew-boy-nigger lovers, you watch 'em now, watch 'em thrill and kill while my good men tall and true take your books and burn 'em and you."

David shook himself loose from this parody and the horrors of everyday that were surrounding Kate and him and concentrated on her and the present. 'What did she want to say? What could that tone imply?'

But now, with her, there was stillness, peace and he was convinced it was because she had silenced the devils within him or at least closed down the 24/7 radio broadcast in his head. Her grace had calmed the beast and he could escape all the memories and torment; he could see his reflection in her eyes and knew that he was okay, maybe even innocent and most of all, deserving of her love.

She whispered, "David, the march up to the church, the one that was to happen on the day after we met, it's happening tomorrow, isn't it?"

He looked at her wondering, fearing where this was going. He nodded yes. His inner elbows flared with heat. His cheeks felt as though they had been struck.

"Why?" he heard his voice quaver, already knowing the answer.

She threw her arms around him again and kissed him repeatedly on his neck. "I've been asked to meet someone there," she whispered. "I need to go."

His stomach, back and thigh muscles tightened involuntarily. He took her upper arms into his grip. He felt tears rise to his eyes and the light became glazed. The afternoon became hazy.

She spoke quickly. "I have to prove to someone that I care enough to go up there."

"It's too dangerous; it's certain the Serbs will attack the church and there's hardly a defence against them."

She pulled herself further away; his anxiety shook her.

He thought, 'This is not a terrorist, a child soldier, a general or drug baron causing pain, it's Kate'.

She felt his concern for her though his body. It was not unexpected but the ferocity of his love dismayed her. She feared his love could entrap her. She had struggled for her independence and now this, an all-encompassing love - real, profound, and devoted to her, but was it too powerful?

"If I don't go up, I'd feel the guilt and I'd fail us anyway. At least this way I may find a story that will do some good."

"Kate, by the time the people leave the edge of town, it's likely the Serbs will have weapons trained on the path or at least snipers. And if not then, they'll certainly attack the church. It will be like the massacre on the day we met."

She locked her eyes shut. She did not want to see such horror again. She knew she was torn. No one had ever loved her like he loved her. His patience, respect and ferocity were fulfilling, exciting and shouted songs of lust and fear. She knew that with his experience he understood more clearly the probability of danger.

With her eyes still closed she said, "I have to go. It's important."

David respected her but he felt tragedy in the air and that he was fated to embrace anguish. His voice almost cracked. "But…but I don't understand. We both don't have to go gamble with our deaths."

"If it's probable death, why are you going?"

"You're new to this; I've been in danger a hundred times. I know what to look for, where to duck and dive. I can get the information for you."

Her set mouth spoke of stubborn independence.

Blood pumped through his neck and temple veins. His face turned slightly red. His throat tightened. He felt a wave of anguish gather in him and then a severe pain streaked the inside of his eyes as if struck by a bolt of electricity. He was shocked and let out a cry, a sound that she could only know as an incompressible curse, a curse not against her but against the unending sadness of life, against all the incomprehensible injustices, against the countless deaths of love, the death of hope and the incalculable struggle to rise once more and to dive into the swirling pool of human existence again and again.

David's elbow became cramped. It was because, in his tension, he had pressed his box of memories ever tighter against his body underneath his burnoose. In an undisciplined descent from order, he jumped the queue and remembered another picture of her. She was tall, slim and elegant. He had photographed her naked, rubbing cream into her belly, reflecting in the mirror in front, her thick dark hair dishevelled, a towel at her feet. She knew he was there with his camera, and even in those first days of their relationship, she trusted him. As the shutter burred she turned to look at him. He raised his head from looking down into the ground glass of the Hasselblad and saw the languorous smile tickle the edges of her lips. He knew that as he loved her she also loved him and for the first time in his life he recognized that he was being loved. This was not admiration, not just sexual pleasure, not a confusion on this woman's part about his minor fame and wealth but rather a love of who he was.

A dull thud reverberated from around the front of the icehouse. David breathed a shallow, steady in and out, attempting to be still and to not be overcome with fear. Somewhere around the other side, two men were shouting at each other in the thick local Arabic dialect. A door slammed, a moment later a shabby customs agent limped away from the ice house carrying a plastic bag with what David guessed was a payment in fish for one of the worker's supposed misdemeanour. He limped towards the distant main gate through the soft haze rising from the warming sea. David figured that he was probably an ex-policeman, injured in the line of duty and given a sinecure for life, a meaningless job on low wages, encouraging him to continually intimidate the workers along the quay. He recalled Marcuse's Theory of Repressive Tolerance: constantly remind people of the presence of authority, constantly harasses and intimidate so they do not forget that the state can do as it will with them.

David looked for a less obvious place to hide. Between the ice house and the main gate, which was hardly visible in the heat haze enveloping the quay, about 25 meters from where David was hiding, was a huge pile of lobster traps left unused for the season. He was certain he could easily lie low amongst them if he had time to safely fashion a cave by clearing some and stacking others.

He waited, watched and returned to his thoughts, remembering she had said, "I want you, I want you in every way and all the time". He wondered why, even now in his sixties, he still asked, 'What can I become?' He heard himself saying over and over in the middle of the night, clouded by obsession and deep-seated fears, 'When is the only becoming the coming of death? At that point, have all of our choices gone?'

The heat was beginning to exhaust both the day and him. He needed to get to cover. A few more minutes of watching and waiting. Because of the coastguard's fast boats, he could not leave port until after sundown, another seven hours.

He looked at the burnoose and wondered what had become of him. How did he arrive at this point in his life, hiding on a quay in a God-forsaken tin pot dictatorship, fleeing from the authorities, trapped by people he had trusted, screwed again by the decisions he had made on the side of what he had construed as goodness. Why was he alone, on his own, disdained by the powers that be, an outcast and yet a man who had helped so many others, who had allied himself with good causes and who had stood up to the money and power boys?

'If I told my story to others, what would I say? A man wishes others not to have to live through the oppression of his own childhood. In his godless, lonely world with no myth of transcendence, no heaven to divert his attention, he believes that only his actions can lead him to living a just life and that a just life would lead to peace. He thinks his work must be in the service of others. He becomes a photographer to expose the filth and to do good in the world. This he believes will lead to a kind of redemption because, if there is one thing that his family had made clear to him, it was that he had no value. As he grows older and sees more of the world and more violence, he comes to understand that he, like most Americans, floats in an ocean of self-referential individualism and that actually he needs to engage in the obligations and opportunities of neighbourliness.'

David pinched his hand and cursed himself under his breath with self-loathing because he knew, for all of his fancy ideas, it was love and nothing more that drove him to the decisions he made.

The sea whispered as it lapped the breakwater and tickled the bellies of the fishermen's wooden boats. Even the traffic on the cliff road above had gone quiet in the heat. No sounds from the quay, no grease covered hands tinkering with engines, no poor sullen men rocking to and fro as they untangled and mended their nets, no arguments over football or the weather, over who had a better wife or whose kids were the most clever; just silence and stillness but for the squabbling gulls fighting over the scraps of fish dropped on the stones of the quay from the passing carts. David guessed that the few remaining fishermen had decided to escape the heat by resting in their flimsy wheelhouses or under their tarpaulin rain covers.

It was time to cross the open space between where he was and the lobster trap mountain, a short but dangerously exposed trip. He unbent his legs, stood and felt the various pains shoot through his right knee, his thigh and his shoulders. He clasped his box of memories under his elbow and moved stiffly and silently away from his shelter towards his next haven, silently tapping his cane.

The heat haze hid him from the distant front gate. He felt assured. He was safe to think about her but suddenly the door of the icehouse behind him rasped open. He did not look but walked on.

"Hey you," came a shout in Arabic.

David kept walking.

"You, monsieur, stop," came the shout again but this time in roughly accented French.

David stopped. He hated violence and yet he remembered he too was human and capable of what most others were also capable of. Culture had been his salvation; it had shown him the richness of life and Darwin's theory - that the fittest is not the strongest but the most intelligent - buoyed him at that moment while he listened to the footsteps approaching from behind. His hand tightened on his cane. Was David capable of all that humans were capable of?

•••

David's brother's return was distressing for David. Joel had filled out; he had become muscular. He had also become more aggressive and more disconnected from anything David understood as important or valuable. David saw a look in his brother's eyes that whispered of a dangerous madness. Joel talked about seeing the walls at night crawling with spiders. He would then laugh and exclaim how the only food worth eating was the "good ol' merican burger".

David was intimidated by Joel's presence but he too had filled out. After working for the photographer for several years he could afford to buy things without his parent's money, which meant without their approval. As they could not care less about what he did as long as he made no fuss in front of the family of cousins and aunts, he felt free to purchase a set of weights to build up his lean musculature. He had promised himself this after he was beaten by the kid in elementary school. He purchased a book on bodybuilding and another on karate and studied them almost forensically. This gave him some confidence in front of his brother but he could not imagine hitting him. In karate he learned that you defend by blocking the aggressor's attempted strike three times and then, if that has not discouraged them, you strike with kicks or punches. But the idea of hurting someone sickened him. He told himself it was only for self-defence, but he would never allow himself to be beaten again, whatever the cost. 'I will not walk silently to the gas chambers.'

"Hey little asshole."

David was in the basement of their house, near the bottom of the stairs that led down from the kitchen, laying out some dried photographic prints to flatten under weights on a table.

"Asshole, that's my table."

David heard the metallic sound in his crazy brother's voice. He knew this was different. He turned and looked up at Joel who was standing on the third step from the bottom of the stairs. "What are you talking about?"

"That's my table. Who said you could use it?"

"Joey, it's not your table and even if it was..."

"Shut the fuck up."

David was at a loss. He walked towards his brother. "What do you want?"

Joel jerked his head forward as he put his right hand into his jacket pocket.

"Ya' know, when I was in Germany, we had these jungle bunnies in our squad. Assholes, they were assholes; one day I saw why I thought they were losers and ya' know why?"

David felt disgust rising. Who was this creature filled with so much hatred and irrationality? He stared at his brother's pinprick eyes and rounded fleshy cheeks, wondering if he had ever really seen him before. He appeared different, strange.

"I asked you a question." He rattled his hand in his pocket as if threatening David with something. "Na, you ain't got a fucking clue." Joel raised his voice and it quavered as it he was losing control over it. He put his right foot down onto the next step and shouted, "Cause they reminded me of you. They thought they were somethin' special cause they were niggers in uniform, that they were better 'n me."

David did not know how to respond. He stepped away, turned his back on his brother and moved towards the table to sort his prints.

Joel shouted, "Look at me. Come here and look at me, I got somethin' for you."

David, surprised by the ferocity, turned again towards his brother.

"I said come here."

David felt his fear rising along with a heady mixture of anger. He repeated over and over to himself, 'I don't want this, I don't want this'.

He took several steps towards Joel who yanked a chrome revolver from his pocket and poked it hard into David's forehead. The shock of the impact was equal to his shock at the sight of the gun in his brother's hand. Suddenly David felt no fear. It was as if all of it played itself out before the event in his imagination and afterwards in his nightmares, but in the middle of this violence he suddenly become serene, as if floating in someone else's story.

"They learned us to kill in basic ... I could kill you right now."

Brought up on TV Westerns, cop shows and films filled with wars and in particular killing the 'redskins', surrounded by an underlying sense of racial violence in his high school, seeing on the news the rising tide of war in Vietnam and the race riots and struggles in the South, bombarded by the harshness of football and hockey violence and the endless propaganda of 'America do or die, better dead then red' and the macho stance of his brother and his friends, David had wanted to avoid violence. If anything he wanted to help create a world of peace, but now this outrage, this lifetime of threat, slaps and scratches and being blamed for their fights and the constant intimidation and the destruction of his world of soldiers and cowboys by the cursed vitriol of this malign human being, this thing called his brother and finally it had come to a climactic moment.

In a lighting move, David swung his right arm up across his body and grasped his brother's gun hand at the wrist while ducking his head to his own right out of range. He quickly pivoted his body one hundred and eighty degrees while forcing his brother's right arm forward. This took Joel by surprise but also threw him off balance into David's back. David reached up and arched his left arm over his brother's head and grabbed his neck. He then dropped quickly and bent forward. His brother flipped off the second step, over David's back and landed hard on his own back on the floor. David leapt over him and dropped with all of his weight onto Joel's belly. He slapped and flayed and smacked and struck his brother's face over and over, shouting ever curse he knew. Blood spurted from Joel's nose. Abel had risen from his grave.

His mother and grandmother, hearing the ruckus, rushed down the stairs. His mother grabbed David's flailing arms. He stopped; he had not known how to stop and only needed this prompt. His grandmother was shocked by the violence. Through David's tear-filled eyes he had a passing fright that he had somehow hurt her. She looked from the gun on the floor to Joel's bloodied face to David, nodded and climbed back up the stairs.

Joel slept elsewhere that night and moved out the next day while David was at school. When David returned home that evening, his mother ignored him and his grandma gave him a hidden smile. He knew she knew he was right about what he had done. Later he found that Joel had sliced all of his prints to ribbons and replaced them under the weights. There was a message scrawled on the back of one of the shards. It said: "I'll get you."

That night his father shouted at David, "It's just a mock gun. For God's sake, you're both as crazy as each other."

David wondered how it was that his father had never taken his side on anything. 'Am I always wrong? Does he understand something I just don't get?'

But for David, the great sadness was that he had no way to discuss things with his father. He thought that if his father could explain to him why, in each case, he had been wrong, how he had been to blame or at fault, he, David, may have become a better person.

During David's third year in high school, his friend Ed moved to Chicago. Ed's father had been given a professorship at the university. They lived in an expensive suburb just south of the city. Ed suggested that David and Helen could come down for a visit during the Christmas holiday. Ed, in his masked voice, told David that his parents were going to the West Indies for a vacation and the house would be empty but for Ed and his new dog, a Golden Retriever called Sigmund.

They would be able to go to The Chicago Institute of Art and to see the famous Second City Theatre Company but David wondered how he would act with Helen. They would be without parents. Would they sleep in the same room and all those other questions he hoped would be answered. David knew his own parents wouldn't care but was amazed when Helen's parents accepted it.

What an adventure. David's mother lent him her car. He picked Helen up and they drove to Chicago. It was so adult. He had a map and Helen guided him as they drove from expressway to highway to interstate, crossing the Michigan-Ohio boarder, cruising across the flat lands of Indiana and into Illinois. Dried brown corn stalks stood upright in the endless landscape like deathly apparitions; farmers' fields stretched for miles on both sides of the highway rimmed with ice filled furrows; huge silos beckoned on the horizon; worn wooden shacks and hunkered down brick houses surrounded by rusted cars and dilapidated pick-ups cried, 'this is the American heartland.' David wondered where were the riches and wealth?

They stopped at a roadside café and each had a hotdog and a malted milk. Helen had a straw pursed in her lips as she sucked the thick sweet liquid through it. She stopped and wiped her mouth with her paper napkin. "David, in June you won more awards than anyone in America."

He nodded.

"There was no ceremony this year was there?"

"No."

"So you didn't tell me again."

"How did you find out?"

She moved her head off to her right as if trying to find an angle on David that made sense. "A friend is going out with someone in your photo class. She just told me the other day; she thought I knew."

David considered this. "I was lucky."

"I don't get it."

"Helen, how would you feel if I suddenly said, 'Oh by the way, I just won more awards than anyone else in the whole United States?' You'd say I was showing off, bragging. There's nothing to say and no one cares except me and my teacher."

She snapped, "I care", and nodded several times as if reassuring herself that to love him was not crazy. "I care, and please don't tell me what I think.''

He understood his mistake and nodded, meaning he was sorry and then continued. "But why should you care? It has no meaning. It's all about good ol' competition and really, I hate competition."

"Then why enter?"

"If I'm lucky I could get a scholarship. I don't think my parents will help pay for college. When I try to speak with them about it they ignore me, they tell me they're busy watching TV or something." He looked at his empty plate. "So I have to compete to get a scholarship."

"Do you really not care about being the best?"

"I care. Yes I care because it tells me what standard I'm at relative to others." He stopped and looked at her beautiful face. "Still, I hate the competition part."

"But without the competition you wouldn't know your standard."

"True." He paused and finished his drink and then sighed. "I know it's not really worked out what I'm saying but I feel that the contradiction is okay. One day I'll understand it ... now it's just gut instinct ... but anyway, I don't think it's important to splash it around."

She took his hand. "You know, there's private and there's private."

"I don't understand."

"What I mean is that you won't let me in."

He thought about what she meant. "If we talk about Thomas Wolfe or Shakespeare, things we study in class together then that's alright because we both know a little about them, but if I tell you about a great photographer named W. Eugene Smith and how he has shown me that photographers can be messengers or how Paul Stand shows me how all people live with the same doubts, pain and insecurity so we are really all the same, do you care or understand? I don't think so because it's not your passion, so I'd bore you and look like I was showing off."

Helen's hurt became clear. "How do you think the rest of us feel when you are always the only one who's read the whole of the Oresteia or Dante?"

Helen shook her head from side to side as though throwing off her other thoughts.

He knew he was supposed to be taking in her disapproval but instead he concentrated on the fluorescent lights reflecting off her long wavy hair undulating around her face.

They drove on to Chicago. After a confused navigation through the city they arrived at a gated property. While David sat at the wheel, Helen got out and pressed the buzzer on the high brick pillar. David could hear the sound of her voice without understanding her words. He watched her. She was self-confident and the curve of her hip was enticing and her breast pushing against her sweater was even more seductive ... she was beautiful and exciting. His expectations for what would happen between them were greater than his interest in Ed's new home.

The gate swung open. David pulled in and drove along the recently planted trees that seemed to march along the road like ordered sentinels. They were still small but overbearing. David appreciated the harmony of similar forms. He had learned that from studying the landscapes of Edward Weston. Out of apparent chaos Weston would see the patterns that revealed either the order imposed by humans or the secret order he discovered in nature. But these trees; they were almost military, too consistent, too proud. David grew uncomfortable as the thin, pale afternoon sun flicked between them, wiping the windshield every other second. He remembered a quote from Henry David Thoreau that 'consistency is the hobgoblin of little minds.' David wondered when man's imposition of rationality crosses over to fascism.

He turned to Helen. "Did Ed answer the bell?"

She smiled broadly and nodded. "Exciting isn't it? His dad must be doing really well."

David slowed the car to a stop. "If this is his driveway, he must be God." He slid his arm around her shoulder and pulled her gently towards him. He kissed her. For the first time she pushed her tongue into his mouth. It was warm and tasted sweet. They looked at each other. She said, "I have a surprise for you."

He looked quizzically at her. She smiled coyly. "Later, when we're alone."

They were all pleased to see each other and although Ed seemed almost sexless to David, he noticed how Ed enjoyed Helen's company. Unlike other boys of their age, he, like David, assumed Helen was their equal in all things. The boy's assumption of her equality let Helen be comfortable in their company.

That evening they went out to a local family diner. They sat in a booth and were waited on by a middle-aged woman whose nametag proclaimed 'Rose'. She had dyed jet black hair pulled tight into a small ponytail and wore deep red lipstick. Her almost gaunt drawn pale face looked hardened and unapproachable, but she took a liking to David. From the start his politeness charmed her and the three of them could do no wrong ... extra French fries and a free fill-up of cokes were laid on. Rose was prone to winks of complicity.

"Ain't from round here?"

David smiled at her. "No mam, we, Helen and I, we're from Detroit."

"Long way from home. Never been there myself but got an aunt up there. Yup, she hates it." She looked closely at David. "Well, don't mean no harm. Really she don't like anybody or anyplace. Guess your city's as good or bad as mine."

David said, "I guess your aunt is like a lot of other people from Detroit. Some of us say it's a great city to see in your rear-view mirror."

Uncertain, Rose studied David for a split second and then laughed. "You got humour son. I like that, you make me laugh. Yes siree-bob, a great place to leave."

David laughed and Rose, Ed and Helen joined in.

Later Ed noticed she hadn't charged them for their desserts.

Helen was thoughtful throughout the meal while David and Ed talked about the slow-motion images of Ernst Hass and what reality meant in a photograph. When at last they paused between the main course and the dessert, Helen placed her hand on David's and asked both he and Ed where they imagined they would be in five years. This unexpected question brought David and Ed to silence for a moment.

Ed leant forward and asked her why she wanted to know.

"Here we are together, but this will pass. And the years will pass and at some point, we'll look back and ask ourselves, 'what was that about? what were those relationships? and could we then have seen where we'd end up?'"

Ed volunteered in his normal self-assured manner. "I'll be in my final year of university getting my BA in psychology."

David was surprised. "Psychology?"

Ed turned slowly towards David and dipped his head as he blinked to assure David he had heard him correctly. "Yes, and then I will go to grad school on the east coast and eventually get a doctorate and practice in some place civilized like Boston."

Helen smiled. "I guess I can imagine you as a shrink."

"Ed, does that mean you'll help people to conform to what everyone else calls normal?" David baited and waited for Ed's cool response.

Ed smiled at his friend. "Is this a trap I see before me?" He paused to gather his thoughts. "That's one way to look at it, but no it doesn't mean artists will be re-programmed into becoming politicians or lawyers." Ed looked at Helen. "And you, where will you be?"

She looked at David as though proclaiming a mutual future. "I want a career but I want kids and a home in a suburb. Maybe a dog."

David was shocked. This was a reality he could not contemplate. He never imagined he would be in this position. He had so forcibly if unconsciously rejected his parents' model it had not occurred to him that he would fall for a girl who would even think about living in Detroit and having a family and a picket fence.

Ed turned towards David more or less for the same reason. Would he confirm Helen's dream? Would he be a part of it and her future?

"I'm more concerned with the pictures I'll enter for this year's competition."

"You're not answering the question," Helen whispered.

"But I am. My future's uncertain but it's based on how I succeed with my picture making. You know that, I explained that to you in the café today."

Ed broke the silence following David's obfuscation. "David, you want your pictures to be about truth?"

David saw the trap now being laid by Ed. He nodded and then smiled, "Here it comes."

Ed obliged. "What about truth in your life?"

"I don't think I can make truthful pictures if I don't live a truthful life."

Ed pressed. "So answer Helen."

"The truth?" He looked at Ed and smiled softly and then into Helen's eyes as if forgetting his clever trusted friend was at the table. He took her hand in his. "The truth is, I would never want to hurt you." He paused. He could see the joy of the holiday, the possible sex and Helen's secret now prancing away outside the diner's window like the doleful plastic reindeer stationed there to remind their patrons it was the Christmas season. He looked across at Ed who

was watching him and then at Helen again. "The truth is that I can't imagine myself being married, staying in Detroit or in any one place for long. The truth is that I imagine I will probably not live past middle age and that I have things to do that will be dangerous. And I guess my truth is different from what you want but when you told us your dream, I didn't know if I was included."

Helen looked at his face but saw an abyss, an empty future because she had come to love him. She realized he was not like the other boys, that he was troubled and angry and filled with talent and he was good looking and sexy and he was gentle and kind and hard-working, and he also respected her. How could she have thought that he would want to settle down and be like the rest of them, like her other friends? He was not conventional and so his life would not be conventional. He needed a bigger stage, he needed New York or even Camus' France, but surely not Detroit. She was mortified in front of both of them. She thought they would see her as a pathetic, unadventurous girl like all the other girls. Good job, nice car, hair salon once a week, pedicures, a stay-at-home with kids, clothes, insurance policies, baseball games for the boys, ballet lessons for the girls, voting Republican, hating the Commies, suspicious of the Negroes, foreigners and anti-war hippies.

Slowly, inadvertently her hand moved to her mouth and huge crystal tears rolled out of her sparkling eyes. She wished she could disappear.

Ed turned away and studied the reindeer. David delicately touched her cheek. "Don't, it's me, it's my fault; it's because of who I am."

She shook her head from side to side and she too looked out of the window at the inanimate reindeer with their blinking coloured lights as she fought for breath and composure.

David, bereft and ignored, went to the counter and paid the check. This was his future - hurting people and being on his own to pursue his dream.

Rose took the money and as she gave him the change, she held his hand for a moment. "Don't break all their hearts."

David leaned close to her. "Is life hard for everyone?"

Rose clasped her lips shut and her eyes moistened. She whispered, "Just be good, son; don't be mean. It'll help."

They drove back to Ed's place without a word spoken between them. Ed showed them their room. Silently Helen went to the bathroom and returned in a pair of pyjamas. They slept in the same bed but he on one side and she far away on the other coast with a sea of grief between them.

David had saved his money to travel to Chicago and to visit Ed. He thought of Chicago as a place of culture, creative opportunity, holding some mysterious force that he would discover in that windy city on the tip of the huge angry lake. He imagined it as Berlin had been to Paris in the beginning of the twentieth century for young European and American poets and artists. He dreamed of the banquet years to come, he dreamed of meeting artists and intellectuals, of discussing and learning and appreciating beauty and of encountering his Tina Modotti. Helen of the picket fences, beautiful and sexy, was not his Tina.

The next morning the phone rang in Ed's kitchen. As Ed strode to it, his long legs churning the chilled winter air of the austere, unheated house, David turned away from Thomas Wolfe's You Can't Go Home Again towards Ed's voice.

Ed held the phone towards David. "For you," he whispered, "I think it's the jerk you call a brother."

David was surprised and concerned. He nodded and took the phone. Ed stood by, watching.

"Hello?" He waited. No response. Impatiently, "Hello". No response.

Ed realized David's confusion.

David covered the mouthpiece. "You sure it's my brother?"

As Ed shrugged, Helen entered. She appeared tired and her eyes were red.

Ed looked at Helen, studying her and said to David, "Fortunately I don't recognize his voice that well. Who knows, maybe not."

David uncovered the mouthpiece. "Hello." he said louder. No response. He shrugged, reached over and placed the phone on the hook. He looked up at Ed. "Sorry." He paused, thinking about what that might have been about. "You know, he's so jealous, maybe he just wants to wind me up while I'm here."

The phone rang again. Now it seemed shrill, demanding, objectionable like his brother. Ed nodded towards it. David picked it up. "Hello". Pause. Nothing. He looked up at Ed but spoke harshly into the phone. "Is this a joke?"

"Ain't no joke Davy. You know when it comes to you I never joke." His brother's silly macho snarl leaked down the phone line from Detroit like acid out of the battery factory on the river.

David looked up and nodded towards Ed, letting him know it was his brother and all was normal.

"What do you want?"

"Nothing, I jes gotta give you some in-for-mation." Joel dragged out the last word as if it carried significance.

David wanted to compliment him on using a four-syllable word so early in the day but he could hear Joel breathing down the phone like a horror film sound effect.

David, thinking this was a windup, became brittle. "If this is about what happened between us, we can deal with it when I get back."

"Naa, not that stuff. Who the fuck cares? You got lucky for a mo."

"So?"

"So, is that all you gotta say when I'm helping you?"

"Quit messing around. What's going on?"

"You really are ungrateful."

David went silent. He felt welling enmity for his brother's mean spirited, bullying and pettiness.

"You got somethin' to say?"

David, gathering all his patience, spoke with a strangled whisper. "What? What do you want?"

Helen and Ed looked at each other. Helen quietly asked Ed if she could make some coffee.

"Well nothing really. Mom asked me to tell you gran died last night."

A chill charged though David's body. Tears of sorrow and rage tore themselves out of his eyes. He gasped.

Ed was staggered by David's instantaneous transformation. He sat down next to David.

"So." slimed Joel, "You got notin' to say about it?"

"How, why?"

"Tripped over the oven door, hit her head and had a heart attack. Yup, massive. Got to hospital but that's it. Jes died."

"Was she alone?"

"Wha'da you mean alone? Doctors, nurses…"

David, hard wired for a bad temper and still short-fused, had enough. His pain fired like sparks into his well-oiled hatred. He shouted in one long howling purple breath, "Listen, you dumb fuck son of a bitch, she was not my grandmother, she was ours. She was ours, ours, get it, ours. What in your fucking little brain makes her mine in the middle of this? You're a thick-skinned emotional coward just like you're a dumb-fuck brute? Or since you can't punch me over the phone you play this crap. Was she alone? Don't you give a crap? Alone, dying alone. Bet you weren't there to comfort her, huh. Probably sitting in a burger joint masticating another bit of pap while our grandmother died alone. What the fuck did I mean? That doctors were around her? No asshole and you know it. I meant was dad with her? Was he there, did he know; did he rush to the hospital or was she left alone? Not with nurses but with family. Left to die alone?" He shouted, his voice cracking with grief, "What's wrong with you? What the fuck is wrong with you?"

Joel, although used to David's temper, had never faced this intensity before. His defence turned as usual into vengeance. "And where were you, huh? Swanning around with your fancy friends in She-ca-ga? Leaving us bumpkins behind...."

"Shut up and answer the question...was she alone?"

He never got the answer from Joel. But at the moment, as he slammed down the receiver, he recognized for the first time, that he had no choice but to leave the Midwest and his roots as soon as possible.

Helen, watching him from a distance near the perking coffee, had never seen his depth of temper before nor heard him swear. She was confused, wondering if she really knew who he was but also concerned for his loss.

Ed looked on like a surgeon, objectifying the emotions, absorbing their meanings, searching for psychological links. Sigmund, with his big eyes looked from voice to voice.

It snowed that day, one of the Midwest's winter excesses, closing roads and airports, stopping trains and shutting schools. The highways back to Detroit were impassable, the great Mac trucks were stranded; thirty car pile-ups were common. David needed to return immediately for the funeral but could not depart until at least early the next morning.

That night David lay awake in Ed's strange bed with Helen on the far side not knowing what to do. David tried to account for how he had become what he then was, a boy about to be rootless. But what were his roots? He had come from immigrants and migrants. He had no sense of community nor had his parents tried to establish one for him or for themselves; he was by gut response in opposition to all that others seemed to hold dear and interesting. The focus of his life had become photography, art and poetry. Virtually no one around him had any interest in these things. Ed had chosen to be a psychiatrist; Helen wanted a suburban existence. He wanted love, knowledge and beauty in his life. But he was the odd ball, the kid with the weird ideas. Maybe even a commie and probably a poof, a queer, a 'faggot, a shirt lifter' to boot, at least in others' minds. What roots were these?

He remembered the only time his parents had gone on a picnic to a local park. His father cooked hot dogs on the cement barbeque built near some benches. David liked the hot yellow mustard and as the others ate, including his older cousin Barry and his family, David wandered to the edge of the woods and after looking around to see if he was being watched, he stepped between sparkling silver birch trees into long yellow grass. He thought that his parents would never notice he was gone. He peered at the fine feathery heads on the grasses and listened to the leaves rippling in the breeze. Shafts of light played through the boughs. He became aware of many more birds singing and the sound of the branches swaying and rubbing against each other. He felt peaceful and suddenly had an image of what this must have been like two hundred years earlier. Virgin, unspoiled by the white men, a land where the Ottawa tribe roamed. He remembered reading that when they killed an animal for food they thanked its spirit. 'How savage could they have been to do that?' He wondered if there were signs of them thereabouts ... perhaps under his gym shoes at this very place there were arrowheads.

As David lay awake in that frozen Chicago night, worried about being too tired to drive back to his city and the funeral, images of his grandma's smile and her huge brown eyes gazed at him in the darkness. He thought without her there were no more roots. Her death was her gift to him. She had cut him free, she had granted him his own liberty. At the same time, he knew his brother was right, that he would be leaving behind the community he was born into. He tossed and stirred and wished Helen would wake and that she would come over to him and they would make love. Again he saw his grandma's eyes and wished he could have been with her, held her hand ... made sure she knew he loved her and that she was not alone. And was this not pure ego? Would she have even known he was there and if so, would she have wished for her angry silent son to be there instead?

Did David belong anywhere? From all that he read he believed his intellectual roots were in central Europe; from the bias of

American history he had been led to believe that England was his true motherland, but emotionally he was rooted somehow in the Mediterranean. Perhaps Spain but he was drawn further east. Not Israel. It held no attraction for him. For now he could only dream.

Early the next morning he drove back to Detroit past stalled and abandoned cars and tractors pulling Macs back onto the highway from ditches and culverts. The land was frozen, the trees as bare as they had been on the way out to Chicago but now with a patina of snow, yet it seemed even more sad and empty. He apologized to Helen for the ruined vacation and missing the theatre and for his disappointing her and then he dropped her home.

When he arrived at his house, the cars were about to leave for the funeral. No consideration had been made that he may have been delayed by the storm. Neither of his parents had spoken to him, had tried to phone him, had offered comfort. Perhaps it was his duty to offer them comfort. He did not know these things. They never bothered to teach him these ways of the world. He had learned about baseball and shaving on his own and about girls and morality without his family's help but he understood that learning about these social nuances required instruction or at least good examples.

That day of the funeral, as usual, he was not in the ambit of his parent's plans. At the cemetery, one of the professionally sad hired hands from the Jewish Funeral Home thrust a yarmulke at him. David looked at it and felt an overwhelming sense of revulsion for the deceit being played out. With no one in the family a practicing Jew, the disinterest his mother had shown in his attendance at the Temple, his father reading the Christian Science lessons and his brother, Godless and insensitive to all but Hallmark card sentimentality, the act of placing this ridiculous piece of blue stitched nylon on his head to show some sort of honour to ... to whom, the vengeful Jewish God, the one that blinked sometime in 1933 and reopened his eyes in 1945, to his family and elders, to the uncaring herd of indolent mumblers, or to his grandmother who would not have cared, who would have held him close to her side and whispered that he should rise above it.

His father had not bothered to greet him let alone be embraced by or embrace his youngest son. Instead he snapped, "You better put on that yarmulke."

'Of all people', thought David. Had his father forgotten the years he had disregarded his son in order to read the Christian lessons? Maybe not. Maybe his father, who seemed more like the vengeful Yahweh than the Christian God of Love, had really never left his roots?

At the graveside he heard little. The sanctimonious rabbi delivered generalized platitudes about a woman he had never met, his mother looked strangely content, his father was about as distant and distracted as normal and his brother, holding the hand of a very fat girl with a pug nose, appeared irritated, lost for a moment in his brooding sentimentality, dreaming of his next burger. Barry's parents were there but Barry was at the University of California in Berkley. David missed him. He thought Barry would know what to do, what to make of all of this. He'd even find wry humour in it.

While David stood by the side of the grave, he was chilled by the thought that in that box were the remains of a person, someone he had loved and had never clearly expressed his love to. Did she know what she had meant to him? Had she been damaged by what seemed his rejection of her? Had his fight with his brother caused this?

He stared at the earth piled along the edge of the open wound in the ground and sought comfort, some stabilizing idea. His mind drifted off to a beautiful lachrymose photograph by Eugene Smith of a Spanish family gathered around a dying man and began to think that is was odd how its beauty brought him comfort at that moment. 'Art's not just transformative of matter but it's a way of filling my spiritual emptiness in a secular, lonely and otherwise empty world.' He shook his head in affirmation. 'In that way art does for me what religion does for others: it provides an understanding of these big questions, it creates a balm for my soul and allows me to feel a unity with others through the meaning of their work. It allows me to cross bridges of time and place, to see within others their humanity; it helps me to feel in communication with other's souls and less alone. It tells me that what I feel, think, care about and believe is also what others have too, and that I can share with them, as I reaffirm in myself, our common caring humanity.' He concentrated on the coffin and the wounded earth. 'I can walk through the valley of death...'

He thought about his grandmother and about Helen. He knew that he was filled with love for them and that allowed him to feel whole and good about himself, and their loving of him created a circle that allowed him to have belief in his self-worth.

'Love and beauty, beauty and creativity, creativity and love.'

On the verge of his grandmother's grave tears streamed down his face and he wished he had held her before she died.

She had liberated him. Her death clarified his life. That was her gift to him. He remembered someone said that we all live our lives standing on the shoulders of those who came before us. 'It is true, she allowed me to see further.'

Part III

CHAPTER 14

The footsteps drew closer and louder. They stopped immediately behind David. He waited for a gun barrel to poke into his back; he waited for his brother from damnation to drool some macho line he'd stolen from an American film, but a hand gently placed itself on his shoulder. David turned, confused and surprised. A small wiry man stood in front of him. Clearly poor by the look of his clothes, a fisherman by his odour, a good, strong face, a smile. They looked at each other. The man said in halting French, "I am Zakkir, father to Ali. He asked me to watch out for you."

"Watch for me? But how…."

Zakkir waved off David's surprise. "My son is secret service man." He nudged David. "Only God knows more than his bosses."

David smiled and relief spread like an infusion throughout his system. He stuck his hand out towards Zakkir who grabbed it in both of his huge hands. They were as hard as wooden planks. Zakkir took David by the arm and guided him towards the lobster traps.

While walking, Zakkir spoke quickly but softly, although a half-century of cigarettes and singing to himself over battering seas had created a voice filled with rusted metal and stubborn durability. "We cannot go now, fast police boats; after dark we go, I come back, you hide here." He moved aside several crates and pointed to what looked like a passage in the lobster trap mountain. David thanked him and clasped his shoulder. He asked this tough, doughty man, "Will you be safe?"

Zakkir smiled. "I know all the right people. It's okay. I know the sea. It's good." He pulled a paper bag from his canvas shoulder sack, pushed it towards David and said, "Here, you will need strong."

David sensed it was food. He looked from the bag to Zakkir's sunburnt face. He smiled and nodded as if to say, 'you've thought of everything'.

Zakkir nodded, turned away and then, without looking at David, asked, "Ahh, you have money for the other side?"

David nodded. "No problem, and for your fuel too."

The fisherman turned again towards David, "Good, very excellent." He gently pushed David into the low, narrow passage he had constructed amongst the traps. "Go. Follow tunnel. I'll be back after sun goes below. Don't smoke." He made an almost graceful feminine movement with his hands. His flesh became wafting air; he giggled and waggled his index finger at David as if scolding a child. "Dead lobsters don't smoke." Pleased with his joke, he laughed, disguised the opening and walked away.

David manoeuvred his sore and tired body through the twisted corridor of traps and discovered a sort of cavern with a swathe of folded canvas on the ground and a pile of fishing nets bunched up as if a couch to lean against. 'This required planning. How long has Zakkir know about my arrival and even if his son knew that I was being hunted, how would he guess that I'd look for his father's boat?'

When he sat, he was delighted that he could see both ways along the quay as well as in front of him by leaning slightly one way or another, catching an eye-line through the densely piled wooden traps. To his surprise, the odour was not unpleasant. It was more of the seashore than rotting seafood. It had the tang of brine and a sweetness of … 'I could name all the lovely things in the universe: moist walnuts, the fingers of a child discovering wonder, garlic warming in fruity olive oil, sunset at Como, Bruch's Violin Concerto, I could list and add them up, I could fight against my romanticism, but naming them all will never equal peeping from behind my curtain, sticking my nose against the bit of schemata and naming you.'

Did David need to explain to himself why Zakkir was doing what he was doing? Did he need to understand Zakkir's motivations? The man was a stranger. His son was more or less a stranger. David had spent less than two hours with his son and although he had liked the lean, tall young man, although he sensed there were things that were special about him, they had not, in an obvious way, bonded. Did their meeting mean more to the son than to David? Could it be some strange inverted sense of inferiority … that a foreigner, an American to boot, had been friendly and kind to him and this had given him creditability or status, perhaps a status that would be admired by his father? Or did they, the father and son, so object to the regime that any way of striking back, fouling their plans, fed their sense of rebellion? He had been introduced to the Sergeant by Dr Suleiman, as if by plan. It all seemed to … to what? Too. And the young man, as now revealed, is in the security services. Was that apparent off-the-cuff visit initiated by the Doctor anything less than a subtle example of a convoluted Arabic culture in action?

He mused about this as he opened the thick paper bag. There was a waxed container of orange juice, several flatbreads wrapped around lamb, tomatoes and chillies, and two slices of a sesame sweet. 'Thoughtful,' mused David. 'Things to calm me. All very well planned.'

'If I were the Sergeant and his father, I'd do the same. I've risked myself and gone out of my way for others and given my money away, but I had to. I could not have turned away and still lived with myself. Are these men, father and son, the same? Or have I become a lobster among the traps?'

He decided he needed to turn this on its head, not out of cynicism but for safety. 'Is there more than I can grasp here? If the Sergeant was seen to be the officer responsible for my capture, could that promote him? Or am I a lure for something else, something bigger? And if not, can I allow Zakkir to endanger himself with me?' He looked at the bread in his hand. 'Why did he ask about the money?'

He thought that his original plan was still the best. Once the sun begins to set, he will scurry to Zakkir's boat, find the key, check the fuel supply, stuff his money into the brown envelope he had purchased, leave it for Zakkir to discover and depart. None of this nonsense of Zakkir taking him.

By then, Ali had climbed up the back of the building and into the first-floor hallway near David's flat. He knocked, waited, picked the lock, entered, quickly looked around, rushed down the stairs and opened the door for the Colonel and several of his comrade crows. By then the Colonel had given orders to arrest the old baker and now realized they had a waiting game to play. He told his men to watch the street as discreetly as they could and decided he would wait with the Sergeant in the flat for David's return. After all, it would be more comfortable; suitable for a man of his office.

The Colonel lit a cigarette and sat on the divan worrying about the death of the Doctor. It was not that he cared for the rich, pompous predator of vulnerable women but he had been, after all, in the part-time employment of the Security Service and under the Colonel's command at the time of his murder. There will be a story contrived to explain the unfortunate death within David's plotting. 'Yes, that's it, the spy was responsible, he had set the old man up as a postman, conveniently situated to receive and pass on information. When approached by the Doctor he panicked, lured the Doctor into the back alley and surprised him in the shadows with his hidden weapon.' But the Colonel was confounded because the Doctor knew which bell to press. 'Somehow he was implicated, and why was it he wanted to first enter the flat on his own? Suspicious,' he thought, 'And did my lapdog tried to cover for him'.

The fat Colonel, satisfied with his cunning, watched the backlit smoke float away from the tip of the burning tobacco and wondered about this spy he was going to arrest. He looked around the room. Nothing special: a radio, a pile of paperback novels in English, several copies of the Herald Tribune, a computer. 'If he is just an ordinary person, having left his balcony door open indicates he's going to return, or did he leave with such speed that he had no time in his panic to close it, meaning that he had been warned. On the other hand, was the man really an agent and clever enough to leave the door open, making it seem as though he would return? Still, the air and seaports and inland road border guards are on alert. Even if he knew of his imminent arrest, he could not get out of our hermetically-sealed county.'

"Sergeant, is your father still a fisherman?"

"Yes sir."

"Does he have his own boat."

Sergeant Ali was taken by surprise and was uncomfortable with this line of questioning. "He has a one-man boat sir, for inshore fishing."

"Where is he now?"

The Sergeant looked at his watch. "Depending on his catch he may be sorting his fish or still out. Hard to say. Depends on the weather."

The Colonel waved him off. He was bored.

Mehmet looked blankly at the rippling tent wall moving more from waves of heat than air. He needed to get away, to find out what had happened. He could no longer concentrate on his actors or crew. He was afraid that if he did not become active in this plot to create a foreign martyr, it would not happen. It is of course a prerequisite for directors to believe that the world does not turn unless they spin it.

He called his first assistant director and the director of photography over. He explained that he was feeling ill and that they could do second unit crowd shots and pick-ups for the few remaining hours and that he would excuse himself. He was sure it was simply a mild bug and he'd be okay the next morning.

He stood up, and as he passed the political officer on his way out, the ferret watched him and seemed to smirk.

As Mehmet got to his car, he wondered if he imagined the smirk. He sighed a deep breath of relief and drove off at speed, still haunted by his premonitions of the burning pyres.

Once in the region where he could receive a signal, he was certain his phone would be alive with messages affirming, in cryptic language, that a foreign spy had been captured. Maybe the radio news would carry the story. He assured himself that all would be well, and he would have a new status amongst the oppositionists in the coming revolution, a revolution inspired by artists and intellectuals as in Eastern Europe against the criminally insane Soviets. What more could he want in life?

He was forced to stop for a pee. As he stood beside his car, just off the strip of empty tarmac, he became aware of his nose. He realized that the land was so flat between the hilly dunes to his back, where they were filming, and the capital on the coast, the only thing between his eyes and the horizon was his nose. He laughed for a second and returned to his car.

When the radio finally caught a signal, there was no news of David's capture. 'Maybe they want to keep it to themselves until they deal with the Americans and the English, or perhaps it's still too early.'

Within thirty kilometres of the town his phone began to buzz. He grabbed it and saw that he had a few voice messages – as he drove he listened. His girlfriend asked him about dinner, his producer asked about the next day's schedule and there was something he did not understand: a man's voice saying, "Red Dragon". 'What was that, a joke, a warning?' He had no idea until he looked at his emails. He found two jpeg files, and, as the cryptic phone message, there was no source address. He pulled off the road and opened the jpegs. There were two snaps, one of the fishermen's quay with boats lined up along it and another close-up showing the prow of a red painted boat with the name "Red Dragon" on it.

For a man used to directing thrillers, he sensed he was now in one, but of someone else's plotting. What could this mean? Did it have something to do with David?

He decided that careful observation was the safest thing he could do. He entered the city, drove to near David's apartment, parked and walked the last several blocks to the café below David's flat. He noticed a suspicious number of parked police cars. As he turned into David's street, he spotted the crows in their oh-so-obvious sunglasses. Discreetly he raised his eyes and saw David's French windows were ajar. Either the secret police were lying in wait or contemplating David's dead body.

Mehmet entered the café, ordered a coffee and sat deep in the shadows looking out towards the street. He wondered how he had become so uncaring about David, that David had become a mere plot point in Mehmet's developing political life and nothing more. As a crow scrabbled by outside, Mehmet panicked, realizing that whatever the jpegs and call may mean, he should wipe them from the phone's memory. Might they not be a set-up or proof of complicity? Or was it a signal that he should check out? Was it wise for him to be by chance sitting in the café below David's flat?

It was now two in the sweltering, airless spring afternoon. The town was beginning to slumber in the heat. It was siesta time, shops would soon close until five, rich men and politicians would scupper off to spend several hours with their mistresses, the sea mist would evaporate and the white sun would bleach the bones of dead fish on the quay and expose the innocent to unanswerable questions while driving dogs into the shadows. Bird song would cease until the starlings would begin to circle and dive through the insect clouds in the early evening and even the gulls would resentfully but quietly squat on pylons, fishing boat prows and rooftops until later in the day when the welcome breeze would return.

The mingled odour of rotting vegetables, gutter detritus and the memory of baking breads with their saffron and fennel perfumes lingered between the buildings and crept into the shuttered bedrooms that protected the dozing salesmen, grocers and judges. It swirled along the promenades, mixing with the tart and heady rumours of drying seaweeds, metallic whiffs of the slaughterhouse on the edge of town and the ever-present fumes of burning oil and petrol exhausts.

In that silence and stillness, when even the children rested, the citizens would have to discover ways to ignore their certain knowledge of who they were, they would have to distract themselves sufficiently to not have to ask questions or, in their most exposed moments, finding neither sleep nor other preoccupations could relieve them, they would, with utter horror, witness in the silence what they had allowed themselves to become. Men would shrink into sullen self-blame and humiliation; women would pray that their children would find a better way than they had and would wish their sons be saved from more violence and that their daughters be spared the attention of the powerful.

Within the searing heat of the day, the Colonel became more concerned that something was amiss. Lazily, without leaving his seat, he looked from the bed to the bookshelves to the rug … ahh he saw one pill and another. He barked, "Sergeant, the computer."

Ali looked at the computer and back at his commander, not certain what his command meant.

"Open it, turn it on, find something."

"Sir."

Ali went to the table, sat down, flipped open the top and hit the 'on' key. The machine buzzed and lights illuminated but only a grey plane showed on the screen. It remained dark, empty; it offered nothing. Ali fiddled with various keys and turned it off and on again. Still a grey screen. He craned his head towards his Colonel. "Sir, this is a Mac. I'm not familiar with them. They are different from ours."

"Let me see it."

The Sergeant handed it to the Colonel who turned the Mac over. "Can you open it, get inside?"

"Sir, if there's evidence, I might destroy it by mistake."

The Colonel looked at his watch, looked at the Mac, rubbed his finger along the fine metal case and then looked up at his loyal Sergeant. "Well said."

After another fifteen minutes the Colonel became more impatient with their inactivity.

His Sergeant plotted.

Down below, Suleiman's body was carted away.

Muhammad hid in a van carrying petrol drums to his tribal land in the impregnable hills. He would never be found and no one would care.

Zakkir smoked a Spanish cigarette in a harbour bar and waited for the other trap to be set.

Mehmet drank more coffee, feeling panic rising, beginning to believe something was amiss, thinking of the red boat, thinking he should do something.

David, among the lobster traps, daydreamed.

•••

Kennedy became president. His brother became the Attorney General. Bullied by the military and convinced by the CIA, John Kennedy accepted that the United States should intervene in Cuba to destroy the pro USSR Castro from turning Cuba into a Communist military base ninety miles from Florida.

David continued to make photographs; his relationship with Helen had restarted but he had as yet not discovered her surprise; he found himself more and more rebellious in school; he continued to work hard for Mr Day and he sometimes longed to speak with his cousin Barry and to see Annie again. He understood how profoundly he missed their stimulating company and he missed being with people who admired his intellectual abilities. School seemed to be too much about grades and about conforming to some set of unstated ideas about what it meant to be a good citizen and meanwhile Alabama and Mississippi were burning, Russia continued to arm Cuba, and the world seemed ill at ease.

October 1962. Finally it happened. David's generation had been brought up on it. In elementary school they were trained to crawl under their desks for safety and now in high school to respond to the one long ring of the school bells by filing quickly and silently to the classroom door, along the hall, down the stairs into the basement under the vast brown pipes that ran along the walls halfway between the floor and ceiling, to sit under the intersecting triangles of the Conelrad warning - the CONtrol of ELectromagnetic RADiation - and not to think of the holocaust, Armageddon, the Strategic Air Command, B29's, ICBMs, Hiroshima, Joseph Stalin and now Nikita Khrushchev, the Red Army and his and Helen's own deaths by fire, or dying with their loved ones from radiation instigated cancers.

Viva Fidel, viva la revolucion which rid Cuba of the gamblers, crooks, hookers, pimps, the American Mafiosi and their casinos, and which entitled all the people to education, food and medical care. But suddenly Fidel, a freedom fighter, was America's enemy and the island of Cuba had become a cauldron of evil military aggression against the United States.

The sightings, the Russian merchant fleet, an American plane shot down, the pilot killed, an act of war, Russian submarines, John and Robert Kennedy working to save America, the free world and civilization and David and Helen trapped, helplessly, as all of their friends, in the sabre-rattling craziness.

On some days war seemed certain. Death or terrible destruction seemed imminent. Detroit, the bastion of Democracy had been, during the Second World War, the largest military industrial complex in the world, producing rubber, steel, jeeps, trucks, tanks and munitions. David's father snarled only one thing throughout the entire crisis, "Sure we're a target". David was amazed at how his father could be both laconic and overstated in the same sentence. As usual, he had offered his son little comfort. It was as if his father was simply waiting for his inevitable death.

By the time the crisis was over, the world had changed for David's generation. Many were convinced that the world's leaders were universally as crazy as were their parents for creating the madness. Much of the rest of the sixties - flower power, resistance to the Vietnam War, the hatred of authority and the disregard of old hierarchies, disdain for the capitalist consumerist goals - were most likely germinated in the minds of the young during those heady days of the Cuban Missile Crisis. It was doubtful that the Cold War leaders wished to create nihilism but they did an excellent job at encouraging it.

On the day it ended Helen rang David and asked him if he was free the following Saturday afternoon. He told her he was and was intrigued ... she had never initiated a meeting before.

He was filled with anticipation all week and on that Saturday, he borrowed his mother's car and picked Helen up at noon. She told him she wanted him to drive to a friend's house.

"What are we doing?"

"Remember the surprise I had for you in Chicago?"

"Well, I remember there was the mention of one."

She laughed. "You know, talking with you is sometimes like talking with a lawyer."

"Why do you say that?"

"You're so exact about things."

He continued to drive and mused about that. "It's because I think I don't understand what people mean. Most people don't ...". He suddenly saw he was heading for deep water. "Oh I don't know."

"Most people, meaning, I guess, me in this case, do or don't do what?"

"Truthfully, I trust my eyes more than my ears."

"So what do your eyes tell you?"

"You're beautiful, and too often when I look in the mirror I see a jerk."

As he drove, she smiled to herself.

They arrived at a house on a street David had never been to before. He parked the car and Helen told him to come with her. At the front door she produced a key and entered. David was confused. He looked at her, not understanding.

"It's my friend Gloria's house. She and her family are on vacation in Wisconsin. They were so worried about the crisis that they went to be near her brother who's at university out there. They wanted to be all together in case, you know, in case it happened."

"When are they back?"

"She'll ring me before they return." She looked at him with an odd expression, redolent with longing and then she whispered, "The house is empty."

"And?"

"Come with me."

Helen led David to her friend's bedroom. She sat on the bed and patted the spread next to her. He sat down.

"I was thinking this might have happened in Chicago and then all those things were said." She was silent for a long moment as though coming to a decision. "I wanted to save myself for the man I'd marry but you ... well with the crisis and all, who knows if we'll even be alive next year."

David was not certain he understood where this was going.

Helen unbuttoned her blouse and took it off. She slowly looked into David's eyes and then she moved towards him. They kissed as never before, as though both of them were liberated by being in a safe private space but also their awareness of each other was forged by the desperation and by the momentary relief from the tension of the previous few weeks.

With her arms around his neck she whispered, "I want you to make me a woman, here, today." She pulled away to see his face. "I want you to; I need you to. Whatever happens in the future, this is what I want now."

He was excited and worried. What was this responsibility? Did it chain him to her? Was this a ploy? He stumbled, "Is it safe?"

She turned away and reached for her purse, opened it and pulled out a small flat foil packet and dropped it into his hand.

He saw that it was a condom and was thrilled and shaken by her careful planning and calculation.

She was uncertain of his response. She stood up and shimmied out of her skirt.

Whatever David's concerns may have been, as he watched her, for the first time, completely undress, his hesitations were burnt to ash by his rising passion for her.

Two virgins discovering the deepest physical expression of intimacy with each other. A bit of fumbling, a bit of concern, pain, blood and relief. She cried.

Although he was overwhelmed by the experience, he could not understand the depth of meaning, the significance for Helen. It wasn't that he was insensitive, simply uncomprehending.

He held her as she cried. It was a wonderful secret and brought him a sense of peace he could never remember having experienced. It is one of those private mysteries that can never be spoken of and only understood through the lived experience and it is a mystery only discovered between two people.

He immediately lusted for her again but he also realized how wonderfully sensual, tender and intimate it was to be able to caress the body of a girl who responded so openly to his touch, even as she lay on his chest weeping for her lost childhood and her initiation into womanhood.

He looked down along her body. The curves were full and beautifully formed. They made love again and afterwards he thought that this act was as close as he could ever be to something sacred. He knew that he would forever feel more comfortable in the presence of women.

Before they left the house, they straightened Gloria's room, Helen put the now bloodied towel she had brought into her bag and then she grasped David's arm. He turned towards her.

"Thank you."

He did not know what to say. He wanted to thank her, to kiss her again, to remove her clothes and make love over and over.

She saw this in his eyes and was pleased. "Thank you for being so gentle. Whatever happens in our lives, this was special and I'll always hold this memory."

He embraced her. She whispered, "I really heard what you said in that restaurant in Chicago and I understand you want something in life maybe I can't yet see but I love you for it."

Tears came to his eyes. It convinced him that women saw things men simply did not and that they were far more practical and emotionally brave. Men stare over the horizon, dreaming of what may be and of what they may become; woman look at what's in front of them and deal with it.

The young of America, unhinged by the October 1962 Cuban Missile Crisis finally revolted against the repression of the pompadoured businessmen, the Madmen of advertising and the military masters. The young of America, that second generation of teenagers, looked their parents in the face and firmly said "We do not want to be you". They were from New York, Chicago and San Francisco but they were also from Kansas, Texas and Podunk and a thousand and one other small towns, farms and industrial cities.

Along with this seeming revolt, folk musicians burst into songs that were heard across the country, filled with naive hope and a belief that things could change and they, with the howl of police sirens, the whistling of bombs, Hare Hare Krishna chanting and the taunting "Ho Ho Ho Chi Minh" became the generation's sound track.

Joan Baez with her operatic voice providing paeans to peace; Dave Van Ronk with his granite-retching drug addled laments; Peter, Paul and the beautiful wistful Mary who seemed so commercial but so seductively providing rhythms for change; Judy Collins, with Leonard Cohen's Suzanne, celebrating the freedom of love and detachment; Buffy Saint Marie's falsetto painfully reminding her listeners how hard others' lives had been and then Bob Dylan giving form to so many young people's aimless ennui and to the sadness of love and departures.

Spanish Boots of Spanish Leather, the Girl From The North Country, Alberta and Farewell Angelina filled David with a wanderlust so real he could look at it in the mirror, reigniting his childhood dreams of rambling across the continent, camera in hand; Hollis Brown, that pain filled, long suffering man, stoked the political fires within him, instigating his desire to understand what was wrong with his country.

While David was still in high school, A Hard Day's Night rolled out of England, and as the sixties tumbled on, the murky murder of John Kennedy made most kids of his generation lose faith in the establishment and the democratic institutions of their country. The sixties of discord, revolt, civil strife, war, imperialist retreats, flared trousers, the judicial murders of Black Panthers, long hair, nudity, drugs, sex, the murders of Martin Luther King, Robert Kennedy, Malcolm X, the disgraceful presidency of Tricky Dickey Nixon, Kent State's slaughter and finally the Weathermen with their violence and, for David, a tragic death of a distant love. David could not for long be a bystander. He remembered his boss, Mr Day, had told him to not join the guilty ranks of the silent.

As if on cue, Mr Busby introduced David to a student a year younger than David, a thin tousled blonde boy named Arnie. Mr Busby told David that Arnie had been suspended from high school for non-attendance but had just been re-admitted and was a very promising young photographer. Would David give him a hand? David was honoured that Mr Busby trusted him.

Arnie was inarticulate, private but polite and had a winning laugh. It was as if, all of a sudden, David had inherited a younger brother. Arnie's father was a big muck-a-muck fund-raiser in some American-Israeli organization that dominated his life and which marked his son, a non-believer and not particularly a strong supporter of Israel, as a useless appendage. David could see that his new friend's self-esteem, like his own, needed nurturing. What surprised David was how he seemed so stable and capable in relationship to Arnie who was close to dysfunctional in all things but making photographs.

He and Arnie began to spend increasing amounts of time together, going to the black blues clubs and small folk clubs in the downtown area. The performers liked these young boys with their cameras who gave them prints of themselves for free and the club owners appreciated the kids' dedication and let them show up and enter without charge. They were accepted by the regulars and witnessed sexual scenes laced by drink and drugs but nobody minded them being around. An old black man put his arm around David, held his other hand as a fist and told David, "Boy, when you can't do this no longer ..." at that he unfurled and straightened his index finger and continued ... "then life jes ain't worth living." David laughed at the good spirit of the story but also understood the lament.

Through Arnie, David was introduced to other kids who were on the social fringes of the school's 'proper' middle class. It was as if a discontented and alienated underground had existed in front of David's nose but he hadn't noticed it. Fair to say he had, for two years, stuck to himself with only Helen and earlier with Ed as his soul mates. Being in the advanced streaming classes, unlike any of these new acquaintances, it was unlikely they would have crossed paths. Through them he met their parents who were musicians, poets, modern dance performers or teachers, sculptors and painters. David was excited but intimidated. They seemed to possess a secret code of assumptions and knowledge he knew nothing about. And there were intriguing girls to photograph in form fitting black leotards; he was growing apart from Helen.

Mr Day asked David to photograph for the first time on his own, various category winners in a ballroom dance competition to be held downtown on the following Saturday night. Overwhelmed and surprised at this opportunity, which would also earn him a significant amount of money, he took a taxi to the arena, introduced himself and waited in the cafeteria for the event to begin. People of all ages began to appear, wearing the most amazing, colourful and sometimes revealing costumes and both the men and women had gobs of make-up on and extreme hairstyles. David began to think he was in a freak show at the carnival or county fair.

As he waited, he began to feel feverish and was uncertain whether from the increasingly odd circumstances he found himself in or from a sudden virus. A man wearing a chartreuse and orange sequined tuxedo leered at David, leaned very close to his face and laughingly announced, "Look darlings, a boy with a man's camera and what a whopper lens." A woman who looked old enough to be his grandmother, dressed as if too young to be a woman, with a face held in place by layers of wax and colour, dropped to her knees next to David, exposing yards of cleavage, and stroked his leg. "Lovely young man. Regardez Freddie, look at the lovely young man." David could smell something musty, unpleasant about her, fumes rising from wet cardboard.

David grabbed his camera, his bag and coat, excused himself and fled to the toilet where he was sick. He was weakened, feverish and dizzy. His eyes felt as though salt crystals were under each lid. Somehow he did photograph the winners, and as was seen the next day after processing, they were in focus and well exposed. Mr Day was delighted.

At the end of the evening, Arnie showed up as arranged and drove him home. As they travelled up Woodward Avenue towards the northwest of the city where they lived, Arnie produced a rolled-up cigarette and told David to take some puffs. David told him he did not feel good and anyway he had never smoked.

"This is different. It'll make you feel better." He laughed. "Well, if not better, at least different."

David lit it from the car lighter and took a puff. He coughed and almost gagged. Arnie encouraged him to try again. David did and in a few minutes he felt physically calmer but the world became dislodged. The street and car lights became more intense. It was as if he could see them through rain spattered windows, each with a long tail trailing behind. And then he had a vision of the ballroom dancers but now they were upside down, spinning on the roof of the car. He grabbed Arnie's arm and asked him to slow down.

"I'm going the speed limit. If I drive slower I'll look suspicious and believe me, we don't want to be stopped by the fuzz."

"The fuzz? The fuzz ..." David began to laugh and Arnie joined in. David could not remember laughing so deeply.

Afterwards, drained and lying on his bed, he felt he had been released from a grip that held him in constraints for all the years of his life. Not only was there a new world without but also a new one within. 'Doors of perception, indeed doors of perception'.

David allowed his hair to grow a little longer. Mr Day didn't mind as he could see the girls admired his romantic young assistant, who, at any rate was always on time and always did more than was required. His father grumped about it but could not find the energy to bother doing more then up the level of his general disapproval and his mother ignored it.

But his new English teacher showed him increasing antagonism. Whatever his contribution was, she challenged him, put his ideas down and seemed to want to embarrass him. Whereas previously he had gained all As on his essays, she marked him with C- and Ds. David never had such poor grades.

One day in class she said, "David, you say in your essay about Intruder in the Dust that you disagree with the idea that everyone behaves differently with different people."

David knew that another attack was coming. "I said something like that."

She raised her voice. "Not something like that, you said exactly that."

"Well okay, you have the paper in front of you, I don't."

"Can you defend your remark?"

David could feel the hatred rising. He was being made a victim of her ire for reasons he did not know. "Am I on trial? Is this some kind of trial? Have I broken some law of English usage?"

"If you won't answer, that means you wrote nonsense and this essay is worthless."

"Is it worthless like the books the Nazi's burned?"

His teacher was caught unawares. She was trapped by his response.

"Is it worthless like Ginsberg's Howl?"

'Answer the question", she snapped.

"People are different in private than in public. But if they vary their responses in public it probably means they are afraid or have no point of view. I read about relativism and it described a way in which people change their views according to the situation for their advantage. To me that's cowardly and immoral ... and weak."

"From your point of view only weak people change their positions?"

"No, because people can learn stuff and grow; they become aware of new things and may change. That's not what I was talking about. I was talking about people who change their position in public, not because they are learning but because it serves them, it is to their advantage at that moment ... it's a form of lying. So if you don't want to lie, you don't change unless you learn something that affects your understanding."

She looked from her desk to the assembled faces and then at David. "Well young man, you have no idea how people live their lives in the real world and since essays on literature are about novels that are concerned with real things, you show very little understanding of what you are reading. This essay ...", she held it in the air, "deserves an E for revealing you have no idea about this book."

David's classmates, who had seen his deliveries about literature since that first day in Miss Mahler's class, were shocked. A wave of disapproval sounded through the room.

The teacher looked around and barked, "Does anyone have anything to say?"

Helen raised her hand.

"Yes."

"I don't get what you're doing. David showed he had thought seriously about ..."

"That's enough or you'll find your essay may need to be rewritten."

David stood up and gathered his books.

"Sit down until I tell you..."

"Who do you think you are? This is unfair and I won't be your victim." He looked up at her. "Don't you worry, I know I have to report to my Counsellor. I'm going before you fail the entire class." He glanced at Helen, turned and walked out of the room.

He was a difficult case for his Counsellor, Mr Mullen, because David was almost a solid A student and won national photographic honours for the school. Mr Mullen was willing to accept that there was a simple personality problem between David and his English teacher but he had heard complaints about her from others, including some of the more free thinking teachers. Although Mullen was himself on the right of the Republican Party, he was nonetheless fair-minded and willing to give David the benefit of the doubt.

All the while David was preoccupied with making pictures of the modern dancers who practiced in the rehearsal rooms at the local sports club. He shot portraits of them, pictures in school of kids in class for the high school yearbook and at sports meetings, but he would not be more than an observer to these events. He felt as if he was an outsider looking in, watching, like an anthropologist, the tribal rites of others. His collection grew and Mr Busby assured him that he was on the right track and that he could, if he kept it up, win a scholarship with his fourth-year portfolio.

At the end of his third year in high school he learned that he had, for the second time, won more awards in photography than anyone else in the country. He seemed unstoppable but he knew his entire future was dependent on creating the best portfolio in the country in his last year.

Meanwhile the beautiful Helen became more estranged from him. He believed that sex was inextricably united to loyalty and love. He desired to be conscious of everything. Life, as always, was complicated and confusing.

CHAPTER 15

As the sun, seemingly suspended forever, eventually sizzled past its zenith, the quay became hell's anvil, so intensely hot that only the devil would entertain sitting there. David shed his burnoose but still poured sweat. His bottles of water were like tepid tea. Vapours rose from the sea wall's massive stones and one by one the fishermen, hearty as they were, appeared from out of their sorry wheelhouses, tucked their tattered nets and oily tools away and dragged themselves out of the quay's distant gate to their small whitewashed houses which lay beyond the shops and cafes, hunkering down, squat and tidy under the flailing sun.

Even the sea had gone quiet. By then the tide was flowing out beyond the shallows. In the environs of the ancient lighthouse, on the southern tip of the encircling seawall, above shallow eddies, the insistent rays of the late spring sun burned the salty seawater into a steamy haze.

The surrounding area had gone so silent that David could hear his heart pounding. He thought of his head on her breast, listening to the rhythm of her life.

He had photographed her torso on white sheets. Kate's body appeared like a luminous sandstone sculpture with its volumes smooth and fully female. Her form was to his eyes and to all of his senses characteristically her, strong and taut but also languorous and inviting.

'And nothing shall remain the same and all things will change.'

'She possessed a transient beauty. How aware had I been of what was then the reality in front of me and what would become of it after the moment I photographed her? Those times still seem so close and real but also so lost in another life.'

He scoffed at himself. 'Indeed how could that perfection have lasted? Not of her young beauty - that I accepted would pass - but rather of our relationship?'

'Is love simply another form of the human plague that plunged all of us into barbarism, century after century? Love played its part in disappointing, frustrating and injuring us and so stoked the flames of hatred and revenge or simply sublimated itself, not into art but rather into a vengeful social pathology. They, she, he, it hurt me, thus I will hurt others. Some city dwellers rose above it, separated as they were from the life and death of the land, of slitting necks and draining blood and butchering animals; they became highly cultured and developed a patina of humanity that helped isolate them from the harshness.'

"Suleiman, for instance," he murmured.

'But the plague had recurred and with it the human tragedy plays itself out again.'

This plague took its personal toll on David who would never forget how, on that tragic day in Sarajevo, Kate insisted on going up the hill to the church. It was against his will and against his advice. He had to go, it was his assignment from his photo agency but she was freelance, she did not have to see what he knew almost certainly would be another atrocity. She refused his offer to represent her in the meeting she needed to have.

They joined the throng in the old town square near the central fountain and began the walk across the river and up the hill. People were excited and nervous.

Kate and David fell in with the locals. They walked side by side. He sensed that it was a special moment and a privilege to be this close to her, to be doing something virtuous with her, but soon his mind was overtaken by practical concerns.

Although exposed to the surrounding hills as they crossed the bridge, there was no attack. David thought the next likely place was on the plateau beneath the church but there, people could flee … too open, not enough of a trap. He became convinced they would wait until people were in the church … a perfectly contained target with enough stone and glass to rip people apart.

He imagined that with every step they got closer to the dome of the sky in this strange country forsaken by the heavens and its benevolent gods. For certain, he thought, 'Only the malevolent and crazy gods would wish to deal with this land of Catholic Croats, Orthodox Serbs and secular Moslems, along with free market cowboys, peppered by a handful of Jews, Gypsies, atheists and artists and always communist purists hoping someone's tanks would roll back in to restore the people's state.'

Meanwhile a heavily armed squad of Serb irregulars skittered their way down a slope above a flat plateau and through what, four months earlier had been a carefully cultivated vineyard.

As he walked, David thought about the dense woods and how they provide thyme and rose petals for tea, a multitude of wild mushrooms, honey and barks for liquors; how their rivers churn with trout, how the mountains offer rabbits, boar and stag, how their cities produce finely beaten metals, how the people live the way of Sevdah … not only was Sevdah their music but it also embodied the meaning of life, of being easy and allowing time to penetrate the moment, to celebrate being alive. And their politicians produce madness, an illusion of some uber-world in which their identity becomes the identity of the region and these malign manipulators spew fear and hatred to sustain their positions. They gathered to themselves illusionists as generals, amoralists as press officers, sycophantic lawyers as judges, and criminals as insurgents as the rest of Europe talked about it, appeased or returned to their long sleep.

While David thought these things, he scanned the hills, worrying that he could not see what would surely be men planting themselves for an attack: another crumb of savagery in the great banquet of hatred.

David leaned towards Kate to speak with her above the murmuring and shuffling of feet on the cobbles and to take in the subtle perfume of her dark hair. "You have good instincts but they're supposed to save animals from danger."

Without breaking her step, Kate explained, "I have to prove I care enough by placing myself in danger." She looked at him as they walked. "Anyway, if it's safe enough for you and her, it's okay for me."

David nodded, accepting but wanting to argue yet knowing he had no right. 'People live their destiny, guided by love, virtue and their fatal flaws.'

He had already protested and failed. He passionately cared about her fate, but he had no right to impose beyond the point he had. He wondered, is life unjust or is it simply a matter of facts?

Margaret, David's reporter, having moved quickly along the streets to watch the flow of people parading up the hill, spotted David in the moving crowd. "David! Yoo-hoo David!"

David waved to Margaret from across the crowd. Margaret, certain of impending danger, signalled for him to join her. David shook his head no and held his Leica above his head as if in explanation. Margaret, who sensibly refused to go up the hill, was left worrying.

The war weary and tattered parade struggled along a narrow path rising ever more steeply uphill at the edge of the old town. On top of the hill was a partly destroyed Orthodox church. In the peaceful but repressive time of Tito and the Yugoslavian state, the church had been a day centre where the young of all three communities met, mingled and contrived to build a country hovering between Stalinism and capitalism. Young men and women eyed each other up, went off to dark corners and by the time of the war in 1992, more than thirty percent of marriages crossed ethnic boundaries. But in the years following Tito's death and the rise of a self-interested oligarchy in need of a scapegoat for the continuing economic failure of the post Tito years, tolerance died in the massacres plotted to turn group against group.

A ragtag brass band with their squawking Serbian horns joined the parade, turning the trudging dirge into a celebration or a prescient wake. The brassy echoes splintered on the valley walls, alerting the gunmen, awakening their vengeful bloodlust, their desire to cause mayhem, to ogle below the effervescences of fire and flying body parts as if viewing a Hollywood film, not remembering that yesterday they shared a common destiny with their potential victims, travelled together in packed troop trains as comrades, admired each other as bathers on the beach, listened and advised as doctors and patients, and held hands together as stalwarts of the middle way against the imperialist tanks of Stalin and the imperialist finance of Washington.

Kate, although by then, in love with David, still did not know him well, but was calmed by his concern and company. "I suppose you're one of those left-brain people: logic, grammar and reason."

He smiled at her. "My instinct says there's a story up there for both of us."

She nodded a 'yes'.

He shouted at her about the din, "And you're like a dog with a bone."

She shrugged. Several locals turned towards them, slapping David on the back and shaking Kate's hand.

"Good."

"Brave."

"Brother and sister, thank you; tell the world."

"Come, report."

Kate noticed David's polite but cool responses.

He understood her observation. "Emotions confuse tragedy."

"Emotions create it."

He looked at her, taking in her raven hair and dark eyes as if a meal to be consumed. "Naa, calculation by the rich and the fanatical create it."

"It's still tragedy."

"True but I leave my brooding until afterwards. I've learned that my anger gets in the way of seeing events clearly when I'm in the moment." He looked for her reaction. She seemed uncertain. "It's no more than a strategy for survival."

Up in the hills above the town, the Serb irregulars reached the woods overlooking the church. They carried mortars and high calibre machine guns. That morning their coffee had been brewed in large aluminium pots with slugs of rakija to fuel their hatred and befog their morality. Not a smooth 45% distilled from the finest local small black grapes rakija, but local hooch tilting 80%. It was enough to churn the mind of a tired and hungry soldier, a young man from a farm or from a coal mine, a student consumed with dreams of victory, or a young dentist whose distorted ideas lead him to believe in his own ethnic superiority. Men who had crossed the line, who killed old people they would previously have greeted with a kind word, who raped their neighbour's daughter and then slit her throat, men who, for fun, burned kids with cigarette butts and then shot them in the head, men who had become pliable, pitiless monsters in the hands of opportunist politicians and priests, all carriers of the human plague.

The parade, led by the out-of-tune band of Bosnian Serbs, trudged up the final hill to the church. These musicians remembered their cultural inheritance from earlier generations who had migrated from the eastern Serbian heartlands, westwards to the mountains and valleys of verdant Bosnia. Although ethnic Serbs, these men and women chose to side with their Moslem neighbours rather than with the fear-mongering generals, rather than with the bandits and politicians who tried to convince them to turn on their friends because they happened to be a Croat or Muslim by birth. Men and women who decided that although Serbian by heritage they were Bosnian by the roots and cords of their kinships and that they believed, as did the once and past country and partisans of Yugoslavia, that religious and ethnic hatred was a disease of the past.

Years later they would ask friends like David, 'How did this happen, when was war declared, why suddenly was I or my neighbour, my brother-in-law or my childhood friend an enemy?" Years later, after the war and its ethnic cleansing, after its massacres and rapes, its mass graves and assassinations, people would turn to each other or to strangers and ask, "Who caused it?" as if an invisible plague had swept upon them. This incredulity would leave them forever wondering about their own sanity and the meaning of being human. War, they would discover, leaves deep scars for several generations. War was the recurrence of the human plague.

The last buildings were left behind as the parade fanned out on the gently sloping plateau above the city. The church, a humble stone building fronted by a ridiculously tall bell tower, reminded David of the overblown white churches of Midwestern towns. But this ancient building, with its massive blue tinted stones, created a greater sense of squatness, emphasizing the overbearing tower.

Inside, under the exposed beams of its one-time roof, there was a makeshift stage where the altar once stood. A string quartet was setting up music stands and a few broken chairs. The parade entered, talking in hushed nervous tones. Kate and David entered. Kate approached the cellist, a lean, dark haired young woman named Vana. They embraced and Kate introduced David. "Do you mind if he listens?"

Vana shook the question off. It meant nothing to her.

Kate turned to David. "Vana heard this story when she worked in Germany."

From among the crowd, a chisel faced, wiry man with Slavic appearance watched them and slowly approached, attempting to overhear the conversation. He was like a snake, slithering through tall grasses, a creature one sees in port cities around the world, a man who would be of no certain address, job or occupation. He had the tarnish of a backstreet bully, a seller of small arms or maybe a pimp; a man who, when flush with money, would wear a gold chain under his shirt, beneath a collar too big for his thin neck, a man who would be exceptionally proud of his shiny shoes with their silver clasps, a guy who would imagine himself a potential film star or national hero.

Vana, like many locals, had been undernourished for months, living off the few truck loads of canned meat and dodgy flour that the surrounding enemy army allowed through as a humanitarian gesture but only after they had taken the best for themselves. Her eyes were strangely empty; she seemed a person who has lost the will to live, a woman who could find no path to her own heart.

In her quietly spoken but edgy English she almost whispered, "I'll tell you now." She nodded towards the sky through the skeleton roof. "Who knows after. When I tell, you should leave."

Kate, worried, looked from the sky to Vana as she continued, "I have…strange feeling today."

David too began to sense the unease. He felt trapped and impending doom.

Up in the hills above the church, the Serb dentist, the farmer and miner among the others set up their mortars but the machine gunners laid in the soft spring grass smoking and joking as they had no clear shot of the church through the trees.

Vana began her story. "I studied ...". She pointed to her cello and waved her hand to mean 'in the past'.

The snake crept closer, listening attentively.

Vana repeated her words as if to reassure herself that they actually left her mouth and had some affect in the cool air around her. "I study at conservatory in East Germany. To pay, I work as orderly in mental hospital. I hear story from crazy old patient, Professor Gottleib." Vana glanced at the other three musicians as they prepared to play. She spat the next words out like a poisonous afterthought. "He was Jew." She glared at David, thinking he may be Jewish and as though accusing him of some awful crime.

"He say in Poland there's village near old Nazi concentration camp where everyone keep secret since war."

David, smelling Vana's anti-Semitism knew his contempt for her and her story was rising. He hissed, "For over fifty years?'

Vana looked at David with impatient disdain. "Everyone there suffer under communists and now under new government for not telling."

Kate was confused. "What's it about?"

Vana struggled, "Phar ... pharama ... medicine; research on prisoners in camp."

David became more interested. "Pharmaceuticals ... the missing Mengele papers?"

Vana and Kate looked at David with greater attention.

David explained, "Witch doctor research: cruel experiments on prisoners during the war made under a madman named Mengele; a lot of them on children and especially twins. The papers went missing in '44 as the Nazis retreated back across Poland. Some pharmaceutical companies think there may be valuable research in the papers. They are willing to pay a bundle for them."

Kate looked quizzically at David. "What's the problem?"

"Some argue that use of the testing will justify and vindicate the torture. Others say it will honour the victims, especially if cures are found within the research."

The snake, having heard, slipped a rubber medical glove onto his right hand.

Vana continued, "Together, villagers hide papers and keep secret ... now authorities are after papers."

Kate was more confused. "But why?"

"The government sees papers as way to get foreign currency from pharmaceutical companies but villagers won't give them."

David half mocked her, "A village of angels?"

Kate flashed him a peeved glance.

He looked at her, confused by her courage and his distemper with Vana's anti-Semitism. "Doesn't make sense."

Kate looked at him for a suspended second. "Life's complicated."

The snake's gloved hand slid into his jacket to grasp a 9mm Glock from his shoulder holster.

Kate turned to Vana. "Why do you think?"

Vana answered but turned towards David as if launching another simmering accusation, but she spoke as though entertaining a momentary religious ecstasy. "Redemption."

Kate was upset by Vana's reaction to David. She was witnessing the age old, untiring quest for fuel by those who endlessly feed the burning pyres of anti-Semitism and the endless catalogue of other prejudice and hatred so carefully written by the scribes of the human plague.

As if to forestall Kate's conclusions, Vana pushed on. "Polish villagers work with Nazis to kill Jews, Gypsies and all others. They were guilty too." Vana pointed to the ground. "You seen killing here. We need redemption example."

David considered this. Kate followed Vana as she drifted towards the other musicians.

The snake's eyes appraised the situation.

Up in the hills an officer, inspecting preparations, walked along the line of his irregular Serb soldiers; each soldier to a man was hyped on spliffs and hooch. He knew he would murder again on this fine, crisp morning but dismissed the thought as he pulled deeply on another cigarette.

In the church, the people of the town formed a crescent shaped audience around the now prepared quartet. The air was filled with fear and expectation and the strains of the tuning instruments. Some looked at the sky through the torn roof.

Kate moved back towards David. They were both worried. The snake crept up behind them.

Kate whispered to David, "She thinks if the press show an interest in the missing papers, the Polish government will lay off the villagers."

"Who's got them?"

The snake leaned further forward, wishing to overhear what they now knew.

"Only the professor knows."

The concert began. The harmonies were a balm to the war weary but determined locals. Kate and David listened and they, as the others, were calmed by the music. They both pulled out their cameras.

High above, the irregular Serb officer listened for a moment to the beauty of the notes as they floated up the slope. He turned to his sergeant and made a resigned gesture as he whispered to himself, "ahh, I've always loved Beethoven". The sergeant replied, "It's late Mozart sir", turned and bawled "Bogdan!"

Bogdan dropped a shell into the mortar and everyone covered their ears as it fired. The officer lifted his binoculars to see its strike point.

The incoming mortar whistled. The people inside the church flinched and stirred, as did the quartet, who continued to play.

David and Kate looked upwards towards the whistling sound. He instinctively glanced at her. Their eyes met. David moved slightly towards her. She nervously smiled. Time stopped. He pulled Kate towards him protectively. She accepted his gesture. Slowly his hands caressed her back. She pressed her head against his shoulder and slowly her hand moved up his back in a half embrace.

The mortar shell struck just outside of the front door. Fire spewed, smoke spiralled out of the dusty crumbling stone and plaster. Fear channelled through the church. The second fiddler wavered but Vana gave him a stern look.

The snake moved into the shadows towards the musicians. He eyed up David and Kate.

Kate pulled away gently and stared at David. "It's too late, isn't it?"

He whispered. "It's okay." He leaned closer and his lips brushed her cheek. He breathed in the perfume of her skin. She faintly smiled. It was inconceivable that she could be harmed while in his arms.

In the dust and confusion the snake slowly raised his gun.

Kate, standing just in front of David, turned away to photograph as David watched her and the locals. Slowly he moved his hand towards her neck as if to embrace and protect her. His hand hovered but he did not touch her again. The snake lost his target.

The Serbian officer in the field above, listened and observed. He put down his binoculars and looked at the sergeant. The officer shrugged. The sergeant turned and bellowed. "Everyone, continuous fire!"

The mortars began the bombardment.

The Quartet continued as the mortars' 'crumps' became serial and the incoming shells whistled, one after another.

Kate looked up, frightened and exchanged a worried glance with David. He weakly smiled and continued to watch her as she photographed. The locals stirred and held each other. The Quartet continued to play.

Shells hit the church. Death, blood and destruction everywhere. Vana, instantly killed; the music stopped but the fiddler resolutely continued. Cries and shrieks arose as more shells rained in, more bodies destroyed, mauled, eviscerated. The snake was knocked over by part of a collapsing pillar. David was blown out of a window. Kate's camera smashed against a wall. Her lens shattered.

The officer yelled an order followed by further shouts from the sergeant. The soldiers gathered their weapons and departed as they came, knowing that they had helped fulfil their nationalist and religious destiny, that in destroying their own church and killing innocent people they had earned themselves a place in heaven or at least a good lunch.

In the church and its surrounding plateau, the air was filled with pain, dust and smoke. Fires burned. From under rubble, Kate struggled to stand up.

The snake, bloodied and concussed, lifted himself out from under charred bodies, fallen bricks and timber. As he moved, it took a moment for his sight to settle. He spotted Kate through the fire and smoke but, as he snatched at his belt, he discovered his Glock was missing. He scrambled amongst the body parts and rubble to find it. To this trained killer, who, as a young man in the service of the

Soviet Army in Chechnya, had participated in terrible violence, the surrounding gore meant no more than the bricks and mortar. Hardened to blood and viscera, he was simply preoccupied with his mission's targets. Perhaps later in life, if he achieved a 'later in life', he might reflect on this, but for then he was, as all adherents to exclusive fundamental beliefs, contentedly justified in his duty. He located the gun, quickly looked around to be certain no one could interfere and took aim at Kate's back. She staggered and tripped. He pulled a slow, steady pressure on the trigger. She lost her balance again, stumbled and fell out of the killer's sight. He eased off the trigger, cursing to himself.

A crowd, including Margaret, arrived from the town. She saw David covered in blood, limping through the smoke and dust. The extent of his injuries was impossible to judge from her distance.

Kate, looking for David, slowly stood up. The killer took aim again, his finger tightened on the trigger.

David, concussed but determined to find Kate, stumbled over a body.

The snake was now certain. He tugged on the trigger that extra millimetre. The barrel exploded, hurtling its bolt of steel towards Kate's velvety, warm toned flesh, towards her delicate soul, towards her unending capacity to love.

Surprised at the unexpected pain, she lurched and tumbled forward. Her entire nervous system collapsed immediately.

The snake crawled away and discovered Vana. He grabbed her head by the hair and satisfied she was dead, let it drop with a disdainful thud.

He exited the front of the church and dimly saw David near the gaping hole blown out of the altar's south wall. He reached for his gun but was inadvertently knocked aside by a huge local soldier who knew David and was lumbering towards him at speed.

David was stunned and entirely focused on finding Kate. The soldier saw David limp through the dust and disappear into the gaping hole in the wall.

The lone fiddler, in shock, continued to play.

Bodies were everywhere; locals calling out, crying, looking for lovers, family and friends. David stumbled over the glass fragments of the blown-out window into the mass of smoke, wood and twisted bodies. He searched and finally spotted Kate. He turned her over.

A low rumbling noise from the sea stirred David out of his memories. Time had passed, the tide was flowing back in, the sun was lower and the heat had subsided to a glowing inferno.

He moved his head from side to side and eventually found a way to look out towards the harbour's mouth between the two curving arms of the sea wall. A red fishing boat was sailing towards the far end of the quay, past the icehouse, aiming for the furthest mooring from the main gate. He noticed it had a small red dragon's head on it and a heavyset man was guiding it into port.

David was uncertain why he found so much interest in this lone boat with its odd ornament. It seemed unusual and more so when the boat was tied up and the heavyset pilot walked across his line of vision and carried on into the mists towards the main gate, without having offloaded fish or nets. The man, with his sunglasses, looked more like a member of the security services than a fisherman, and yet his build and limp reminded him of the customs agent with the bag of fish. Something was not right.

A few moments later a figure appeared, quickly walking, half running from the main gate towards David's end of the quay. At first David was unsure. The shape of the body, the heavy but still graceful movement seemed familiar. As the man became clearer, emerging from the mist that still swirled around the inner harbour and occasionally floated across the quay, David became certain it was Mehmet.

Why? How would he know? Was this a set-up, a trap, a part of an elaborate plot?

Mehmet drew nearer but seemed to be concentrating on something beyond David's hiding place. Mehmet darted past, oblivious to David, and ran towards the red boat with the dragon's prow.

David felt trapped, uncertain about what to do. Should he let Mehmet know he was there? Should he try to melt into the mist and re-climb the stairs?

Mehmet jumped onto the red fishing boat and seemed to search for something.

Why that boat and not Zakkir's boat? Was Mehmet here to help David?

Mehmet stopped and looked along the quay. David turned and saw a brown car speeding towards his hiding place and towards Mehmet.

Mehmet appeared confused and frightened as though trapped. He peeled off his jacket, dipped out of sight, bobbed back up, ran and dived off the rear of the boat, now without his shoes and swam like a champion.

The car skidded to a halt. A tall man flung himself out. He darted to the boat, jumped onto the deck, pulled a pistol and fired round after round. Eventually he stopped. Using a grappling hook he pulled Mehmet's dead body onto the boat and fiddled with something in Mehmet's right hand.

As he did this, Zakkir ambled into sight, spoke with the shooter who climbed out of the boat and handed Zakkir something. David waited, frozen into inaction. Mehmet dead?

Zakkir arrived in front of the lobster traps. He shouted, "Monsieur David, come. You come now."

David stirred. 'What was going on? What had happened to Mehmet? Why had the soldier shot him? Why had Mehmet suddenly appeared?' His mind whirled as he collected his things, grabbed the burnoose and stiffly climbed out of his safe little cavern.

As he appeared, Zakkir took David by the arm and pulled him impatiently towards his boat. David noted that Zakkir was wearing gloves. Gloves in this heat?

"Come, we must go now. Quick. Now it is safe. The rat has been trapped."

"But … he was a friend … I mean, why kill him?"

"No problem now, my son fix all. Come with me."

David saw that it was Ali, the lean, good-hearted Sergeant, who had shot and was now dragging Mehmet's body onto the quay.

Zakkir quickly made ready, unhooked the ropes tying his fishing boat to the quay, started the engines which coughed and produced a deep liquid chesty rumble, shoved the gears into reverse and puttered backwards into the inner harbour. He jammed the gears into forward and swung the wheel around which turned the salty sea under the hull into cream Chantilly. Off they motored towards the lighthouse, open water and safety.

David turned and watched as best he could from the moving boat as the Sergeant searched Mehmet's pockets. David peered more closely and saw that the good Sergeant was placing things into Mehmet's pockets.

The penny dropped from a great distance and clanged like a pounding bell in David's head. Instinctively David looked at Zakkir who had taken note of David's focus on his son's action. David's eyes travelled south and saw that Zakkir had a bulge under his blue canvas jacket, just to the left of his belt buckle.

David's mind did bounding leaps. 'The Sergeant had to know Mehmet was going to appear. He had things in his possession that, planted on Mehmet, would incriminate him in my getaway. Zakkir shows up, offers to take me to safety but is carrying the gun he was handed by his son with Mehmet's fingerprints on it. Zakkir expressed interest about me having money.'

'Zakkir kills me, returns to harbour, gives the weapon back to his son who plants it on Mehmet. Zakkir goes home, the Sergeant calls in his foiling of the plot. When, eventually my washed-up body is found, Mehmet's bullet is lodged in me. The Sergeant is publicly rewarded with advancement; the father and son privately share the cash they knew I had.'

David looked up at the Zakkir. "Like all fishermen, I bet you can't swim."

Zakkir visibly relaxed and smiled broadly, revealing his remaining, tobacco stained teeth. He shouted over the increased noise of the engines, "As a boy, I learned good. Strong, I am strong swimmer even today."

David moved from a squat to a crouch, as if getting more comfortable.

"How long will it take to get to international waters?"

"Out of the harbour past the light house, two hours."

Although it was painful, David flexed his leg muscles.

"How do we go?"

Zakkir moved away from the wheel, leant forward off his balance and waved with his right arm in the direction David thought was due north. "There."

David sprang up, rushed Zakkir and, with his elbows locked across his chest, hit him from behind with his full weight. Zakkir was knocked flying, face down onto the deck. David landed on the stunned man, grabbed him around the neck with his right arm, pulled him up and pushed him into the port gunnels.

Although shorter than David, Zakkir, built like a pit bull, was able to push back. He tried to grab the gun under his jacket which gave David the opportunity to release his arms and using both fists, punched Zakkir on either side of his upper back, with all of David's weight and force. Zakkir's knees painfully smacked the gunnels, his feet flew up from under him and he flipped into the sea.

David grabbed the only lifebelt and threw it towards Zakkir who immediately bobbed back to the surface. Although he would be sore the next day, with bruised thighs and a wounded pride, he'd be okay. The foundations of the lighthouse were no further than twenty meters away. David was certain he would be able, with or without the lifebelt, to reach it safely.

David darted to the controls, increased the engine's speed and left the lighthouse, the plotting old man, the good Sergeant and the dead Mehmet behind.

As David held the wheel, suddenly shaken by the mystery and the enormity of what had just happened, he carefully took the map, compass and binoculars from his straw bag.

He needed to concentrate on clearing the twelve-mile limit of maritime sovereignty while watching the swell of the waves and hoping that there was enough fuel to cross the open sea to safety.

That insecurity and sense of destabilization many others experience in the face of violence or death, David always felt more poignantly at sea. As the adrenalin charge from the fight receded, he began to feel exposed, cold, frightened and alone. Once, as a child, he had almost drowned. Since then, never had he felt comfortable in the water and here he was in a rickety fishing boat with only thin wooden boards between him and a watery death and now, because of his generosity, without a lifebelt.

The sun set.

Tugging from deep within his reserves of steadfastness, he demanded clarity of mind against exhaustion, muscular strength against stiffness, and mental concentration in the face of contending emotional challenges. With these and luck he would persevere.

The little fishing boat plied out into the open sea. The moon played across the water.

'Concentrate. I must get into international waters as soon as possible and then I can think, muse and worry.'

He set down his compass on the peeling wooden surface behind the wheel and occupied himself with sailing due north. He studied the map and thought that he would be okay, and although going due north was not the shortest route to the nearest landfall, it was simple and at least he'd land in a country for which he would not need a visa. So far, so good and then he remembered that he had not thrown Zakkir the cash in the brown envelope to pay for his boat.

•••

Several times in his final high school year, David attempted to speak with his parents about going to university. It became clear that his father had no interest in the subject nor did he show any pride in the fact that his youngest son would go on to higher education. His mother glanced at the cover of the brochures David had got from the several universities he was interested in, she would immediately turn to the fees page, murmur "ah ha" and drop the brochure onto the arm of the couch as though relieving herself of a heavy burden. Neither of his parents made an offer or hint of assistance nor did they ever ask him what he wanted to study.

It finally struck him that they really were not interested, did not care and would not help in any way.

David's world seemed even emptier. He was not only abandoned by his parents whom, he assumed, would be happy enough if he would finish high school and then leave them in peace, to disappear somewhere far away. He suspected they would be okay if they never saw or heard from him again. He began to wonder why they had children. Clearly neither he nor Joel had brought them pleasure nor pride. Why bother? He took little comfort in deciding that there was something seriously wrong with them.

Beyond his being certain of the void at his core, he was concerned with what he could do to advance his life. He knew he'd have to leave home, to leave the Midwest and to find a way to survive with his camera, but he craved being educated. Helen was going to the University of Michigan in Ann Arbor where most of the other bright kids had been accepted. Being an in-state institution, they need only pay for their maintenance, books and transportation. Helen would find a guy studying medicine or law, have sex with him and maybe remember David once or twice and eventually she'd get her suburban home and picket fence. David did love her and felt close to her in many ways but he also accepted that she was not what he needed nor wanted in his dream of an adventurous life. She was beautiful, seductive and smart but the romance stumbled at the borderlands of vision and poetry. She was not Annie of the books nor Tina Modotti.

In his continuing research he discovered that he could attend the local city university for free and although he could not study photography or journalism, he could study his second love, which was history. History for him was a stepping-stone to understand what there was to photograph and how to interpret it. But he wondered if his parents would kick him out after his high school graduation, where he would live and how he would pay for it. His only real opportunity and his dream was to win a complete scholarship to one of the journalism universities. For that, he would have to produce the best portfolio in the country in his last year of high school.

But now, what to photograph? How to convince the judges he was worthy of the scholarship? He believed he had to do something that was important, but he feared he did not understand the world well enough.

With the emotional centre of his life being slowly eviscerated, the romance of the poets and singers of his imagined banquet years seemed both real and far away to him, caught as he was in a struggle to understand why he made photographs, what purpose his pictures could serve, how he could live within and relate to a social and political world whose values he could not abide.

He asked himself what was central to what he wanted to know and to photograph. Eventually he thought that every layer he examined led to another more profound one beginning with individual's attitudes, then social constructions and finally he asked himself where was the soul of America? What hands and faces, what forests and roadways, what logos and scripts, tools, dams, trucks, lipstick, what body parts and pin ball machines made the breadth of the land and the lives of its people visible?

His disillusionment with his parents, with his coming separation from Helen, with Ed's distance and his own inability to feel part of society, forced him to examine his reasons and rights to document others ... he began to believe his pictures wouldn't work, wouldn't connect or address anything meaningful because he was too much an outsider to others' lives and dreams. He needed to go searching for America, to turn the abstractions in his mind into concrete images of people ... but he had lost the will to photograph people's everyday struggles because his confidence in his own mission had been undermined by staring into his own empty future.

He knew he could not sit still so he began to shoot artefacts, landscapes, things which were signs of labour and people passing, but not the people themselves.

He saw that everywhere he looked, the world tripped over itself with things to be photographed: textures, patterns, colours and inventions, tools of the trades, artisan's work and factories, cities, celebrations and festivals. There were the lakes and the air and fairs, moonlight, flowers, leaves and stones, insects, fans berries and melons, shellfish and coloured wire. A chair, a calliper, an old jug, a tin can.

'Would this make a meaningful portfolio? Would the judges look at these signs of life and understand the metaphor or would they disregard it as inessential?'

Soon he found solace in individual portraits: faces like road maps; expressions like facets of a prism; the chosen shot becoming the truth of how that person was and would always be seen; a portrait fixed in the viewer's mind.

'But what are these portraits? Truth, revelation or an index of the sitter? Are they sociology, history, psychology, art? Why only these portraits? The general audience is attracted by heroes: movie and sports stars, or 'personalities' so why these unknown people? Elitist, class-ridden and money dominated society insists on hierarchies - the 'us' of the right accent, bank balance or beliefs and the 'them' of the mob.'

He drove himself to a frenzy searching for answers. While his new friend Arnie was supportive, he was a person of instinct rather than intellect. David finally said to himself, 'I insist on seeing the humanity of people.'

He re-looked at the books of Paul Strand. Through his portrayal of people and cultures around the world, his work was an example to David about how the universality of humanity existed as something touchable that could be revealed in photographs. Strand's work was a visual poetry of photographic beauty created through consummate technique and an engagement with intelligence. It was almost ethnographic, which inspired David to believe that his own intellectual interests were of value and not an academic encumbrance.

David was nonetheless a teenager, adrift in a world that provided him few safe moorings. One day he asked himself, 'When I look into a mirror, whom do I see?'

'An immature kid and as most kids, he lives inside a narrow world. He's imbued with the surrounding culture, attitudes, assumed truths and social norms. He knows only what's been told him and what he's seen. But he senses, deep in his dreams, a distant yet potentially richer life. In this world that surrounds him, there must be a reason to point the camera, a place to focus and a point of view. Instinctively he knows what's in the frame is important and what's not important must be excluded. He develops a practice to reduce his images to simple forms and lines, framing out or printing down what is inessential or distracting.'

David saw reproductions of Michelangelo's Prisoners in the Florentine Academia. He began to understand that artists need to liberate the subject from its surroundings to the point where all that had to be shown was revealed, knowing that the next chisel stroke would take away a part of what was essential and therefore must remain. That lesson in reductiveness was learned against the Midwestern arabesques – the superficial decoration and embrace of bling which surrounded him. He understood that it had no meaning other than to shout about wealth in a shallow culture.

In his parents' home there was little culture and less discussion about the outer world of chaos. There were moans about money, relatives and life; there were innuendos about the 'neeegros', 'Polacks' and 'queers'; so David asked, 'How can the kid escape the darkness?'

David began to see that in his own city the factories were closing, buildings were crumbling and men like his father were disappointed and bitter. He began to wander the streets with his camera to behold and grasp the city's death, to participate as witness, to have a role or identity – that of the truth teller, the messenger.

As the city died he wished to make sense of life. Like all kids, he wanted to live and to matter and he wanted his portfolio to speak to the judges of something important.

Arnie's father caught him smoking marijuana. Arnie laughed at his father's rage. The hypocrite was more concerned with his own precious drug - Israel, than with his own son. Arnie laughed and his father sent him up north to a military academy. David was devastated by the sudden loss and the waste. Several weeks later David received a letter from Arnie in his bold round handwriting, telling him that he had walked out of the school the second morning he was there, caught a Greyhound to New York, was staying with a friend and that David was welcome to join him anytime.

Arnie said he was going to take his portfolio around to show people and that he hoped to get a commission. David was stunned and jealous. His response was ungenerous and irrational. He understood that Arnie was plugged into ideas and an imagination that were beyond him but he was not as technically accomplished nor as articulate as David.

During the 60s, in that age of youthful self-assurance, when the rising generation seemed so certain of its rightfulness and its solutions for the future, David found unacceptable the answers of his peers. It seemed to him that hairstyles, music and other manifestations of the youth culture, supposedly his culture, were hollow, easily absorbable passing fashions. Nor could he believe in their political answers. They were of style, not substance or form. The same rebellious strains that led David to react against the conservative society around him also reared up against the 'alternative' culture. The fragmented movement offered a reaction to rather than an analysis of the status quo, and it offered no political plan for change.

'Why are wars fought? Why are so many people hungry? How could the centre of one of the finest moments in Western art become the home of Nazism? Why had the many revolutions and liberation struggles around the world turned into states of hideous repressive regimes? The Students for a Democratic Society, the Weathermen, the Hippy movement, the counter culture do not answer my questions'

He looked elsewhere. He read Thomas Mann, Herman Hesse and took drugs. He tried peyote, LSD, Mescaline, eventually opium the dream weaver, and always grass and hash. They unleashed storms, horrors, tongueless creatures crazily calling for help, rasping chimera grasping away his sleep, creating night times of constant restlessness. But there were no compelling answers.

An acquaintance loaned him Trotsky's History of the Russian Revolution. He thanked her but doubted it would interest him. Many revolutions had turned into a succession of murderous events. Those artists he so admired from Mayakovsky to Eisenstein had been side-lined, 'disappeared', committed suicide or were murdered; a foretaste of the rest of the century in which politicians, bureaucrats and religious maniacs would relentlessly massacre artists in every part of the world. If there was any crime he was to find particularly disgusting and irrational, it was this unending assault by his species on its own creativity, an assault equal to harming one's own children. David was to become an observer and at times a participant but for now he needed to sort out his portfolio, finish his fourth high school year with good grades and find a way to resolve his overpowering sense of emptiness.

One day, in early spring, David's Civics teacher spoke about the responsibility of individuals to stand up and be counted. Dr Kaufman, a large framed, rotund man, was intimidating in stature but gentle. David raised his hand.

"Yes David."

"Can a law be wrong and if so, is it wrong to break it?"

"That's a great question. We know from repressive states like Nazi Germany and the Soviet Union that laws can create evil outcomes. So what do citizens do? Often peaceful protests wind up in violence but does that make the protest wrong?"

There was silence.

David raised his hand again and was acknowledged by Dr Kaufman.

"The protest will be wrong in the eyes of the law but the same people making the evil laws are also making the anti-demo laws."

Dr Kaufman waited.

"If the members of the Boston Tea Party had not disobeyed the English tax law and thrown the tea overboard from the ship in the harbour, there may not have been an American Revolution."

Dr Kaufman smiled at David's analysis. "Excellent example but this leads us to a moral problem: do the means justify the ends or vice versa?"

Helen, who had been watching the exchange as if it were a tennis match, raised her hand.

"Good, someone else, We need communal participation. Helen."

"Can a law be accepted as a law if it's immoral?"

"That depends on the nature of the state ... in a repressive dictatorship, where people have little or no say in what laws are passed and enforced, then yes but you're asking larger questions here."

Helen's huge eyes opened even wider, as they always did when she realized she had discovered something.

"Larger question ... ahhh."

Dr Kaufman turned to David. "Do you get it?"

"I once worked for a man who had fought and had been badly maimed in the Spanish Civil War. He used to quote a Russian named Trotsky, usually with blame but once he said that Trotsky talked about what he called 'the great excess of history' when people have been so disappointed or were so hungry that they had no choice but to revolt. In those times, all laws are swept away."

A heavyset kid at the back of class said loudly, "You're saying we should destroy America because we got maybe a bad law or two?"

David tuned and saw the threatening look on the kid's face. Heavyset, blunt and menacing like his brother, like the safety patrol oaf, like the kid who didn't like his trousers, only now David knew his strength and his fury would protect him. As his mind raced, he thought that in the context of a class about 'standing up and being counted' he had no choice.

He leapt to his feet, turned on the oaf and spoke loudly. "The world's filled with people who threaten with a loud voice or a kind of physical threat when they misunderstand or don't like what's said. And then, once they've bullied the rest of us, they make laws that suit them and their group and then steal our lives from us ... from the people who've been too frightened or too preoccupied to speak, and that's how democracy dies."

Dr Kaufman watched this with some pleasure. When David seemed to finish, he asked David to sit down.

David looked from the kid to Helen's beautiful face to Dr Kaufman. As if by explanation he stammered, "I was standing up to be counted."

Dr Kaufman smiled, went to his chair behind his desk that seemed too small for him and sat down. He looked at his meaty hands and back up at the class. "Our country is entering a difficult period. It will either spell the end of the republic and the beginning of empire as in ancient Rome or we will restore it to the vigorous health it once had."

He thought for a moment and then began again. "A man named F .J. Turner, a chronicler of the American west at the end of the nineteenth century, spoke about a need for a revival of the old pioneer conception and of the obligations and opportunities of neighbourliness. This he said was a part of the spirit of the pioneer's 'barn raising' and in that rests the salvation of the Republic'."

David's arm darted into the air.

"David."

"I saw an article that said that guy Rockwell, the head of the American Nazi Party, is going to speak at an open-air rally in Hamtramck on the weekend. If we stand up to be counted, if we're against laws that allow people like him to speak, should we try to stop him?"

The class foamed with fear and excitement. David was incomprehensible to most of them. He was at best an oddity and at worse an undefined and dangerous troublemaker but not one of them could explain what they meant by that. It was an inchoate fear of difference that, in most circumstances, strikes down the unexplained as a threat. 'Let's kill it first and ask questions later.'

Dr Kaufman, frowning, said, "David, you're still a minor and as such, I think you must take advice from your parents."

That weekend, David asked his mother if he could borrow the car to take some pictures for his new portfolio. She looked at her younger son with unresolved pride and handed him the keys.

David drove to a modest house in the suburbs mentioned in the newspaper article. There were police cars parked up and down the block. He drove past, around the corner and saw there was a paved alley between the two sets of backyards of the houses facing outwards to the streets either side of it. He parked near its entrance, took out his camera and nervously walked along the alley towards a gaggle of tough, foreign looking men. Something was odd about them. He studied them as he walked and thought that they looked poor and that their pockets were strangely bulging. They reminded him of somebody, but he could not remember who it was. They eyed him up but didn't bother to ask anything. He saw they were gathered in the alley behind the back fence of a squat red brick house. Its high back porch had a flag draped from it with a red field, a white circle in the middle and a black swastika inscribed on it like a swathe of pitch. David was shocked. This was America.

'Don't give into the fear, concentrate.' He took a light meter reading from behind the fence and set his camera's aperture and shutter speed to be ready. He judged the distance to the porch, set the focus distance on his semi-telephoto lens and then hesitantly lifted the camera to check it visually. It was only then, through his viewfinder, did he realize that in the shadows of the porch were a group of very tall blonde men dressed as Nazi Storm Troopers just like the ones who burnt the books in his worst dreams.

Now he was concerned; who were the toughs behind him? Supporters of the Nazis or... he didn't have long to wait.

With the Storm Troopers standing to attention, the mob behind him still hanging back, David opened the gate, waited to hear if anyone would shout at him and in the silence he walked into the backyard. No one said a thing. There he was, ready to photograph this horrible creature.

Suddenly Rockwell, a tall fit looking dark haired man walked out of the shadows to the end of the porch where the flag was draped. His right arm projected into a stiff Nazi salute. David shot several exposures. As one, all of the men behind, piled into the yard, some though the gate and others over the fence. David whirled around and photographed them. Immediately the men began to hoot, catcall and howl abuse, with some shouting in a foreign language. David's fear disappeared. The shouting rose, becoming more like agonized screams. David kept shooting. He heard a noise from behind him on the porch and turned again, shooting wildly as he did. Four of the Storm Troopers were bounding down the stairs and several more came charging from around the side of the house towards the screaming men and David. There were no police to be seen. David kept shooing but was trapped between the mob and the charging Storm Troopers. Whistling noises, unlike sounds David had ever heard before, zinged passed his ears. The Storm Troopers fell back;

one hit the ground, another shouted out in pain. David shot more. Suddenly a huge hand pulled David to the ground from behind and dragged him towards the line of protesters. What was happening? Was the mob attacking him? Was this the temple all over again? David regained his feet, in a whirl of impressions. The man who pulled him to safety had a tattoo on his left wrist, Rockwell had retreated into the house and David's rescuer's big mug, unshaven and puce with anger was near David's face. He said, "The bastard's gone without saying a word or we kill him".

David croaked, "What was the noise?" The man said, "Those were stones passing your head. You only worry about one you don't hear."

This was David's introduction to the real world of civil violence.

He got home, processed the film and immediately made contact prints. He was amazed, thrilled and a little shocked. But there they were, the final images he needed to round off his theme on his city, a city violently abused by the harsh industrialists, the police and the Nazis and racist organizations that so often did the employers' dirty work - breaking up union meetings and stirring racial hatred.

David showed the portfolio to Mr Busby. He looked at the pictures slowly, one by one and then at David who was trembling with expectation. This was the first hurdle towards his scholarship.

"One thing I've said to many students is if you can't make 'em good make 'em big." David was heartbroken until Mr Busby added, "But with these pictures about the Nazis, well they're already so excellent. If you make 'em big, by gosh, I'll eat my hat if you don't walk away with all the honours and all of the scholarships."

David blew the pictures up, the largest prints he had ever made. They were filled with inky shadows and blurred motion, which expressed the horror and violence, not only of the event and the Nazis, but of the condition. He remembered the conversation with Ed about the blurred bullfight images by Ernst Hass. This pleased him; no knowledge was useless, no knowledge was wasted. The more he knew, the less he had to reinvent and, as his grandmother had taught him, he could stand on the shoulders of those who came before him.

These were his first pictures of the human plague.

David swept the board that year and was offered two scholarships to different universities, both of which would provide partial tuition for their photojournalism courses.

One rainy June night he told his parents. His father left the room without a word. His mother said, "All those extra costs to travel up and down the country when you can stay right here, get a job or study for free if that's what you wanna do."

"But this is an honour."

"Honour, schmoner. Costs money. Your father will never agree."

"But mom, it's what I've been working for all these years."

"Talk to your father. He'll put you straight."

David sat back on his heels. He saw all his hopes draining away. He saw his postcards burning, he saw his father shaking him by his arm. He knew, no matter how much money he'd make working over the summer, he could never afford those distant schools on his own and he knew he should always have seen this coming. He was beyond disappointment and anger. David looked closely at his mother and realized she had no idea who he was and what he needed and further, that she didn't much care.

He got up slowly and went to his room. He looked at the two letters of invitation he had received and slowly tore them up. He lay back on his bed and thought of his future. He knew he'd embrace a wider world, he believed he would find love but that he'd die alone.

CHAPTER 16

The tiny fishing boat had thus far proven doughty, like Zakkir. David was certain that by now he had made it into international waters. Freighters loomed out of the mist and passed nearby with their foghorns moaning.

David looked through the fog at the few stars and the stalking moon. 'There is a man alone on a small boat at sea and the sea is very large. There is a boat alone under the stars and while the man on the boat alone at sea under the stars shares those shards of light with many others at the same moment, the man is still alone in his boat knowing that there and then, whatever fears he has, he is alone on the boat under the stars shared only at a distance by others whom he could, in another life, at another time, embrace.'

He remembered he had thought in the past that he would die alone, and after Kate he knew that to be probable.

Even in the chill of his wet clothes, he perspired. He became feverish and mumbled to himself. Was he going to be seasick? He had never been before. He remembered a gnarled Greek sailor who told him to sail the Aegean only on a full stomach. "It keeps the bottom of the gut steady against the waves, especially those which move from side to side."

David looked away from the far horizon in front of him, the place he knew he would bump into the European coast, distracted by something off his port side. The faint moon darting in and out of the clouds allowed enough light to see the sea was turning crimson. It was as though, from below the surface, a dark matter was boiling up with effervescent bubbles. The boat churned forward on its small engines but rocked in the blood. David steadied himself and watched the spinning compass. He saw the moon scudding again behind clouds as though teasing him. He tried to keep his course. He remembered that when the Iberian navigators were more than a degree out they might find themselves smashed against rocks rather than moored safely in a port.

He remembered the spreading pool of a rebel's blood. He watched it become the spreading pool of a young Egyptian woman's blood in a gold leaf covered passage of an arcade. The many faces of the many people he had seen die uselessly began to emerge from the billowing moon-painted highlights in the clouds.

The sea was rising although the wind was still calm. The tips of the waves frothed; they became furious and darted into more angular shapes. They transformed into galloping white horses and one by one they metamorphosed themselves into images of Kate surging through the choppy sea. David, becoming dizzier, gripped the wheel while the breeze, as if by some command, became a rising wind and through it he heard a woman's voice singing:

"How did I come to love you
how did you come to touch me
how did we come to care?

Like the sweeping hand of a clock
chance became a bloody snare
how did I come to love you
how did you come to care?'

The wind increased. Tankers passed across his bow. David stared in bewilderment at the spray of the sea in their wake, the strobing running lights, the frigid metal hulls; he saw the night close around him, he saw the blood in his eyes, he saw the sky soaked in bile. He was on the deck, his back plastered to the rotting wood.

'Is my fate the same as that of the world? Is this world of people as unhappy as I am and have always been? Should I surrender; give this game up, hand over my life to the sea?'

His eyes looked wildly around, his hands grasped and scratched at the flat deck.

'What does surrender mean? The vanquished surrender before their victors. Women surrender to men. Did Kate surrender to me? I dove into her body as into a warm lake. I dove into her body. My god, I dove into her body. Never claiming control over her being, which was private and sacred; I left it for her to reveal if she wished it. I made no demands. I had no desire to insist. I created no guilt as if to say, "you must surrender your private world to me". I didn't ask for ownership. There was no surrender because there was no conflict. She was a lake, I was a stone.'

In the spume and spray of the sea and wind's violent effervescence, mist became smoke, pulsating waves became the crump of falling roof beams and the slashing of the spray across the bow became a cacophony of pain. Kate, lying in David's arms, looked around with glazed eyes. She was surprised and murmured, "Shouldn't be."

David gently touched her lips with his fingertips. Through tears he whispered, "Your lips, they're warm, you're okay, your lips are warm."

Kate extended her right arm, blindly dug in her bag, extracted a load of film cassettes and thrust them at David. She murmured, "Selma."

David was confused, "Selma?"

Kate, breathless, began to pant. "The papers, he'll pass them on ... the old prof ..."

She was startled. She looked past David through the blown-out wall. A white horse stood behind the crushed and smouldering ceiling beans splayed like matchsticks over broken glass and bodies. Kate's eyes pulled back to David. She was turning white. Blood was draining from her face.

David darted a glance at the horse. He could not miss another moment of her life. He looked back at her and bent closer to her.

Her eyes wandered off. "He'll pass them ... help save ...".

David caressed her cheek and held her more closely.

Her eyes froze open.

David's heart missed several beats, as though it was preparing to stop.

Kate stared. Kate was dead.

David cried out, "But your lips are warm!" He grasped her even tighter to him, stood and released a guttural moan that spoke of all the agony of existence he had thus far witnessed. He carried her through the bodies, smoke and fire to the entrance of the building where he staggered and fell. He was bleeding from his lower left thigh. Grasping her protectively, lovingly, he rocked her like a child, he held her and rocked like an old Jew in mourning and then he passed out.

David dreamed. His old New York Jewish friend was sitting on a park bench eating a huge sandwich out of a brown paper bag. He was half smothered in autumn leaves. Others drifted down. The old man put the sandwich down and looked at David. "So you still ask the same questions. Well, we don't really know what it is that brings us to love another. It happens and thankfully it is still a mystery. The point is that you truly love at least one time in your life. And you know, my little David, whatever the American myth, life is still a struggle and a vale of tears. Happiness is not the goal; understanding who you are is what you want."

David gazed at the old friend as snow began to gather on the fallen leaves. The old man looked from one shoulder to the other and then at David.

"Fancy stuff huh? There are those among us who need only to be loved. In your case my friend, you need to love and to be loved. In matters of the heart, you're an egalitarian, indeed willing to be self-sacrificial, to give more than you receive, to please before being pleased, to offer the best pickle on the plate to the loved one, to give her the best as a matter of commitment and politeness. For you politeness will always be a necessity in a loving relationship, not as a matter of manners but as a matter of care."

The old man looked at his snow-covered sandwich and ran his hand over his snow-covered pate.

"Bet you didn't expect this." He laughed. "Okay, so answers. You embraced the notion of a faithful and enduring relationship, one that would pass through the heavy breathing period to a constant exchange of ideas, affection, humour and shared experience. When you first saw Kate, all these things poured through your mind as if an aura around her announced a premonition of enduring love. In the midst of the massacre in the woods, you experienced a presence unlike you had ever previously encountered. For the first time in your life you thought you had met your Tina Modotti. Well, that's something huh?"

"This woman, where is she?"

David picked and twisted at the crisp material between his fingers. 'Are my eyes open or closed? Where exactly am I and where's Kate?'

Footsteps. 'Perhaps she's approaching. No they're gone.'

He sensed a presence, a woman.

Evening light spilled through the windows of the ancient hospital ward. Nurses in winged hats fussed about. In the middle of this, Margaret sat next to David's bed. Slowly he opened his eyes and stared towards the ceiling and then glanced around. 'At that door, guarding this place is a UN soldier. Something's happened.'

David tried to concentrate but his head was filled with voices and sounds: cries of people in pain, the rustle of forest pines, the whining horses, Kate whispering: "He'll pass them on David, he'll pass them on ... it's in the papers ... redemption." He heard his name spoken by her as if she was describing something jewel like, made of precious beauty and of great human value. She spoke the word "David" followed by a soft breath. 'I know her lips are soft and warm. I know her lips are warm.'

David's opened eyes began to connect to his brain. It's not that the world was blurred but rather drained of colour and had no apparent substance. Slowly his eyes moved to his left. He saw a shadow, a woman perhaps. 'That's it; Kate's sitting nearby. She seems concerned.' And for a moment he was ignited by the idea that she could be attending him for some reason. Perhaps he has lost a segment of his life and now they've come together, that they were to be lasting lovers. He began to focus more. Margaret. He reached for her hand, wondering where he was and what was going on. She thinly smiled and whispered, "You'll be all right; nothing permanent but you're in shock and concussed."

He weakly turned the corners of his lips up and then lost himself in a time-space hole. 'What was I thinking a moment ago? It was so satisfying. It provided a kind of radiance. There's a sense of something missing.'

He moved his toes and then his fingers. 'All there.' He began to grasp he was in a hospital. 'A hospital. Why? A hospital.' Suddenly it came to him in a sickening wave. Sweat and fear, nausea and palpitations, an onset of panic and horror. He darted a look at Margaret.

She slowly shook her head 'no'. "She was killed ... by a bullet ... shot in the back. Suspicious. No one knows why."

David tried to take in what she had said, closed his eyes and passed out.

Later, after he recovered, he was to solve that mystery of her death, but for that moment in the hospital, he wanted oblivion.

Hours later the sun tugged itself above the horizon at the far end of the Mediterranean, that end where the Phoenicians claimed the huge jutting rock south of Biblos was God's head guiding them back home from their long sea journeys. There above the land of Canaan, the earth twirls towards the light that, at that craggy point, is first admitted to the Mediterranean and then spreads like tungsten bars above its hidden myths.

David's boat bounced on the playful currents, slowly swaying towards a sandy coast. His skin was whitened from the salt and his clothes stuck to him. He awakened from his nightmares and felt the gentle pitch of the sea beneath him. The sky was lightening with the dawn and he began to orient himself, to discover where he may have been in a psychic rather than in a geographical place. For the latter he was certain Africa was to his right; beyond the crown of his head, out in the mist, through the Gates of Hercules, across the vast Atlantic are the Americas; and above his toes are the Biblical lands. Confidently he knew that should he sit up, the salty marshes he'd been searching for would be in front of him. By then he was certain that his greatest threats were the traps hidden within himself rather than those set by the likes of Mehmet and the Sergeant. Would he seek revenge and perpetuate the human plague, or would he seek understanding and forgiveness? Had he at least come to answer his last remaining questions, and could he therefore find peace?

Slowly he began to feel his fevered blood and moved his limbs to remember they were a part of him. He began to pay attention to the sounds calling across the water. As if in a game filled with ruses and Kafka-like rules, he insisted upon staying where he was, flat on his back, viewing only the patch of sky above until he had accommodated his mind to the labyrinth of emotions which were beginning to bedevil him.

But his concentration strayed again, and he wondered if he needed to know what cause would bring about his own demise. Sickness can determine an approximate time; an accident would be a surprise and suicide might be well planned or suicide might leap upon a man at a moment of despair, something unexpected and vengeful.

He remembered discovering that among the Nazi assaults upon European civilization, one of the consequences was that many people, including numbers of well-known artists and intellectuals, recognized that they were utterly alone and that there was no person or institution to care if they lived or died; that these people were in an existential hell, a universe in which neither the surrounding society, their God of heaven nor their mothers of the earth gave two hoots about their survival. They could neither run nor hide. This aloneness sapped their will to survive. Capitulation to hunger, hard labour or border guards' bullets was more painful and less dignified than their taking possession of their own fate. Many committed suicide in despair. This self-destruction of once-vibrant human souls ranks amongst the greater crimes of the fascists. David still wondered if European civilization had ever recovered from what it had done to itself.

And now David lived in his silence and asked himself if any of it mattered? We live a limited existence in an infinity of non-existence. He sensed desperation overcoming his diminishing hold on his game plan. He looked for an escape, a mental bolt-hole. Greatness or infamy, a pain-filled or joyful passage were both a matter of luck, a drawing of the cards influenced a little by one's place at the table.

But the despair beginning to envelope him took him nowhere. He was still on his back, alone in a small boat somewhere, he suspected by the bouquet of herbs carried on the early morning breeze, close to landfall.

'I wanted to do good but I screwed it up; I wanted to understand the world but have wound up the tool of more clever people; I wanted to hold onto love but lost it.'

He knew he had experienced love, which he cherished as an incomprehensible but stunning jewel. But he believed through his own actions, although innocent, he had been at least partly responsible for the destruction of Kate and for love itself. Now he was old and tired and only left with a desire to play out the end game of regret and death. Slowly he was realizing that he was committing himself to oblivion and in a hidden corner of his increasingly tormented mind, he had decided that within this was a justifiable logic. He was, in short, still a victim of those he had struggled against.

Suddenly he rose from the deck as if startled into an awakening. He had got up with ease as though young again. He surveyed the nearby landscape. It was so flat that the horizon between the sea and the land was, in the soft light and rising heat haze of dawn, almost indistinguishable. The spring sea grasses played in the strong but already warming fingers of the rising sun and the dew-drenched salty swathes from the previous summer's burnt out marshes sparkled like rhinestones. The last time he was on this marshy plain he had seen piles of raked salt and here and there a small mountain heaped by the poor and encrusted Andalucían and Moroccan day labourers.

His aching eyes searched both ways along the west-facing horizon to determine where the opening to the river's freshwater mouth was. He studied the sea's surface colours as best he could from his low vantage and noticed a slight warn brownish tinge and thought there it was.

David returned to the small, worse-for-wear shack that housed the wheel, flicked the engines over and moved off southwards along the shore searching for the river's mouth. He wondered how it was that he actually arrived so close to his destination and rippled with a tiny satisfaction that his reckoning was correct.

Slowly the boat chugged up the river. These ends of the earth's waterlogged flatlands slowly revealed proof of human habitation - rusted cars, piles of industrial detritus, several unpainted cinder huts and then a warehouse, a truck garage, a bar and finally houses. He noticed the salt smeared souvenirs of Zakkir's life pinned to the peeling wall of the wheelhouse. There was a greying snap whose metallic silver base was slowly oxidizing but its surviving image revealed a pretty young woman, slightly blurred, whose dark eyes reflected an exterior world of white walls and a shimmering sky but which also, in that indescribable way that still photographs isolate a moment in time, revealed an interior world of desires, maybe even lust.

David remembered the deep brown skin of Zakkir, his grizzled face and the faint air of fish which mingled with motor oil and sea spray on his clothes and perhaps on his body, and wondered how this young woman would have responded to Zakkir's lust as his sinewy body and his rope rasped hands grasped her when they tumbled for the first time on a bed. Maybe that's it, he thought while still staring at the girl's face: that existence for most is without love, just a life of lusts and duties performed in order to survive. That's why most people dismiss culture, that's why the fascists and the God-fearing disdain the intellectuals: lust, avarice, anger, envy, gluttony, greed and sloth oppress ideas and relegate them to a narrow band of consideration. Ideas create ideologies and the people knew ideologies lead to being imprisoned, expelled, castigated, starved, tortured or disposed of by people like the Sergeant, employed to quell questioning, revolt and even unconscious resistance.

But where was he? Why was the river so rough, why was it dark again? Had he fallen asleep? Had he reached a safe haven only in his dreams? Were these huge waves with their churning white heads of foam not just illusions or, oh my God, was he now awake from a delirium and still at sea?

The water still churned and the hull smacked the surface again and again. He wondered if the brute cruelty he was fleeing from had been more transparent and more truthful than the every-bickering Europe he was now so desperately trying to reach with its pall of verbiage and layers of manners and rules that incarcerated most people in an inchoate miasma of confusion, self-doubt, incandescent frustrations and, more to the liking of the cowardly leaders, a life of seeming helplessness in the shadow of faceless bureaucracies and unresponsive corporations. Forms, procedures, call centres, queues, questionnaires, box ticking democracy, the fog of sound bites and always "yes" meaning "maybe" and "maybe" meaning "no" had worked so well to diffuse and ultimately disillusion the people of Europe. The onetime social democrats had found a soul rending but non-military way to curb discontent and revolt. Was this the end of history?

As the spray lashed across David's face and the taste of the sea stung his lips he understood how useless his life had become. He was still the outsider, only interesting to the establishment had he allowed them to claim his person, his photographs or his ideas as theirs through showering titles, wealth and reputation on him or by waiting until he died, then having their plaudits consign his work into the acceptable canon when he could no longer shout "no, you are distorting and lying, I was in opposition and I believed in my opposition".

'My own history rendered me meaningless and the world's history had destroyed the only person I truly loved. I still remember all the evil of the world, but I've witnessed heroism, solidarity, kindness and astounding beauty. I heard the Ode to Joy, I've seen Rembrandt's self-portraits and Michelangelo's Prisoners. My pictures have done some good.'

He suddenly realized that underlying everything he did had been a search for truth, the kind of truth that erodes all the bastions of safety and all the posturing of denial.

'I recognized that virtue, love and redemption could only exist in an intellectual and emotional environment of truth. All defences, falsehoods, pomposity, all anger and violence would dissolve away in the flora of truth. I'm certain we are inherently decent social and loving beings distorted by our own lies and those of others. It is not redemption I need; it's truth.'

David looked at the ever-higher waves and thought how beautiful they were. Their phosphorescent glow in the intermittent moonlight reminded him of her.

POSTSCRIPT

Two days after David disappeared the Colonel was arrested and was never seen again.

The Sergeant, responsible for stopping one of the plotters, was promoted to Captain.

Zakkir recovered from his sore thighs and wounded pride but, having lost his boat, lived miserably, occasionally working for his fellow fishermen. A year later he received a check for $3000.00 from an unknown source.

The smiling woman from the key shop received extra monthly support from the secret police.

Annie became involved in the Weathermen, a radical group who believed that violence against the US government would stir people to revolt against the system. She was blown up in a bomb factory accident in New York.

And David, that's another story.

ABOUT THE AUTHOR

Robert Golden is an American born photographer/filmmaker working for many years in the UK. During the 1970's he co-authored and photographed a series of books and editorial articles about what turned out to be the demise of the British industrial working class. Having been born in Detroit he was sensitive to these issues. At the beginning of this century he shot 26 films around the world about food and culture and realized that he had photographed and filmed two bookends of the homogenizing processes of globalization, the first in industry and the second in agriculture and food production. Out of this came an exhibition called HOME:

https://www.robertgoldenpictures.com/the-demise-of-the-english-working-class/

that is about how jobs, community, family, customs and traditions are destroyed by globalization. This is like a distant wind that sweeps across people's lives, destroying much in its wake; a wind people can feel and see the results of yet have no real idea what the source of it is.

He has written many film scripts, poems, a few plays, and has reached a point in life where he believes the novel is the form he can use to explain/cope with/resolve/express certain issues, hence having written A FORGETTABLE MAN

David's story will continue in the soon to follow
A VENGEFUL MAN

WriteSideLeft
2018

www.writesideleft.com

www.ingramcontent.com/pod-product-compliance
Lightning Source LLC
Chambersburg PA
CBHW072030220726
48293CB00016B/620